From Russia With Tassels

A HANNIBAL SMYTH MISADVENTURE

MARK HAYES

Salthomle Publishing

Saltholme publishing
11 Saltholme Close
High Clarence
TS21TL

Publisher's Note: This is a work of fiction. Names, characters, places, and incidents are a product of the author's imagination. Locales and public names are sometimes used for atmospheric purposes. Any resemblance to actual people, living or dead, or to businesses, companies, events, institutions, or locales is completely coincidental.

Book Layout © 2019 Saltholme publications

From Russia With Tassels:
Mark Hayes -- 1st ed.
ISBN 9781695471528

This novel could not have been possible without the help of C.G. Hatton, Amy Wilson, Andy Hatton, and many others, for all the proofreadings, editing and most importantly the ceaseless encouragment and advice. I offer my heart felt thanks to all of them

The Hannibal Smyth Misadventures Series

A Spider In the Eye
From Russia With Tassels
A Scar of Avarice (novella)
A Squid on the Shoulder (coming 2020)

Other Novels

Passing Place: Location Relative
Cider Lane: Of Silences and Stars

Also features in the following Anthologies

Harvey Duckman Presents Vol 1
Harvey Duckman Presents Vol 2
Harvey Duckman Presents Vol3

Dedication

As ever this novel is for my children; Sarah Louise and Aaron James. Neither of whom are children anymore.

It is also for Clive 'the badger' Weldon and 'Magic' Mark Adams, the two friends I would turn to first for help, if I was the kind of person who ever turned to anyone for help, rather than pretended to be stoic and just say 'I'm fine…'

And finally, it is for all the people who pretend to be stoic and just say 'I'm fine…' You don't have to, there are always friends willing to listen, and happy to hear from you, so don't follow my shockingly bad example. Talk about things if you need to, lighten the load on your shoulders, know that's it okay to say, 'I'm not fine…' and learn you only need to smile because you want to.

Not because you feel you should…

Contents

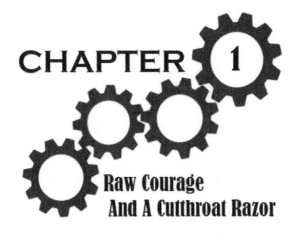

CHAPTER 1

Raw Courage
And A Cutthroat Razor

So, let's recap a moment, shall we? Just to take stock of all this. You know, to save us from confusion and what not, after all, it is easy to lose track of those little details since last we spoke. So where were we…? Oh yes, Nepal.

As you will recall… There was I, high in the Nepalese mountains, where the air is thin, and it's cold on the warmest day. Sat beside a brazier of hot coals, for which I was grateful. In a cell of stone and iron, for which I was not. And before me, as the mist burned off in the weak spring sunshine, I witnessed the disturbing vision of a rebel air fleet in the making. My own stolen craft, The Jonah's Lament, frankly the least of them, small as it was beside two pirated passenger liners, being hastily refitted as vessels of war. And then, of course, there was the Russian craft. An Iron Tsar. A thousand feet of death and thunder. A beast of an airship if ever there was one.

It was a fleet that I knew, for all my passing grasp of international politics, could plunge India into chaos and by extension the whole British Empire. Indeed, the whole world come to that.

As sights go, it was a disturbing one, I'm sure you would've agreed with me had you seen it as I did. Though the full extent of the chaos to come… why of that it was just the merest glimpse. A glance at the future, without full context. A looming threat gathered on the mountainside. Had I known then, in that cold, cramped cell, the full truth of all that would come to pass. Why, I dare say I would've been a damn sight more than merely disturbed by the sight of that fleet. That man can never perceive the truth of the looming future and can merely speculate upon what might come to pass is I think either a blessing, or perhaps the truest cursed of mankind. But such heady thoughts weren't foremost on my mind right then.

What was on my mind, what disturbed me, was simply this, I was the man The Ministry sent to stop whatever vile machinations were underway in this remote Nepalese valley. I was their foil. Their pawn, if you will, in whatever greater game was being played. The piece they had moved across the board to counter whatever Herbert George Wells was up, out here, in the back of beyond.

Me. All but alone. Hannibal Smyth. A man, as you've doubtless learned, who is happy to admit within these pages, and with a certain degree of self-loathing, to being at best a liar, a thief and on occasion a murderer. A man condemned to the noose by the courts of his own nation, and as you may have surmised from the first of these volumes, one with all the moral fortitude of a Tory politician with a bag of cocaine in his pocket, standing in the doorway of a Whitechapel brothel.

I'm not, to put it bluntly, the stuff that heroes are made of, but perhaps you think, as many do, that heroes are not so much made, as forged by adversity. What is that old chestnut, *'Cometh the hour cometh the man'*. Perhaps, therefore, you think that this cell deep in the Himalayas would prove the furnace in which my pig iron character would be forged anew. The anvil upon which the steel of my inner nobility would be hammered. The plunge into cold water that tempers the blade. Oh, what a romantic soul you must be if this is the case, but if it is so I thank you, and pity you in equal measure, for thinking of me thus.

In the past, or so I have read on occasion in the odd journal at train stations when the bar has yet to open, men have come to Nepal seeking self-knowledge, seeking insight into their existence, into the balance of the universe, searching for ancient wisdoms of the kind found in secret rooms in temples of stone, and all that stuff. For reasons which I for one have never understood, such wisdom is always to be found far away. Huddled close to the burning coals, snow drifting through the bars of my cell, wisdom, I considered, seemed more likely to be found at the bottom of a good pint of porter in a tap room off Leicester Square. But, right then, the bars and brothels of dirty old London were, for me at least, indeed very far away. Which I supposed just goes to prove the point.

In any regard, such delights as the old main drag had to offer were, I suspected, forever denied me now. Convicted felons pressganged into the service of the crown by The Ministry, that ministry, the one that did the things other ministries didn't like to talk about, well such fellows as I tend to be persona non grata, even in Soho. My chances of carousing with my old compatriots in the main bar of *'The Ins and Outs'* were therefore slim. Besides which, I suspect that even if the committee had not rescinded my membership of the old club upon my conviction, they would've by now, my subs had lapsed. Being a convicted murderer was one thing after all, but not paying your dues and failing to cover your bar tab… Well some things are unforgivable.

But putting the matter of my tattered reputation on one side, let's get back to our little recap, shall we?

So, there I was, in a tiny cell, on a mountainside, in sodding Nepal, while this fellow Wells was waltzing around in the orange robes favoured by the native monk fellows. Here was a man who for all the world looked like a bank manager's assistant, playing some damn fool game of dress up. A typical middle-class civil servant, gone slightly off his rocker, as men of a certain age are wont to do once in a while. By rights he should have been chasing around after some young piece of skirt behind his wife's back and trying to recapture his youth in a desperate attempt to regain that wide-eyed naivety of his younger years. Or following some new found mad passion for collecting butterflies, or rare books or some other such pursuit. Because that is what middle-class middle-aged men do when they realise they had wasted the best years of their life. Or worse barely noticed their passing. What such men generally didn't do, leastways one hopes, is become hell-bent on bringing the British Empire, if not the whole damn world, to its knees.

Though I guess insurrection and piracy is a step up from bird watching as a hobby.

I will not lie, not to you, not here, not right now, what after all would be the point in doing so? So, I will not lie about this, I found the whole idea somewhat terrifying. Not so much because of the scale of it all. Plots to bring down the Empire were, let's be honest, far from uncommon. It was every rebel's dream after all, and if the British Empire was good at anything then it, like all the empires that preceded it, was good at manufacturing rebels. That and stamping all over the rebels to make some more. Rebellion has always been a growth industry in the Empire, much like making bullets and gun running.

Before my unfortunate conviction I knew an arms dealer by the name of Redwood, an arse of a man, in truth. Indeed, if ever a man made you itch just to look at him, it was Johnathon Redwood. He was, among other things, a proud Englishman, and one given much to perversities in his boasts of that pride. He used to supply me with crates of munitions, bullets for small arms and the like, along with a list of drops to make to pass them on further down his chain of suppliers and supplies. Conveniently you see, as I was a gunnery officer on a RAN airship and it was part of my job to log the munitions kept on board her, as well as keep track of our supplies. As such it was an easy matter to store a few extra boxes at the back of my magazine for a week or so before loading them off onto a truck in the early hours one dog watch when the ship happened to have made port wherever Redwood wanted his boxes shipping. All, of course, for a reasonable consideration for services rendered. I can't say I ever asked who all those boxes were ultimately for. Can't say I cared much in any case, just as long as Redwood or one of his men passed me a brown envelope for my troubles.

I only met Redwood himself a couple of times. One time was after I'd had some slight trouble in the Baltic states because my contact never showed up to collect several boxes of rifle rounds. Unfortunately, this meant I'd had to keep them on board for a few more weeks than planned. Which wouldn't have been an issue, but the annual inspection of the ship's magazine was due any day, and so I had the looming spectre of the fleet's auditors to contend with. Basically, I needed shot of the crates, lest my little side-line be discovered. Caution, always my watchword when dealing with those on the grey side of the law, informed me just ditching the boxes out over the North Sea wouldn't be well received. So I got in touch with Redwood's man, and word came down to me that I'd been invited to dine with the man himself at his club to discuss the matter. Dine turned out to mean a cup of insipid tea and a slice of poor-quality Battenberg, but that was beside matters.

Redwood made a show of peering down his nose at me, but then he was a man with a nose for peering down. That and sniffing, he was, it seemed, perpetually on the verge of sniffing and had an unpleasant air of assumed superiority about him. Which is to say he assumed his superiority over just about everyone who didn't at least hold a minor baronet. Which was strange as Redwood himself held no such title, just the pretensions to a class he could only aspire to and almost certainly never gain.

Our meeting it transpired was nothing more than a fan to the man's vanity, it could have been handled by intermediaries had not Redwood been so bloody fond of his own voice and enamoured of the high opinion in which he held himself. Things should've been all sorted out in a few brief words, Redwood's man would be at Heathrow to collect the crates and store them while my inspection took place. Then I'd get them back and reroute them to a new location, with a few extra considerations shoved in an envelope for the additional inconvenience on my part. This seemed all to the good from my point of view. But as I said, Redwood had a certain vanity about him, and enjoyed the chance to stare down his nose at the likes of me. So, tea at his club it was and a lecture for my troubles on the international arms trade, both on the level and illicit.

"You see, Mr Smyth, I am a patriot. I believe that no British soldier should ever face the indignity of being shot by some shoddy foreign bullet."

"Perish the thought," I replied dutifully, and he sniffed at me once more, a one nostril flaring kind of sniff. I suspect he was wondering if I was merely the toady kind of chap, or if I was taking the saint, as it were. In fairness, I was doing neither. Mostly I just wanted to get on my way, so I sipped my lukewarm tea and resisted examining the slice of Battenberg too closely.

"Yes... well, you see some of those shoddy foreign things might only wound a man. Leave him bleeding for days rather than kill him outright, unlike a good honest British bullet, which will do the job properly. I for one believe the British infantryman deserves better than a slow death of a foreign field; a good clean death is what's called for. Bullets that do the job right, British bullets, finest bullets in the world, that's what they deserve to be shot with."

"Oh, I agree," I said. '*Of course, being wounded by some pesky foreign bullet does imply a chance you might not actually die, wounds, after all, can be treated,*' I thought but decided against voicing that observation.

"Exactly, which is why it is our duty, nay our honour, that we seek to spare our fine British servicemen the fate as being shot by inferior bullets."

I nodded in reply, feeling it wasn't my place to suggest that most of them would prefer not to be shot at, at all.

"Good British lead in a British brass jacket, made on a British bullet press, with British gun powder, by quality British manufacturers. That's what the British soldier deserves both for his own gun and for the guns being shot at him. Some of these foreign bullets will jam in the breach, or misfire. Why I hear sometimes they damage the guns themselves."

"That's dreadful," I agreed, deciding it not overly pertinent to mention my personal opinion was that if I were facing down a rebel soldier and his foreign bullet jammed his gun or perhaps even blew up in his hands, then such an event would please me a great deal more than being shot by good old British lead. I didn't want him to think me petty…

Redwood sniffed at me once more, sipped his tea then continued with his diatribe. "Yes, it is indeed most dreadful, not least because those are in all likelihood guns we sold to the rebels. You see, we have the nation to consider, Mr Smyth. British guns do not misfire, of that, I can assure you. Not if they are loaded with well-crafted British bullets. Our reputation must be preserved; we can't let these bally rebels use shoddy bullets and make our guns look bad now, can we? Our reputation is paramount, Mr Smyth. We are British after all. One nation, one Empire, proud and strong, by the grace of God and the Queen. So, if our British menfolk are being to be shot at with British guns, then I make it my business to make sure it will be British bullets that they are shot with. I consider this a matter of duty, Mr Smyth, duty."

"Oh, I agree, Mr Redwood, duty is everything," I said though duty to oneself outweighs duty to the nation every time in my humble opinion.

Mostly, however, by this point in the conversation I was wondering how much longer I was going to have to suffer listening to the damn fool. Any man who could cram the word 'British' so many times in so few sentences was clearly a basket case. Besides which the Battenberg was beginning to leer at me.

"Exactly," Redwood said, smiling a smile that had all the warmth of an icehouse. "Duty, Mr Smyth, duty. And our duty is clear. It commands us to keep on supplying these rebels with the very best British bullets, provided, of course, they can pay the going rate for them. Very good, Mr Smyth, very good…"

I realised then, having met the man and discovered how much of a loon he was, my wisest course of action would've been to sever all ties with him. Besides, I will admit, I felt it was morally bankrupt to go around supply rebels with bullets and guns in the full knowledge they'd be turned upon British lads and lasses in uniform. Men and women, I served with, after all.

But there was the matter of those brown envelopes, and well, if it wasn't me, someone else would be doing it sure as a politician lies. At least I was doing it for the purest of motives. Those of money and self-interest. Rather than some bastardised twisted sense of patriotic duty like Redwood, though doubtless there was plenty of self-interest and money in it for him, and power I'm sure. Redwood was all about money and power, and he had ambition aplenty. I wouldn't have been at all surprised if he went into politics at some point, he was just the sort.

If you're wondering why I'm bring all this up, when I should be telling you about a cold morning in a cell in Nepal, well let me just say I recognised the markings on a stack of munitions crates, piled up a few feet from my cell. I even recognised the lot number. So, whatever was going to happen, it would appear Redwood may indeed get his oh so patriotic wish.

I, for my part tried not to dwell on the irony that would be involved should someone decide to assemble a firing squad for my benefit...

But not to digress further.

On that particular cold morning in the mountains of Nepal, the scale of matters I'd been dumped in the middle of was, as I said, only just beginning to dawn upon me.

For all I was far from a willing agent, I was The Ministry's man by want of the sinister device they'd placed in my eye. I was still an Englishman born, and while I didn't feel the mad patriotic fervour that gripped the likes of Redwood, the emphasis here on the mad, I was still a proud Englishman. I believed in Britain, I believed in the Empire, for all its faults. The Imperial system both spanned the world and tied it together. And sure, while those who lived under the yokes of the other great powers probably suffered more than those in the tender embrace of Old Brass Brazier's ample bosom, the world worked. Peace, while not perhaps assured, at least held strong. Nations prospered.

Yet here in the mountains, Wells, with his small but growing fleet, was a man who despite all the odds might well have the means of pulling all that down. So, who had The Ministry sent to foil this mad man's plot, sent right into the heart of his base?

Me, your own, ever trustworthy, honourable, reliable, steadfast, dashingly heroic, Hannibal Smyth… a self-confessed liar, blaggard, coward, thief, smuggler, arsonist, and convicted murder.

On balance, things weren't looking good. To be frank, I'd no idea how I was going to get out of all this alive… I was after all alone, locked in a cell and armed with nothing but the cutthroat razor in my boot and my own raw courage. So mostly just the shaving implement, which was in dire need of sharpening.

Of course, things could always get worse. My proverbial Bad Penny hadn't turned up and threaten me with her own bespoke brand of violence and then knocked me unconscious. No one was taking pots shots at me. I wasn't hurtling towards my death aboard a rail-bound super bomb. I wasn't being operated on by mad scientist types or assaulted by samurai. I wasn't, to pick a random example of things that could possible happen with my luck, falling headlong into an ocean from a burning airship, half hoping the fall would kill me and spare me a choice of fates between drowning and shark bait.

No, that joy was still very much in my future. But it's nice to have something to look forward to, don't you think…?

CHAPTER 2

From Russia With Tassels

"So, Mr Smyth, we meet again," said a voice with an Eastern European accent I didn't recognise. It was later that first morning, as I was starting to feel the chill as the brazier died down and I was feeling miserable with it.

"Erm… no, I don't think so…" I ventured as a reply. Then looked up to take in the owner of, what to my admittedly not entirely educated ears, were Slavic sounding syllables, and my eyes widened just a little when I did.

He, whomever he may be, was wearing a Russian Fleet uniform of the deepest blue. A uniform hung with more gold braiding than any sane man wanted in his life. It also had little epaulettes on the shoulders with gold braid curtains that draped down six inches or more. A gold sash crossed his chest from left shoulder to right hip, this too tied off with tassels. Tassels seemed a common theme. Braided loops hung from his right shoulder around his left arm, while the thin tramline decorations down each leg of his trousers to his highly polished black boots were also braided and ended in tassels that hung at his side. All finished off with a dualist's half cape that hung over his right arm, attached by tasselled brass buttons front and back, and a bicorn hat trimmed with black eagle feathers, and as you may have guessed; tassels.

I pitied anyone who had to actually try to walk around, let alone fight, in such a getup.

"Oh, but I think so, Mr Smyth. Were you not the British agent who tried to steal the plans for the new Iron Tsar's weapon systems in St Petersburg last autumn?" he asked, though the way he spoke all the W's sounded more like V's.

"No, that wasn't me. I've never been to St Petersburg, in the autumn, or any other time of year," I said and shrugged, while wondering to myself how anyone would expect to be taken seriously dressed the way he was. That said the rumour mill in the RAN mess had it the Tsar himself had had a hand in designing his officers' uniforms. Which, given the apparent strange mania for tassels in his get up, seemed to be firm evidence, if any was really needed, that the centuries of inbreeding among the European aristocracy was still producing raving loonies.

"I am not sure I believe you, Mr Smyth. Indeed, I have it on good authority that you are also the British agent reported to have had an illicit encounter with the Young Tsarina before stealing the plans for a new Tesla plant on the Movska. It has been said the agent in question left the young Tsarina with child..." he said with a distinct note of chiding in his voice, doubtless at the scandalous nature of such a liaison.

"Not me, I'm afraid... that must've been some other British agent..." I replied while thinking to myself that it was, '*One who seems to be having a great deal more fun than you, Harry old boy.*'

"Ah, so you admit you are a British agent…." He said and triumph flashed in the man's eyes as he said this. I swear he even waved one finger in the air to punctuate at his masterstroke.

I didn't bother to rise to this, I just stared back at him. My face doubtless a mask of incredulity. It wasn't as if I'd been skilfully outwitted here. I was locked in that cell precisely because I was a British agent, for God's sake. I was starting to wonder if the legendary insanity of the Tsars was infectious. Perhaps the man was some distant cousin of the Russian royal family, though I knew that was unlikely to be fair, because the Tsar had married most of his distant cousins and had the rest of them shot.

In some cases, both.

Now I know it is possible that is just my British bias showing through. Our delightful tabloids are always full of stories of Russian insanity. Perhaps I am guilty of putting too much faith in the 'honest' men of Fleet Street.

So, let me put that bias aside, have a little honesty here, just between us, and admit that what is reported as the insanity of the Russian royal family is not dissimilar to eccentricity of our own. Besides, let's face it, the houses of Sax-Coburg and Romanov are so utterly entwined these days it's hard to figure out who is a first cousin and who's a third. Though, as I grew up in the gutters of London, the job lot of them seemed like thirds to me.

An awkward silence descended between us, and I soon realised he was going to say nothing more until I did. In the end just to move things along I asked what should've been a simple question.

"You have me at a dis-advantage… Captain?"

His rank was a guess, it was hard to tell looking at his uniform. The rank insignias may have been removed, unless rank was dictated by the number of gold braids, which it could have been for all I knew. He was certainly an officer, however, because there was no way rank and file airmen could afford to dress in such impractical garishness, or would wish to. I for one would have hated to go climbing about an airframe that get up.

That said, having had a few moments to really take him in, he did seem a little too overblown to be an actual officer. It struck me he was trying to act the part. Mimicking the mannerisms of his betters, if you will, and getting it subtlety wrong while doing so. I could've been wrong of course; but it was the impression he made on me, but there were other clues as well. His uniform didn't look cut for him. It hung a little too loose on him, sagging in places where it should have been tight, as if it had originally been the uniform of a larger man. Unless of course, he had lost a fair amount of weight since the uniform was made.

'*And height*,' came a stray thought, as I noticed his trousers had been turned up two inches or more.

"Yes, Captain Smyth, I believe I do," he replied, smiling at me once more and showing too many teeth. He had an off-putting friendliness about him. Not that this meant a great deal. Russians are renowned for seeming friendly right up to the moment they shoot you in the face or so I'd been told. But that was perhaps my British bias showing through once more…

"What I mean, sir, is we haven't been introduced," I carefully explained, feeling slightly frustrated. So much so that I almost missed the obvious slip. Almost. But it did strike me, a moment later than it should have, that if he was a real officer, he would've likely recognised the rank insignia of a British uniform. At the very least he certainly wouldn't have mistaken a first officer's uniform for a captain's.

"Yes… That is true. Indeed, we have not," he replied, still smiling, while I just got all the more irritated.

"I mean…" '*Oh for God's sake…*' "Who are you?" I asked him a tad snappily. This whole situation was rapidly dissolving into farce. I would've half suspected he was doing the whole 'I do not understand your English nuances' routine just to wind me up, but in truth, he didn't strike me as bright enough for that to be the case.

He smiled at me again, then clicking his heel together sharply and offering me a courteous nod, he informed me. "I, sir, am Vladimir, the new captain of the Sharapova, our fine Iron Tsar yonder." His voice holding a touch too much pride in those words.

I raised an eyebrow at this. The 'new' part was a bit of a giveaway. As was introducing himself by his first name, rather by his title and surname. No captain I'd ever known would've breached the social protocols in such a way. Adding it all up, I weighed him as a junior officer who'd jumped sides. That, or, like as not, one of the rank and file who had seen an opportunity to leapfrog to a new standing in life. Some leap that would have to be as well, from able airman to pirate captain, it did certainly explain a lot about him though. It also explained the rumour mongering about the Tsarina as well. That was just the kind of story the engine stokers and rear gunners of this world love to gossip about. Whereas a true gentleman would've only thought it.

I'm admittedly far from a true gentleman, and, well, who doesn't like to gossip about unobtainable woman of noble birth putting it about a bit with those lower on the social strata…? Why, the British tabloid industry was built on those morally questionable, but tantalisingly believable, grounds. Indeed, if The Times and other gutter rags like it didn't have 'Duchess of Basingstoke and the Gardener' scandals to print they'd have to start printing actual news, and nobody wanted that.

"I see, well, Vlad are you here just to annoy me or do you actually want something?" I asked, which was somewhat ungentlemanly, perhaps even a tad cattily side. Blame spending a cold night in an open cell and then having to deal with a buffoon. Vladimir was clearly nothing more than one of the monkeys. I suspected I was going to get nowhere until I was talking to the organ grinders, and the only 'where' I was really interested in getting right at that moment was out of that cell. Closely followed by out of Nepal and as far away as I could get from this whole mess. Luckily, as it transpired, this was the reason I was being forced to converse with the tasselled buffoon before me.

"Indeed Mr Smyth, I have been sent to escort you to the war room," Vlad replied but showed little inclination to open the cell door. By this time his accent was really grating on me as well. It wasn't so much the 'V's which should have been 'W's, as the strained nature of his English and his attempts to sound aristocratic. But I swallowed that irritation, hoping to move things along a little with some gentle prodding.

"Very well, best jump to it then, Captain, don't you think?" I said, trying to make my words sound like an order. I was sure now I was talking to nothing but a jumped-up scrotum of a man. A man used to taking orders from his betters and, begrudgingly or otherwise, obeying them. That kind of thing becomes as much a habit as much as issuing orders to subordinates. If I am honest, that was a habit I'd had to learn. I wasn't born of the officer classes, and the men of the ranks can spot an upstart like me a mile away. As such, I'd learned quickly to make it plain I was giving out orders, least the rank walk all over me. After a while, it became second nature to get an order in quickly to establish who was in charge whenever I had a new crew to deal with in the hope they never cotton on that I was not born to it.

No one, you see, likes an upstart. No one wants someone to carve a better lot for themselves. A man risen from the rank, why he was an insult to everyone who hadn't. And sure, most rank and file airmen may hate the officers who came from the upper classes, but at least they were men born to it. Some toff-nosed twerp of an officer giving you gip, well that was to be expected, and hating them, well that's just what you did, it didn't mean anything. But here's the thing, toff-nosed officer types hadn't started out in the gutter with you. They hadn't climb out of that gutter while you just languished down there among the other turds. Toff-nosed twerps didn't rub your nose in the fact you'd never amounted to more than just a lowly airman shovelling coal into a boiler, while they swaggered about thinking they were better than they had a right to be.

Which, in case you have ever wondered, is why I changed my name to Hannibal from plain old Harry. Harry was a boiler stoker's name, after all, not a name for a toff. No one would ever call an heir to the throne Harry, would they?

In any event, my attempts at a tone of authority must have worked on Vladimir, because he snapped his heels at me, and all but saluted when I said jump to it. Which confirmed all my suspicions. He might be playing the captain, but play-acting was all it was. He'd just treated a prisoner as he would a superior officer. I had to squash down a smirk as he took a key from his pocket and unlocked my cell door. So, I found myself thinking that Vladimir was nothing more than a comical clown of a man. One who would last a few weeks at most as the new captain of that beast of a Russian airship. Before long some bastard less fond of tassels, with a stick not so firmly inserted up their backside would decide they should take charge of the Iron Tsar.

Pirate crews weren't made up of the type of men to take to 'boiler stokers' who wanted to play at being nobility. It was generally to rid themselves of toff-nosed twerps that crews turned pirate in the first place.

Of course, that's not the first time I've been wrong about someone. But I digress…

Still stifling the desire to laugh at the clown, I brushed myself down. There were a couple of bored-looking local guards, with billy clubs, listening to this whole affair a few yards behind Vlad. I assumed they were my actual escort because if I were in charge, I wouldn't have sent this idiot to fetch a bucket of water, let alone a prisoner. They looked on disinterestedly as I stepped out of my cell. Though I had little doubt, they would've jumped to it the moment I did anything they perceived as threatening. So, I did my best to be as non-threatening as possible because they didn't look the types to go gently with their clubs if needs must.

Fully expecting to have my wrists clapped in irons, I held out my arms with a certain resignation. This was hardly the first time I'd been escorted out of a cell to face a judgment of one kind or another. But Vladimir just smiled at me and to my surprise asked in brisk officious tones, "Can I take it, Mr Smyth, I have your parole?"

I stared back at him a moment, thinking, '*You have got to be kidding me*'.

Parole, if you don't know, is an archaic principal at best. It's the kind of thing you might hear in a radio play. Or read of, in some fatuous novel whose heroes were officers and gentlemen. But no real officer would've ever offered a prisoner parole in this day and age. Even if they didn't have a cell to throw you in, which he did, or they happened to be married to your second cousin, which I am almost entirely certain wasn't the case, because I don't even have any first cousins I am aware of. If I did, I suspect they would be plying their trade 'selling cockles' down the east end docks. There're a lot of 'cockle sellers' in my family tree. However, very few of them ever sold seafood… But, putting my potted family history on one side, the fact the Russian offered me parole just confirmed all my suspicions. Vladimir was no more a born officer than I, and he was a damn sight more naïve than I'd ever been.

To be fair, it wasn't like I could actually make a bid to escape. I could hardly steal an airship and fly it myself without a crew, and sure as Victoria's not a virgin, I couldn't peg it out of there either. I was deep within the highest mountain range on Earth and not even vaguely sure whereabouts in that range I was. And just to put the icing on the cream bun, I was a white British officer surrounded by enemies of the British Empire. In short, I was target number one for every Tom, Dick and Koresh for hundreds of miles around. So, in all fairness, of course, Vladimir could trust me to my parole. It wasn't as if I was likely to be going anywhere.

"Of course, Captain Vladimir," I replied, smiling back at him, almost tempted to ask for my weapons back. If he was daft enough to offer me parole, he might be daft enough to hand them over to me because that's the form, don't you know, or was back in more trusting times. The weapons an officer carries are generally purchased by them, you see, or family heirlooms in some cases. As such, it is considered unseemly for one gentleman to refuse another his property, just as it would be unheard of not to take one at his given word. If you have a man's parole, well he is sworn not to attempt to escape or to take up arms against you. So why would you not hand him back his sword and pistol…?

Perhaps it is due to my coming of more modest stock. Being as I am a 'cockle seller's' son from the East End. But to me, the whole concept seemed utterly insane, but that's the aristocracy for you. Every one of them, one grape short of a bunch.

So if he was daft enough to offer me parole, well I would happily swear on my dear mother's matronly honour to respect it and fail to mention she would have been the first to scoff at the idea of her having any if she was still alive. She'd have suggested I pick the idiot's pocket while I was at it, I don't doubt.

Unfortunately, it occurred to me the local guards would likely have objections if I asked to be rearmed. Parole is a very European concept. Your average Asiatic considers it far wiser to just kill your enemies if they are foolish enough to let themselves be captured. If only as an attempt to keep the gene pool clear of the kind of stupidity that leads to officers getting captured. European aristocracy could learn a lesson or two there, if you ask me. Centuries of careful inbreeding has left them with a prevalence for weak chins, haemophilia, and having it off with their second cousins, all of which are still common enough traits of the upper classes. Unlike more prosaic traits, such as general sanity and an ability to tell their backsides from their elbows, which are somewhat less common among the upper house brigade.

I probably sound like one of those disgruntled followers of Karl Marx and that failed ideology of his. Though why they were so convinced they could dethrone the Tsar with a slapdash army of resentful factory workers, escapes me. It's not as if the Tsar's armies were off fighting a war somewhere making them unavailable to clear the streets. A Cossack charge, I could've told the bolshies, puts paid to even the most ardent revolutionary's fury. Added to which the Russian aristocracy were more than willing to let loose with machine guns, to prove a political point. Let's be honest here, the Tsars have never been shy when it comes to killing their own people to maintain their supremacy. Though I'm sure Watt Tylor and those at Peterloo would point out the British ruling class could be equally forceful when it came to preserving their position at the top of the pile.

There is, in my opinion, no point fighting the aristocracy. They're in charge for a reason. Even if that reason is that they've all the men with guns on their side. Besides, what happens if you actually manage to get rid of them? You only have to look at France for the answer to that question. They kicked the aristos out and cut off the heads of a generation with madam guillotine. Yet within a couple of hundred years they were back in again. And let's not even mention Oliver Cromwell's little experiment. I mean, what's the point of parliament deposing the monarchy if it invites them back a generation later?

Cockroaches have nothing on the resilience of the upper classes.

In any case, I may consider most toffs to be a waste of good air, but the alternatives don't bear thinking about. Giving every Tom, Dick and Hank the vote in America worked out so well in the end, as we know…

But I digress, and political rants are not really what you're here for, so to move along a little…

My parole given, Vladimir escorted me, with the guards in tow behind us. He led me out of the cell and into a paved courtyard full of activity. Dozens of men were milling about, all either busy or busy looking like they were. It was reminiscent of an upturned ants' nest rather than anything you'd expect to find in a peaceful mountain monastery. A damn sight more weapons and uniforms on show, to start with. Dozens of different uniforms. Russian, Dutch, Indian sepoys, British, Japanese, French, even one or two from the formally United States, most of them a tad ragged unlike that of my tassel fixated companion.

There were, dotted about, other uniforms, dark sea green uniforms with strange insignias I didn't recognise, which looked like a stylised squid creature. The wearers of these uniforms, unlike the others, weren't just milling about. It was clear to me they were the provosts of the encampment. Nasty-looking buggers to a man, each wore a breathing mask that only covered the lower part of their face. Given the thin air at this altitude, it was perfectly possible these were for practical purposes. But it lent them a sinister look, which did nothing for their charm in my opinion, not least because the masks reminded me all too much of The Ministry and its Sleepmen. Those bastards had given me quite a complex when it came to uniformed thugs in breathing gear…

It wasn't just the masks and the uniforms that lent them a sinister air. They also carried odd bulky guns, loaded with small viciously barbed darts that reminded me of harpoons. They seemed impractical but sure as Albert's piercing I wouldn't of fancied being shoot with one.

Besides, even if their masks, strange uniforms and stranger weapons didn't mark them out as the thugs in charge, I've enough of a military eye pick out the key strategic points around the encampment. This wasn't overly difficult as that was where the squid-bearing guards were standing.

There were some actual monks as well, of course. You know the kind I mean, all decked out in saffron robes and carrying incense burners. Generally, they were wandering around seemingly oblivious to everything else, following rituals that had probably been repeated for hundreds, maybe thousands of years. Rituals that weren't to be put on one side just because a small army had decided to camp on their doorstep.

Our route climbed an ancient staircase up from the main courtyard. It was a good twenty yards wide and climbed steeply up the side of the mountain. One young monk was sweeping away at it with an old-fashioned twig broom. Well, I say sweeping, in actuality he was brushing aeons of accumulated dust up into the air. The breeze then blew it back down behind him to settle on the steps once more. A seemingly pointless task if ever there was one, but perhaps it was one of those Zen things that one hears about. Something along the lines of: 'If the dust is not swept, how then will it settle?'

All the while, as we walked, my new Russian friend was talking, with those misplaced V's grating evermore on my nerves more with every passing step. He was, as my old mum would have described him, full of himself. Well she would have said 'That bleeder's enamoured of his own piss and wind', but you get the point, he was playing his assumed role for all it was worth. In his mind, if no one else's, he was the dashing, heroic airship captain. As we passed by, he would call out to various men by name and ask how things were going. Exercising his ardent desire, to be seen as a man in full charge of events around him. He wanted me, along with everyone else one suspects, to see him as, well, as he put to me, 'A big cog deep in the throbbing virile engine of Mr Wells' grand enterprise'.

As descriptions go, I believe that one says rather a lot about our dear Vladimir, and what passed for the inner workings of his mind.

While I was only half listening to the prattling fool, I was still struck by just how free he was been with his information. Considering he believed me to be a British spy, which in essence of course I was, Vlad had little in the way of tact and even less guile. He was telling me all kinds of odd little snippets. Had I paid any attention to what he was saying, there would've been many things I'm sure would be of interest to my government. He was, it seemed, a simpering fool, gesticulating all his masters' secrets away, to an enemy agent. I found it all rather incredulous. I mean, what kind of fool tells a known agent of an enemy power all his plans when they are at his mercy? It's tantamount to just asking that agent to pull off some daring if unlikely escape with the aid of the secret gadget he has hidden in his shoe, only to return and scupper all those plans. Win the day. Save the Empire. And importantly get the girl…

'Does he not read crappy spy novels?' I wondered.

Luckily for him and his masters, however, I wasn't taking a blind bit of notice. Frankly, I didn't care a great deal by this point.

"So, you see, we are prepared and ready to…" he was saying as we finally reached the top of the stairs that ran up the outside of the temple. I was a tad out of breath by that point, and too busy cursing Buddhist builders for their love of steps to pay much attention to anything, so didn't notice a familiar figure waiting for us at the crest, until she spoke, or I may have tried to hide the wheezing.

"Putin guard that mouth of your…" a female voice chided; one I knew well.

The voice in question belonged to Saffron Wells. Whom in other circumstances I would've been delighted to reacquaint myself with. Though I suspected the easy comradeship we had shared on The Empress of India was in the past, and unlikely to be renewed. Which was a shame as she was as delightful as ever to look at.

Except, that is, she still wore that strange monticule device, that was the twin of my own, which looked ugly and out of place amid her delicate features. Noticing the device, I realised to my mild surprise I'd grown so used to my own I'd almost forgotten its existence. Something I found decidedly odd, now it was brought to mind, and I had to stop myself from touching it to assure myself it was still there. Unlike the currently dormant spider it was holding in check, something also mirrored in the delightful Miss Wells' eye. That I found harder to forget. Remembering all too well the feeling of it crawling around in my eye when it was awakened.

The expression on Saffron's face was as stern as her words. It was clear to me she didn't think much of the Russian Captain. I noticed too, as I looked between them, that Vladimir's pride was ruffled. I swear his moustache grew stiff as a board, and his eyes, narrowing like slits on a gun port, were as stern as hers. Vlad wasn't a man who appreciated being chastised by a woman publicly. Indeed, I suspect he was too hidebound to appreciate such things in a more select environment than on a temple's steps. From his reaction, I suspected he wasn't a man who took kindly to a woman holding any authority over him. An attitude I've always found strange. But then I like nothing more than a virile young madam taking charge. Indeed, I know a few establishments where men have been known to pay quite a lot for that privilege…

But I digress once more…

"Madam, what I say is of no matter, for I have Mr Smyth's parole," Vladimir snappily retorted, then began to explain, in that superior manner men of his predilection adopt when they are explaining things to women. "As I have his parole, he is honour-bound to speak not of anything he sees or hears while I grant him liberty."

Miss Wells gave Vlad a withering look, snorted at him, then, presumably on finding a dark humour to the situation, the side of her mouth curled up into a smile, and she just started laughing at him. A response which as you can imagine really ruffled his feathers. Indeed, he visibly fumed.

"Did you hear that, Hannibal? You're bound by your honour to hold your silence," she told me, still laughing, then added, to salt the wound, "By your honour…"

I'll admit the way she said that was a little too snide for my taste, though I could hardly blame her for dismissing the idea. I tried to rally some small pride all the same.

"So, it would appear, Miss Wells. Thus, honour bound I am," I said, pulling off a small bow as if we were conversing at a Harrow tea dance rather than atop a windy staircase in Nepal.

As you're doubtless aware, Saffron knew the full value of my honour. Which is to say she wouldn't have given you a bent farthing for it. All the same, it still grated on me having this thrown in my face. More so when it was thrown by her. For, as we are being honest, she was a woman I'd rather held me in good opinion, for reasons as old as humanity, and to do with the perpetuation of it. Sadly, there was scant little hope of that between us anymore, if there ever had been beyond my fevered imaginings. Her parting words to me that last night on The Empress made this abundantly clear. My response did at least prolong her charming if cynical smile, which was something, and she took my words in jest, responding in kind.

"So, it would, Mr Smyth, but appearances can be so deceptive, can they not?" she replied coyly.

"With all due respect, Miss Wells, I would not expect you to fully comprehend such matters. But you must understand when a gentleman gives his word, he is indeed bound by it," Vladimir retorted, failing to mask the undertone of anger in his voice. I wasn't sure who he was defending, himself or me. But the venom with which he pronounced 'Vells' did his argument few favours. Saffron visibly winced at his pungent pronunciation, and her eyes narrowed in a way that I'd become familiar with on that journey to India where I'd first made her acquaintance. If I was to pick a word to describe that look, I would have said dangerous…

"He's calling you a gentleman now, Hannibal, did you notice that?" she said with more snide than humour.

I shrugged in reply; there seemed little point defending myself against the veiled barb. Vlad was doing such a bang-up job of digging a hole for himself, I saw little need to pick up a shovel and help. Besides, Saffron could be cutting when she wished to be, and I was happier with him on the receiving end of those cuts than myself.

"Mr Smyth is an officer, so by definition, he is also a gentleman, Miss Wells. You clearly do not understand these matters. But honour and its demands are the core of what it is to be an officer and gentlemen," he informed her, oblivious to the implications of her words, or oblivious to the possibility she was correct. Indeed, Vladimir seemed entirely oblivious to the idea that any woman could be better informed than himself, or indeed had the capacity for intellect.

'Never trust a man who thinks women are all ditsy little airheads. A man like that, you shouldn't even trust to pour your gin,' my old mum used to tell me, and my old mum would let anyone pour her a gin if they were paying for it.

From the looks Saffron was giving Vladimir, I suspect she and my old mum held much the same opinion of men who were dismissive of their sex. Given what she said next, in fact, it couldn't have been clearer.

"Putin, you're a conceited arse and a bloody unmitigated fool," she snapped at him, showing little of her breeding, but a whole lot of her annoyance.

"I protest. I shall not be spoken to like this," Vlad retorted angrily.

I suspect had Miss Wells been a man he would've challenged her to a duel on the spot, for he seemed the type for damn fool gestures. It also struck me that a 'damn fool gesture' was probably exactly what it would be. If I were a betting man, which I most assuredly am, I would've backed her to gut him with his own ornately jewelled sabre. Vladimir was a pompous peacock of a man, whose self-image of virile manhood and intellectual superiority was built on the feeble foundations of his vacuous vanity. Whereas Saffron Wells, when circumstance demanded it, had the eyes of a killer. Beautiful eyes. Eyes which were as pools of dark desire. Eyes a man might wish to fall into most assuredly, but they could also be murderous eyes with damn all pity for fools when she wished them to be. These were the eyes staring back at Vlad right at that moment.

"Your protestations, I assure you, will be given all the consideration they're due, Mr Putin. But right now, I suggest you go look to your ship and make sure your crew is tolerably up to scratch. I'll take charge of our 'oh so honourable' Mr Smyth from here," she replied, an edge to her tone sharper, I'd wager, than his sabre.

Vlad stiffened even more at this, the Russian showing no intention to be relieved of his charge and said as much. "I was ordered to bring him to your father, Miss Wells. I shall do as ordered."

"And now I'm ordering you to go get gone and get your ship in order. Leave bloody Smyth with me, and step to it. Now, Mr Putin!" Miss Wells said, her face a mask of a vengeful Kali in the making, and a tone that was utterly unforgiving. "Unless you wish to answer to my grandfather…" she added, correcting him on her relationship with Wells senior.

The Russian wanted to argue some more. I could tell by the darkening of his brow, the narrowing of his eyes and how the veins on his neck were pulsing. A tense moment passed between them, and for that brief few seconds I thought he might react with more anger and less judgement. But then Vladimir clipped his heels, pulled off a bitter, resentful salute to Miss Wells. Then he nodded vaguely in my direction, turned and started back down the steps without a further word.

I found myself chuckling at him, though I'd the good grace to wait till he was beyond earshot. I'd enough enemies to worry about. If he was fool enough to think me bound by honour, then he might also have the makings of a foolish ally at some point, and lord knew I needed some allies.

"Irritating misogynistic chutiya," Saffron muttered after him as he marched stiffly down the steps. I still not sure what a 'chutiya' is but in this context, I could guess… It's just one of a choice number of Hindi swear words I was learning to recognise. Which is proof that travel broadens the vocabulary if not the mind.

"He does seem rather hidebound and a little stiff around the collar, but he isn't a complete fool," I said to her. Though I wasn't entirely sure why I was defending him, because in all honesty, I was entirely certain Air-Kaptain Vladimir Putin was just as foolish as he appeared to be.

"The man is an utter idiot, Hannibal, lanata hei. He chose to trust you for one thing. Even that cretin should be able to see you've no more honour than a cobra," she said, the snap still in her voice.

'Lanata hei' for those interested in the study of languages translates roughly as 'fornicating in the houses of daemons', I believe. Though there is a coarser translation.

Then she barked out something else in Hindi that I didn't recognise, so probably not swear words, and my two native shadows came forward holding a set of irons between them.

"As you say, Miss Wells," I said with a degree of resignation, holding out my wrists. So that was that for the freedom of parole, though I was hardly surprised. I was reasonably sure Saffron knew all about Harry Smith. So, expecting her to trust me, well, that would be too much to ask. It's not as though I trusted myself.

As the guards locked the restraints on my wrists, Saffron smiled at me, an almost pleasant smile, just one that lacked any real regard.

"You're a twister, Hannibal. A snake in the long grass. Why my grandfather thinks you'll be of any use to us, I don't know. Any more than I understand why he trusts that damn Russian. But just so we are clear, my dear Mr Smyth, I don't trust you as far as I could have you thrown. Which at this moment is a very long way, all of it down."

Saying this she led off and we walked away from the steps following a narrow path that ran along the side of the main building. When we rounded a corner, I realised that on the other side of the path there was a drop of about three hundred feet. A neat little wall, edged that side, separating us from that vertical crevice. The wall would have been a comfort, had it not been merely a foot high and purely decretive. The path itself was very narrow.

To take my mind off that prospect, I tried to focus my thoughts on what her grandfather could possibly believe I'd be useful for. I rather hoped whatever it was, I would prove to be up to the task, or could at least convince him that I was. Not least because Miss Wells' threat about how far she could have me thrown was suddenly very clear.

Later, I was to discover that the narrow path wasn't actually the usual way to the chambers I was being led to. Indeed, it was a little used path to a less used side door. Saffron just had a quirky fondness for showing people the view the first time she took people to meet with her grandfather.

I did mention those murderous eyes, did I not?

CHAPTER 3

Call Me Gertrude...

"Sit if you please, Mr Smyth," Saffron's grandfather said, pleasantly. There was nothing in his tone to suggest it was an order or demand. Just a mere pleasantry. The kind you'd expect from one English man, of a certain class, to another.

Mr Wells had welcomed me into a room that had all the trappings of a gentleman's study. One much as you would expect to find in any Englishman's home. The walls were liberally dressed with framed photographs and pictures. The shelves, of which there were many, were full of oddities and books. High-quality leather-bound books that covered an array of subjects. Medical texts, treaties on astronomy, a study on the indigenous peoples of the Upper Volta, a book on butterflies with careful illustrations by a spinster in the Lake District and texts on engineering, all sat on walnut shelves next to bare frame wooden models of airships. There was a stuffed stoat cunningly posed to hold a tesla lamp. Some oddities under glass bell jars. A full set of the Encyclopaedia Victoria taking up three shelves. While a collection of the works of Shakespeare, Wordsworth and Coleridge lined another. A well-heaped fireplace was smouldering away steadily, with a pipe rack sat on the mantelpiece above it, next to a large carriage clock which ticked just loud enough to break any ominous silences that befell the room. Even the chair I was ushered into was good old Wentworth oak with green leather padding, the kind of chair that used to grace the smoking room of my old Gentleman's Club '*The Ins & Outs*' in Soho. It was one of a pair that were placed in front of the fireplace at the right angle to allow conversation while enjoying the warmth of the flames. Between them lay a finely crafted occasional table, with a tea tray upon it. On which sat a fine bone china pot and two cups resting on matching saucers. Alongside those were a sugar bowl and milk jug, which, if I've half an eye for things of value that are easy to fit in your pocket, were made of finest Sheffield silver.

All of this, therefore, couldn't be more out of place inside a Nepalese monastery. It was a room whose owner you would expect to find begat in Harris Tweeds rather than, as my host Mr Wells was wearing, saffron Buddhist robes. Indeed, he looked like he should be kneeling over a mandala. At least, as much as any English man ever could…

The guards, in their squid insignia uniforms, half-masked faces, and armed with those strange harpoon gun weapons I'd seen earlier were, I must admit, also a bit of a distraction. In general, most Gentlemen's studies are bereft of guards. I found it detracted from the atmosphere of gentle refinement a tad. Though as I was still wearing handcuffs, hadn't shaved, and had spent the night ostensibly sleeping rough on a mountainside, I suspect I didn't fit the ideal of gentlemanly refinement either.

All in all, considering my circumstances and his handy thugs in uniform, when I was asked to take a seat, I considered his words to be more an instruction, than a suggestion. But at least Wells was being civil about it.

So, I sat.

I half expected to find myself restrained in the chair once I'd done so. I'd been sent to find him by his enemies after all. Or at least it was the reason I'd ended up where I was. I doubt somehow even at its most conniving The Ministry had planned for how this had actually come about. Surprisingly, however, I remained restrained only by the handcuffs, though in fairness, that was more than enough.

Wells took the other seat and poured tea into each of the bone china cups.

"Milk? Sugar?" he inquired of me, his tone as even and placid as it was the first time I'd made his acquaintance him a couple of days back on The Jonah's Lament.

"Yes, and one," I replied, bemused. I'd not been sure what to expect when I was marched off to be interviewed by HG Wells, but I hadn't expected to be taking tea with the man.

Wells served us both, then leaned back into his own chair, regarding me, holding the cup handle in one hand and the saucer beneath it with the other. It struck me he was wondering what I would do next. He'd a certain air about him, perhaps that of a dispassionate scientist examining his subject. Or, perhaps more favourably, a sportsman considering how best to tackle some new challenge.

I returned his gaze evenly; if we were playing games, then I was happy enough to play along for the moment. So, I leant forward to take up my own cup and saucer. The chains on my wrists made it a more difficult task than it would otherwise have been, but I managed. I briefly considered using this as an excuse to ask for them to be removed. HG seemed to be treating me amiably enough that he might have agreed. Miss Wells, on the other hand, was still hovering nearby. Close enough to intervene if I got any wild ideas. She would've doubtless refused such a request and at that moment seemed anything but amiable towards me.

The tea, I'm glad to report, was excellent, even if drinking it proved a clumsy task involving some juggling on my part. Restricted as I was by chains I had to raise both cup and saucer together, like a child who had been told not to spill. Which was mildly embarrassing but one perseveres.

"I suspect you are wondering why it is I wished to see you, Mr Smyth," HG commented while watching me drink. He was polite enough to refrain from smirking as I did so. "You may also be wondering what exactly that eyepatch you're wearing does?" he added, almost as an afterthought.

I finished the last of the tea, maintaining what dignity I had, and sat back once more, taking a few moments to consider my answer. I ignored the former, believing it to be rhetorical. As for the other, well, that seemed obvious even to a luddite like me.

"Well, the latter I presume blocks signals to my lords and masters in The Ministry," I replied, and if he couldn't hear the bitterness in my voice, I'd have been surprised. There was a lot of bitterness. Over the last few weeks, I'd been much abused because of The 'bloody' Ministry after all.

"Indeed, Mr Smyth, you're quite correct in your surmise. As I understand these things, the device they implanted you with communicates with them from wherever it is in the world. When it does, they can see what you see, among other things. The eyepatch prevents this communication, to a degree at least. Sadly, it's a far from permanent solution. But I presume you understand why we consider it a necessity that you continue to wear it. I would prefer to not have knowledge of my location in the hands of our mutual friend 'M'."

"Of course," I replied, then added as civilly as I dared, "You've gone to some lengths to hide your activities, I would be remiss were I to endanger you. Besides I prefer the Ministry's device to remain dormant, I've no fondness for it or them all considered." Which was certainly true. They could go hang themselves for all I cared, but then so could Wells and his crew, whatever they were up to.

"I'm sure that's the case, Mr Smyth, I can see why you may feel presumed upon by them. But now... Hannibal... May I call you that by the way?" he asked, which struck me as mildly ridiculous in the circumstances. How could I object in any way that meant a damn? I was his prisoner when all was said and done. If he decided to call me Gertrude, I'd be in no position to object. But as we were playing at being gentlemen, I thought it best to play along.

"If you wish, Mr Wells. I'm sure I've no objection to informality," I replied.

"Well Hannibal, let me say you've no idea of the lengths I and my friends have gone to, to keep your masters at The Ministry in the dark regarding our intentions. It simply wouldn't do for you to place them in a position whence to scupper those plans. Rather a lot depends on them. More than they can imagine certainly, more than you could imagine too I'd venture. Even though I suspect you're a somewhat enlightened soul in some regards, certainly more enlightened than our mutual acquaintance 'M'."

"Oh, I'm sure each of us likes to think we are enlightened souls, Herbert," I replied, because two can play the name game, then I shrugged with false modesty and went on, "However, I'm but a humble airman and servant of the crown, little more."

I was being played for whatever I was worth by Herbert George Wells. He wanted something from me that much was clear. Otherwise I wouldn't be sitting in a room with him sipping tea. Not when he had perfectly good cells outside. But if he was going to play games with me, I'd be damned if I wouldn't play them in return. Besides, in this I had an advantage, I'd been playing up to being a gentleman for most of my adult life.

Wells, however, was no more fooled by me, than I was by him, and he was less able to hide it, the slightest of cynical smiles crossing his face betrayed that much, a tell that would've cost him if we were playing poker. This, however, was a different type of game, and I was far from sure of the rules, which is a problem, because if you don't know the rules it's harder to avoid getting caught when breaking them.

"Oh, my dear Hannibal, you're not as humble as you claim. Indeed, I would venture you're anything but. Do humble men escape the noose? Indeed, do humble servants of the crown face the noose in the first instance? And if so, do the likes of The Ministry take an interest in them? My dear friend 'M' is not a man known for his generosity of spirit. So, tell me what did the Ministry offer you for your part in all this? Your freedom, some rich reward, a new name and a new life perhaps?"

I laughed and found myself wondering if that was truly what Wells thought. I suspected not. I suspected he knew full well the kind of offers The Ministry made. He was still playing games with me, perhaps to discover how much I'd tell him. Yet all considered I saw no logical reason to lie. Not that I expect to be believed exactly. All I expected right then was that I'd soon be returned to my cell and left there to rot. This pleasant little tea party was just an interrogation by another name, of that I was sure.

It struck me then, Wells and the detestable 'M' had a great deal in common. More than either of them was ever likely to admit. For one thing, they were both very fond of verbose wordplay, that and turning your answers back on you. As such, I found myself wondering what else the two might have in common.

I took a moment to breathe and wished I knew by what rules this game was being played. Then I went with the simple truth. "They offered to delay my sentence, nothing more than that. Offered is stretching it some; my choices were, limited."

Wells smiled. A smile that said it knew all and understood. A smile that was genteel and mild of manner. A smile I far from trusted.

"Limited perhaps, but I am sure most inviting to a man facing the drop. Some may even say generous, considering your circumstances."

"True enough," I allowed. I could hardly disagree after all. Limited options once more, you might say.

"As you say, Hannibal, it is indeed true enough. It does, however, present me with a problem. I'm loathed to kill a man when he has been given no choice in the part he plays, but what use do I have for you? A convicted murderer with few talents of great note?" he said, as conversational as ever, which frankly I found a tad chilling. I got the impression he considered me as no more than a mayfly, unimportant, a mere inconvenience even. Yet I saw something in his eyes that suggested this was partly an act. He wanted something from me I was sure, or else why go through this charade at all, rather than throw me over that convenient cliff outside. Oh, I'm sure you are probably thinking in terms of morality, but morality is no lover of causes, and Wells was a man who believed in his cause. Unfortunately, I'd no idea what that may be.

"I am sure I could offer my aid. I must confess I have little love of the Ministry considering the position they placed me in. Or the Empire come to that. If I may be frank and use coarse language, I am one of its bastard children, condemned to serve, as I've little other choice," I told him, all of which was certainly true.

A bastard child of the Empire, it's as good a description as any. I was orphaned at ten, placed in the state's care and by luck as much as the judgment was sent to Rudgley School on a scholarship from the state orphans' fund. I was trained to serve in the Empire's armies and only my aptitude for calculating trajectories and weight to power ratios got me placed me in the naval college at Newington after Rudgley, rather than sticking a rifle in my hand for a short career as cannon fodder. I was hardly the first to tread such a path. Old Iron Bun's armed forces thrived on making soldiers out of the dispossessed. The military was always a way out of the gutters, even if that way generally led to dying in another gutter for your troubles.

"True enough, I am sure, but you're 'M's pet now in ways you don't even understand," Wells said.

I thought to protest this, but he waved a hand at me to stem any protestations.

"As I said, ways you don't know. Indeed, ways I don't know for sure myself, which is why I need your help. You are, after all, not the only one here that has been gifted with one of William Gates' toys."

The penny that had been hanging in the air so long started to drop. I glanced to my side and saw Saffron still standing there. The same eyepatch device covering her left eye as graced mine. HG's great-granddaughter as much an unwilling agent of The Ministry as myself. The implication about my value to him was suddenly obvious.

"You want to try and remove it?" I said, more statement than a question. I was to play the canary in the coal mine, it seemed. Or guinea pig in the lab perhaps would be a better analogy. Why put his granddaughter at risk when he can try prying the spider out of my eye first. I suddenly had a bad feeling about where all this was going. Which given I had nothing but bad feelings about everything to start with isn't saying much, I guess. But as experience has taught me, no matter how bad things may seem, they can always get worse. That damn spider was always going to be the death of me, one way or another, though as it happens, I wasn't entirely right in my assumption of his intent.

"In time, Hannibal, that's true if we can do so safely, but not just yet. What I have in mind is something far simpler than that. You see, I suspect you are not so much The Ministry's spy but a trap. An unwilling one, but a trap all the same. 'M' expected that you would be able to get close to me. Rightly, as you can see, for here you are. I'm not sure exactly how the trap works, but I know that's what you are. I'd like to know the nature of that trap. As such I intend to walk right into it. I'd like you to help me do so."

"I'm not sure I understand," I replied. Which was an understatement. It would be closer to say I had no idea what he was talking about. How was I a trap? More to the point, what made 'M' so certain that I'd get close to Wells? I'd never understood that part. They'd a use for Saffron, that much was clear. Using his great-granddaughter as their pawn made sense. But me? I was nothing to him, so what made me useful to them in this? How could they use me as bait when he'd no reason not to just kill me? I'll admit that the list of things that made no sense was almost endless, but at that moment that last mystery seemed at the heart of the matter.

Wells just smiled once more, that strange condescending smile, the smile of someone who knows something you don't and feels no compunction to tell you.

"I am sure you don't, Hannibal, or is it, Harry… I'm quite sure that you are an unwilling participant in 'M's schemes. 'M' is rather fond of using unwitting and disposable pawns, it's one of his faults. He has never learned to value every piece on the board equally. But perhaps I shall have a chance to explain the whys and whatnots to you in time. Though that will depend on many things, not least what happens in the next few minutes." He said, all cryptic and Machiavellian. He was more like 'M' than he realised and just as fond of playing the 'I know things about you' card. But so what? He knew my real name. But that wasn't much of a surprise. It didn't seem to be much of a secret from anyone anymore, if it ever had been.

"But as for right now, Hannibal, I'm going to ask you to remove your monticule and look directly at me…" Wells said, to my genuine surprise.

"What? But won't that mean The Ministry will be able to see, well, everything?" I asked, my surprise doubtless evident in my voice.

"Yes, I'm rather expecting they will. It will be interesting, don't you think? They may have assumed both you and my dear Saffron here are dead, with their transmissions blocked. But I suspect they are watching, and likely believe you've been turned. I'd posit therefore their first action on regaining a signal will be to use the device to try to kill you, or perhaps something unexpected and that Hannibal is what I wish to find out." He told me this with a chilling evenness to his tone.

I don't know about you, but I've never taken warmly to people who talk about my impending death without a hint of passion in their voice. Give me some enraged bastard swearing to high heaven they will have my guts for garters any day. At least enraged bastards who want to kill you care if you live or die. It's an odd distinction to make I know.

"You're serious, aren't you…?" I stated, with a certain degree of anguish. I was, I don't mind admitting, more than a little scared for my life. Which is something I'm distinctly fond of. It hadn't occurred to me The Ministry might react in such a way. Not until that moment. Suddenly though, it seemed a very real and terrifying possibility.

"Quite serious, I assure you, but I also suspect that on seeing me they'll decide not to kill you too quickly. Not if they want information, which is the question is it not? Have they aimed you at me to gain information or for something other reason?"

"You want me to risk my life because you're curious what they'll do?" I said. Trying to keep both fear and anger from my voice. I now knew Wells was no better than 'M'. A man happy to use me as a stick to poke at The Ministry just to see what they'd do. So, I was angry but more than that I was disappointed. I think I'd hoped Wells would turn out to be an idealist. God only knows why, it's not like I felt any great need to believe in something. Believing in something never gets you anywhere but an early grave.

"Yes Hannibal, but I assure you the risk will be worth it," said, like he truly believed this to be the case.

"Well, that's okay then…" I replied, retreating to sarcasm because what else was there to retreat to, when all was said and done.

A feminine hand reached over from behind me and took a hold of the monocle. I struggled on instinct while HG looked on impassively, raising my hands, only to find them dragged down by the guards as Saffron pulled the eyepiece away from my eye. My vision swam with the influx of light. A sharp pain shot through my head. My left eye seemed to explode with sensation. It felt like it was burning. My vision blurred. I screamed.

And then.

It stopped, as quickly as it started, and I found myself able to focus once more. My gaze locked on HG Wells. I wasn't sure if I'd only imagined it but I felt as if something was studying his face, looking at him with my eyes, or one of them at least.

Then more pain. The pain I remember from before. A build-up of energy that then flashed a burning image of a letter 'K' across my retina. Followed by another agonised burst which left the faltering afterglow of an 'I'. I felt anger rising within me as the pain built up and then flashed to the almost inevitable 'L'. There was more though, my pain centres were alive. Pain and an unnatural rage that followed in its wake. As the second 'L' flashed across my eye, I started to struggle against arms that clamped down on mine.

Reason fled. What was left was only anger, only rage. More letters followed, I ceased to even see them, though their meaning must have registered somehow. A seething red, burning anger became all there was. Anger, that I'd been thrown to the wolves. Anger at my masters in The Ministry, anger at the Empire, anger at the Queen, anger at the world. Anger and rage. But focused, all that pain, all that anger focused on a single point. Centred on the small mild-mannered man before me.

He was the cause of all my woes, he was the reason I was here. All my resentment, all my bitterness, all of it. It was on him. A wave of adrenaline swept through my body. Burning in my muscles, aching at my core and all I could see was the smiling face of HG Wells. All I could see was the epicentre that hatred. The devil I must destroy. Must kill. Eradicate. End.

I must've torn myself free from those restraining me. White rage fuelling strength I shouldn't have had and leapt forward. My every intent, my every fibre, crying out at me to kill the smiling bastard before me.

This was nothing like the rage I felt when I killed Hardacre. This wasn't some frantic action of self-defence. This wasn't kill or be killed. This was just rage. Pure, primal and simple. Focused entirely on HG Wells.

I would kill him and damn anyone who got in my way. Damn the Ministry. Damn Wells. Damn the bloody Queen. Damn them all and damn me too.

Nothing mattered, nothing but closing the gap between us. Putting my hands around his throat. Throttling the very life out of him. Ending him once and for all.

Those around me fought to bring me down. Hands grabbed at me and grabbed again as I kept tearing free. I roared with anger, the sound coming from deep within me. A scream of senseless animalistic rage. Anger. Hate. As intense as any I've ever felt.

More than intense, it consumed me and became all consuming.

I tore free once more. Threw myself across the gap between us. Arms outstretched. My whole being focused on ripping the life out of the man before me.

Ending him…

CHAPTER 4

The White Room

You know the drill by now. I woke, not knowing where I was and not remembering anything beyond the moment I've just described. I can't think of any reason why that would surprise you…

It didn't surprise me one bit.

When I re-joined the world, in those hazy moments between consciousness and the lack of it, I was greeted by familiar vibrations – the comforting sensations of an airship in flight. Airmen like myself are much like sailors on water-bound…

Do you get the feeling I've told you that before?

The circle of time, the wheel of life, 'All of this has happened before, all this will happen again, and no one will have learnt any damn lessons from the last time…' and all that.

But this was what happened, just as when I awoke on the Empress of India after The Ministry dumped me on a flight to the subcontinent. After that fit of insane rage, I couldn't explain, and being subdued by guards who lacked any compunction to spare the rod preventing me murdering Wells, I did indeed wake to find myself in a comforting, familiar environment. Except for being in an empty white-walled room, with a pounding headache, and wearing a straitjacket. That was a new one.

I was told once, somewhat later in life, that the worst thing you can do if you find yourself in a straitjacket is panic. If you panic, then you thrash about within it. Do that, and all you succeed in doing is making it tighter. Which, no doubt, is the point. But as I said, I was learned this later in life, and in fairness even had I known this at the time, waking up in one of those things is something that doesn't inspire much in the way of reflective thought. It's okay to tell someone they shouldn't panic, but that doesn't stop them doing just that when they wake up in a straitjacket.

So unsurprisingly, I panicked.

In fact, I thrashed about for a good few minutes, and sure enough, succeeded only in making the restraints tighter. That and bashing my head against the wall a couple of times, which didn't do anything to help with the headache.

Eventually, with that first wave of panic out of my system, I calmed down and took the safest option available to me and sat myself down against a bulkhead. There I tried to get a grip of myself and to think.

But mostly I waited, letting the comforting subtle vibrations of the airframe seep into my soul.

Then, I waited some more.

While waiting, I tried, as much as I could with my head ringing like Big Ben at noon, to figure out what had happened when they pulled off the monocle. Which, unsurprisingly, was strapped to my head once more. It wasn't until the ringing in my head started to dull down that fragments of memory started to return. When I'd made my move to murder Wells, his guards stopped trying to hold me back and started laying into me. I remembered a shock of familiar white pain. It didn't need much of a guess on my part to realise I'd been struck with charged batons. I'd had enough run ins with the Met to know what that felt like. Dear old London's police were rather fond of their Tesla truncheons when it comes to chucking out time down the old main drag. So, in fairness, it wasn't the first time in my life I'd been subject to a static charge or two, wrapped around a length of hardwood.

Clubbing me down with Tesla batons was the humane option, as I'd been raving like the Earl of Sussex on a cocaine binge at the time. Though it felt like they'd been distinctly inhumane. I was, however, still alive and given the other options that had been available to Wells guards, well, that may have been mercy, for all it was a mercy that left me feeling like I'd been beaten like a ginger stepchild.

This was why I wasn't entirely retrospective about my predicament right then. The more clarity returned to me the more I was aware of the pain in my much-abused body. There was this deep burning sensation, akin to after catching your finger on a cigarette, but it encompassed most of the right side of my chest and back. There was a smell too, the smell of burnt carbon on a Tesla coil, and now I wasn't distracted by the initial wave of panic even the slightest of movements made that pain flare up. With that pain came the memory of jarring impacts, and the crackle of discharge. I remembered a loud snapping sound that came from somewhere around my rib cage. Judging by the pain I now felt in my side, that had been the sound of a couple of my ribs breaking.

Even then, as they dragged me down, rage, anger and hate were flooding through me, and I still struggled against them all in my mad desire to get to Wells.

The last thing I remembered was HG staring down at me. A weirdly quizzical look on his face. A look of concern tinged with inquiry.

And then the world went it's all too familiar black.

But then, as I said, I wasn't overly surprised at that last occurrence. Frankly, almost everything seemed to end with me plunging into a dark state of the unconscious of late. So, the resultant blackout was to be expected.

But, everything else aside, the worst of it had been the rage. A rage I'd felt without knowing why. A rage that came from the external. From elsewhere, rather than inside me. Taking me over. Making me lose my grasp on self. Swamping me with a hate so intense I could taste it, literally, as I must've bitten my tongue at some point. I could still taste blood in my mouth. And amongst all the other pain I now felt there was this final resounding ache around my left eye. The eye now once again hidden by that strange half mechanical eye patch. The eye inhabited by something stranger still, that abominable arachnid of The Ministry's. Their spider. The thing I realised now had taken over my mind back in that room…

What was it Wells had told me? 'You're 'M's pet in ways you do not even know…' Well, I guess I knew now. They couldn't just see through my eyes. Not just send me messages with retinal burning bursts of light. No, they could take over me completely. I was just what Wells said I was, 'a trap'. Those begotten bastards in Whitehall could tamper with my mind, make me do things, fill me with that unbridled rage, make me their dog, their rabid, crazed, killer dog, and unleash me at their will.

'*Well Harry*,' I thought to myself, '*The straitjacket makes sense, cause you're down the bloody rabbit hole now.*' Either I was mad, or the damnable Ministry could turn me so at will. I would've put me in a straitjacket as well.

But there was the one question I had left, why I was still alive? I was clearly The Ministry's loaded weapon. A gun pointed right at Wells. If I was him, I wouldn't have put me in a straitjacket and thrown me on an airship. I would've thrown me off that cliff his granddaughter had walked me past earlier and had done with me.

I guess I should've been thankful that I wasn't at my own tender mercies. Though right at that moment I was struggling to be thankful for anything.

Time passed.

The gentle vibrations of the airframe lulled me towards sleep. To pass the time I pondered for a while on the question of where they were taking me, what might happen when we got wherever that was, and what would happen next.

That said, I could've hedged a reasonable guess. That strange sense of repetition was still with me. I half expected the next thing to happen would be for a maid to come knocking at the door of my cabin. Well for cabin read white-walled cell obviously, but still 'different day same knickers' as it were.

Of course, the last time the maid hadn't been a maid, but the woman I'd come to think of as my own personal 'Bad Penny'. Which, while that may not her real name, suited her all the same, after all she had a habit of turning up in my life just like one.

Of course, some reoccurrences could be said to stretch credulity, I'm sure you will agree with that. I mean what were the chances that my 'Bad Penny' would choose this, of all moments, to turn up again…

I found myself laughing at this thought. Which was when there came a sharp knock at the door, followed by the sound of a key being slid into a lock heavily. Which made me looked up just in time to see the door handle start to turn. Then the door was pushed open and through it stepped a familiar figure.

CHAPTER 5

Turning Up Like A...

"Arh, Mr Smyth. We meet again," said Captain Putin. Still bedecked in too many tassels. The latter I will admit came as no surprise.

I groaned a little at this opening line, repetitions once more, albeit not the one I'd been expecting. Though if I'm honest my visitor being Vladimir rather than my favourite 'Bad Penny' came as something of a relief. Coincidences can be stretched too far, and I'd started doubting my sanity as it was.

"Vlad old chap, good to see you. I'd offer to shake your hand but, well I seem to be a little constrained right at this moment," I said with all the false joviality as I could manage and risked a smile.

Not that I felt much like smiling, and there was every chance I looked a mite manic doing so. What with the straitjacket and everything else. However, irritating swine though Vladimir might be, I saw no great advantage in alienating him right at that moment.

In reply, Vlad laughed, in that strange half sincere way of his. A laugh that said, 'Yes, I see the humour you are exhibiting so I will laugh with you because that will put you at ease…' Whenever he laughed like that, I always found myself wondering just why he wanted to put me at ease. It also caused an odd kind of itch on my neck, around about the line of my jugular. At the time I put this down to good old-fashioned baseline paranoia. But the thing about good old-fashioned baseline paranoia is this, just because you've a tendency to believe everyone is out to get you, doesn't mean that they're not. The inner lizard brain is sometimes bang on the nail, and Putin's laugh always made me wish I was wearing a stiff high collar, preferably one made of steel. But I digress…

"I must apologise for the constraints, Mr Smyth. Komandir Wells insisted we use them until we could be certain of your state of mind after the… incident," he said, while noticeably remaining in the doorway, showing no intention of remove them, or getting too close to me. Instead he just peered at me through narrowed eyes.

"Well yes, I can see why that might be considered wise, but if you could see your way to removing them now, I would be much obliged. I've this terrible itch on my nose, and it's damn hard to scratch it in this getup."

"Of course, I would be only too delighted to do so, but tell me first, you have no homicidal thoughts, yes? No desire to attack anyone? I am told you were quiet, adamant, in your desire to do harm to our mutual… benefactor."

"I'm fully in control of myself. I assure you," I replied and tried to suppress my irritation, both with him and, if you're wondering, with my nose, which really was itching, quite damnably if I'm honest.

"Of course, of course, but you see my dilemma, yes? I am thinking it is entirely possible that this is exactly what you would say, if you were still under the influence of your Ministry... Yes?"

I took a deep breath and held my tongue for a moment. The last thing I needed right then was lash out in anger. Though the way Vlad kept leaving a pregnant pause before finishing a sentence was getting right on my nerves, which wasn't helping matters. So, I took another breath and tried to keep myself calm and measured despite the urge to punch this cretin. An urge that had nothing to do with spiders in eyes controlling minds, and a whole lot to do with Vladimir being what in polite circles is the word used only to describe hitting someone in the face, and in less polite circles has a more vulgar meaning, in reference to a ladies', well, bits.

"I assure you, Captain Putin, I'm in full control of my faculties," I said after hypothetically counting to ten. "So, if you would be quite so kind as to unstrap me from these constraints, I'd be very much obliged."

Vladimir sucked air through his teeth like a builder about to double the price of his quote. Which boded ill for my prospects, as such sucking of air always does. So, no surprise there.

"Again, that is very much what you would say if you were, in fact, they, is it not Mr Smyth? I regret I cannot in all conscience release you from your constraints until I am sure. As captain of the Sharapova, I have a responsibility to my crew. I am sure you, as an officer yourself, can understand my... position."

"Oh, for the love of Sticky Vicky's brass nipples, man. I'm perfectly fine," I vented.

"Sticky Vicky, who is this Sticky... Vicky?" he asked with what I at first assumed was genuine confusion on his part.

His eyes narrowing still further, he continued. "I must say she sounds like an interesting... girl. But your emotional attachment to her aside, I am not sure I understand what relevance they have to our... dilemma."

Now in utter fairness, such vulgar references to Her Royal and Imperial Majesty, Queen Victoria of Great Britain and its Empire, 'may the sun never set upon it', were probably not in common parlance in the Russian Air navy. But all the same, I was sure by the end of that sentence he was having me on.

"Captain Putin, will you please just get me out of this bloody straitjacket," I snarled with frustration.

"Well, now you're sounding irrational once more. I am afraid therefore I shall have to... decline."

"Oh for..." I started, what would have been an epic rant, but it was not to be.

"Release him, Vlad, I'm sure I can keep an eye on him," said a voice from beyond the open doorway. A voice which even in my state of advanced agitation I recognised. Indeed, I recognised both the voice and the sinking feeling in the pit of my stomach that voice inspired. It was a feminine voice, with a strong hint of the American about it and a voice which told me I hadn't escaped the curse of repetitions and coincidences just yet.

That's the thing about bad pennies; they just keep turning up.

"Madam, while I have been instructed to follow your directives regarding our mission, command of this craft is mine and mine alone. I shall be the one to decide if Mr Smyth remains restrained or otherwise," Vladimir responded brusquely which reminded me once more that the position of captain didn't quite fit on his much be-tasselled shoulders. No actual captain, in my experience, would ever feel the need to assert their authority so directly. Or indeed feel the need to reinforce it quite so often.

Of course, it really didn't help that my personal Bad Penny was a woman. Captain Putin, as you no doubt remember from earlier, had a problem with women giving him orders. Some men do, though I find a woman being in charge in certain circumstances quite invigorating. Particularly in certain clubs of my acquaintance down Soho.

That said, in the case of Bad Penny, my experiences with her taking charge in the past had been somewhat of a less than entertaining variety. I still had residual bruises on my head from that night in Calcutta almost two months ago, though I'd been hit on the head a few times since, which frankly didn't help. The bruises on my balls had, however, thankfully eased quite a while ago.

If I'm entirely honest, the idea of remaining locked in the white room, even trussed up like a debutant at the annual Stanstead Fetishist wine and cheese party, now held some appeal. Given the other option was Bad Penny keeping a close eye on me.

She, however, had other ideas.

"Really Captain Putin, Saffron already told me you gave Mr Smyth his parole. Are you the kind of gentleman who would revoke an agreement so readily?" she asked him. Though I'd be remiss if I didn't make passing mention of the note of condescension in her voice.

Vlad, bless his Muscovite wire wool socks, became rather stiff and straight-backed at this point, and retorted with, "Madam, he attacked Mr Wells. His parole is, therefore…"

"Oh please," not giving Vlad time to answer, "We know Hannibal was not in control of his own faculties at that moment. Do you seriously think our dear Hannibal here would be capable of attacking Wells of his own volition?" she continued, managing to be condescending to both of us in a single sentence.

"Regardless, we cannot be sure he is in control of himself at this time," Vlad insisted, irritation evident on his face, his moustache bristling as if it had a life of its own.

Penny stared up at Vlad. It was almost comical to watch, even from my position. Even though he was not a substantially tall man himself, Vlad was almost a foot taller than she was. With all his bulk, some of which I attributed to the heaviness of his greatcoat and the excess of tasselled accoutrements, he looked bigger still. Penny was petit and lean, more obviously than usual, dressed as she was in tight-fitting jodhpur trousers and a closely tailored shirt. While these clothes may not have been particularly lady-like they clung to her in ways that…

Well, I'd be more a liar than I am if I said I didn't wish that night in Calcutta had gone differently.

Logically then, Vladimir should've been the one intimidating her. But I can tell you honestly, that is exactly the opposite of what was happening.

"I have neither the time nor the inclination for this discussion, Captain Putin. That man there would no more attack our benefactor over a cup of tea while surrounded by guards than he'd charge naked into the Winter Palace yelling 'Death to the Tsar'. Hannibal is not a man to risk his life for anything other than what he holds dear, and the only thing Hannibal holds dear is his own bloody hide. So, I'm damn sure Hannibal Smyth wasn't in charge when he attacked the boss."

I couldn't disagree with her. I mean I wished I could. But she was quite right; I wasn't about to risk my life for any man's cause save my own. Still, if I had a preference, it would be to not hear that from someone else.

Vlad, trying I was sure not to take a step back from her not so looming presence, was about to disagree with her, but she cut him off with a raising of her left hand.

The mechanical one, over which she was not wearing a glove. The strange and cunning workmanship of that limb as apparent as ever. My memories of that hand, and the strange things it could do came back to me, all too sharply. The heat of the night in a Calcutta hotel room. A night shared with a beautiful young woman. Which would have been a vastly more pleasant memory I'm sure, had it not been for the razor-like blades that extended out of the fingers of that mechanical hand. Not to mention its powerful grip, which even now I find hard to think about without a twinge of phantom pain in the place no gentleman, or any other kind of man come to that, wants to feel such pain.

"So, we're clear then, as Hannibal wouldn't have attacked the boss. Not in a room surrounded by armed guards. Not outnumbered six to one. Not if he'd even a modicum of control of his own faculties. Which he plainly has now, so he can be released, correct?"

"Well, yes, but…"

"But, Captain Putin, but?"

"Yes, but…"

"But, Vladimir, but… What you need to realise right now, at this moment, right here, is this. While our good friend Hannibal here wouldn't have attacked Wells, in his own office, surrounded by armed guards, outnumbered six to one, with no logical chance of success…" she said, running roughshod over the objections he was failing to raise.

"Yes, but…"

"Yes, but, Captain Putin, I would've," she said, and he finally came up short, which was good because he was starting to sound like a steam-punt with an erratic engine with all his 'Yes, but's.

He stared at her a moment, his eyes locked on hers, as he tried to hold out against her stare, a contest he was bound to lose in my opinion, then finally he said. "You…"

"Yes, Vladimir, me," she said, a leer to her voice, her teeth all but bared at him. I could see a glisten, like light catching metal, at the end of her fingertips. I thought I was probably imagining it. For a second…

"I…" he said, uncertain of himself.

Those finger blades I was hoping I was imaging, let's just say I wasn't. And I'd a queasy reminiscence once more of my own close encounter with them. One extended out an inch or more from her finger, and she reached forward, hooking it round the nub of one of his tasselled braids.

"I indeed, but what more, what's very important in fact, and what I need you to realise, my dear Captain Putin, and why you are going to do as I instructed and release Hannibal to me, is one simple fact. Which is this. Had it been me who attacked the boss in that room then the only person who would've walked out of there alive would've been me…"

And with that she, for want of a better word, snapped her fingers, and one of Putin's tassels fell rather neatly to the floor.

The Russian's face became somewhat ashen at that point, and while I can't speak for Vladimir, if you're asking me, well I would've told you this much, I believed her…

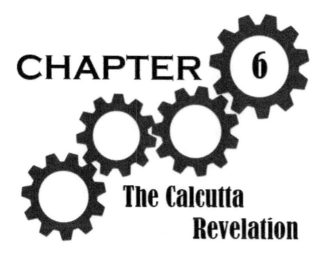

CHAPTER 6

The Calcutta Revelation

"So, you still haven't plucked it out then, Hannibal?" Bad Penny said, referring to my eye. The one languishing behind the mechanical eyepatch. Her words were full of all the nasty humour she could summon. But then Bad Penny always did have a nasty sense of humour in my experience.

The last time I'd heard her voice quoting that particular piece of biblical text to me, it hadn't gone well for me. So, despite my restored liberty, I wasn't exactly pleased to hear her quoting it again now.

We were walking the ship. Vladimir had conceded to her demands, and released me, with a modicum of grace, to the liberty of his craft. Though he told me very firmly not to interfere with the crew's business while I was aboard. Then he'd left us to it with a tad more speed than grace, claiming he'd been called to the bridge. Oddly or not as the case may be, I'd heard no tannoy announcement to that effect. I did notice he left without claiming his tassel that lay like his shame on the white room's floor.

Then my female 'companion' unfastened the straitjacket, without any messing about with buckles. Something I found just a tad unnerving, what with her finger-blades slicing through leather an eighth of an inch from my flesh.

Freed, I almost bent down to take the tassel myself, as a kind of keepsake, a trophy you might say, or if I'm entirely honest because I thought I'd show it to a few crewmen and embarrass dear old Captain Putin. He was after all an utter prig of a man and too stiff-necked by far and doubtless it would infuriate him. Passing fancy though that was, he struck me as a man worth infuriating…

"Leave it there," Bad Penny said firmly enough that I didn't even think of arguing. Then, as we were leaving, she retrieved it herself and stashed it away in one of her many pockets. I guess she liked to take the odd trophy herself. So, I found myself once more thinking back to that night in Calcutta and considered how lucky I was she didn't decide to take a trophy from me at the time, given threats I remember her making about bits of me, not just my eye either…

We walked for several minutes, through the bowels of the ship. As tour guides go, my Bad Penny was less than forthcoming. She was silent for the most part, brooding on something, I suspected. Though I'd no clue what it was at the time.

I had, it is fair to say, more than one question on my mind. Where were we headed? Why was I aboard? What were we going to do when we got there? I say we, what I meant was them.

What I was going to do when we got wherever we were going was to find a way to get off that damn airship and as far away from Wells, Putin, Bad 'bloody' Penny, The Ministry and even for that matter the otherwise delightful Saffron Wells, as I could. If I could find a nice beach with a bar that sold drinks in hollowed out coconuts, then all the better.

But somehow, I couldn't see that happening.

"So then, Hannibal, what do you think of Putin's ship?" she asked me, breaking her long silence. It was a question that took me off guard and one I suspect she didn't really care about. Her voice had an edge to it which made me suspect she'd other concerns on her mind.

Not for the first time, I found myself wondering about 'Not-Really-A-Maid', as I'd thought of her once. I still didn't know her actual name. Though I was reasonably sure it wasn't Justine Casey of the Calcutta Gazette, as I'd briefly known her for the first half what had promised to be an interesting evening in Calcutta, until it wasn't. Now I thought of her as Bad Penny, which was as good a name as any for her anyway. My own personal Bad Penny, whom like her namesake, kept turning up…

Generally, not long before I lost consciousness.

"It's a fine craft. A tad austere but it's built well. I'd hate to fight her," I said, with the utmost honesty. As I mentioned earlier, the Russian ship was a brute. A ship built for war, not beauty. Its interior was stark and utilitarian. Save for the plethora of Imperial Russian eagles which seemed to be painted everywhere, there was something depressingly grey about the interior. It was, however, built in a way my dear old mum would have described as akin to 'a brick shit-house'.

My mother had a way with words…

My comment elicited a snort of derisory laughter. It was clear she was less impressed with the ship than I. But whatever her own opinions, she kept them to herself, and we climbed down to a gantry that led to a second gun deck, which doubled as crew quarters. A line of bunks was running down the middle of the deck between four sets of heavy twin-locked half-inch cannons, on either side of the craft.

The crew were elsewhere, which meant that wherever we were going, we weren't expecting trouble, at least not right at that moment. Which at least implied we were heading to some safe harbor, which I took as a good sign.

Really, you'd think I'd know better, wouldn't you…?

I managed to risk a look through the gun ports, but I could see little other than clear skies. So, we were out of the mountains. Airships for all their wonder start to struggle at high altitudes, so they fly through mountain ranges, navigating between peeks, rather than over them. This revelation caused me to wonder how long I'd been out. At least a day, perhaps more, which explained why I felt so hungry at least. '*Sedated and bungled onto an airship again, Harry old lad, that's getting to be a bit of a habit…*' I thought bitterly, while my stomach growled.

"Is there a galley aboard this ship?" I asked, knowing there would be, but hoping she'd take the hint.

"We're going there now. Nice to see you're thinking with your guts again," she replied and I couldn't tell if I was being disparaged or not, though I suspected the former.

The galley turned out to be at the back of the lower gun deck, and all but empty. A crewman was peeling potatoes and dropping them into a large pot at the back of the kitchen. A sight so common I barely registered his presence, beyond the passing thought that if he was the chef, personal hygiene didn't lay high on the list of the chef's qualities.

"Потребность в корме." Penny said in surprisingly fluent Russian. Which, of course, I understood not at all.

The unhygienic one grunted a reply and nodded towards a pot, gurgling on the small Tesla stove at the back.

My companion shoved a less than clean bowl in my hand and pointed at the pot. Hunger did the rest, so I lifted the lid. A sickly-sweet smell and a gush of greasy steam washed over me for my trouble. What lay within I was even more uncertain about. Brownish stuff with lumps of sausage that wouldn't have passed the muster at a British breakfast table. Some horrendous continental sausage at that, of the kind they put real meat in and not enough fat. Had I been less hungry I would have shoved the lid back down in an instant.

However, Bad Penny peered over my shoulder and smiled the most genuine smile I'd ever seen cross her lips. "Solyanka, fabulous, I'll have some myself," she said with genuine relish. But, as I reminded myself, she was an American, a people who'd take any cuisine and adopt it as their own.

I watched with something akin to horror as the thick stew with gravy you could slice glopped itself into my bowl, but hunger was the deciding factor, so I grabbed the cleanest looking spoon I could find and made my way to the furthest table from the 'chef'. Not wishing to offend him if I started retching.

The food tasted better than it looked. Not that this was saying a great deal. If nothing else, it rid me of my hunger. I could go for days on a bowl of whatever that stuff was, particularly if the only option on offer was more of the same. Once the initial desire to eat had been sated, I sat back and asked her one of those questions which had been bugging me since she walked into the white room.

"Why on earth are you here? Last time we… met… was Calcutta and there you were looking for Wells. Clearly, you found him." I paused a second and remembered a previous speculation of mine. "…Or her, whichever of them it was you were looking for. But that doesn't explain why you're here, on this ship going… wherever the hell we're going?"

She smiled a smile that suggested while she knew a lot more than I did, she wasn't necessarily about to tell all. Though, in all honesty, that was hardly a surprise to me. Everyone involved in this messy affair knew more than I did and none of them seemed overly forthcoming with the bean spilling.

Still, there was something about that smile. It reminded me of someone she'd been, for a brief time at least. That delightful young woman at the hotel bar who I'd convinced to go back to my room in Calcutta. She was still that petite, blonde who was exactly the kind of woman I'd normally be pleased to find smiling in my direction.

She also had no glove on her mechanical hand, which was an all too unpleasant reminder of what occurred later that night, which was about as far from what I'd hoped for at the bar as it was possible to be. So, I reminded myself to be careful around her, no matter how much she smiled in my direction.

"Me? I'm exactly where I should be, Hannibal. Unlike yourself. If it had been up to me, I would've locked you up and thrown away the key. Or just thrown you off the side of a cliff, but the boss see something in you the rest of us don't," she told me, still smiling. I noted though, beyond her obvious disparity of my good self, she'd an edge of distaste for old HG in her voice. I remembered it from that night in Calcutta. The same slightly disparaging tone she always used, no matter which man she was speaking of. Yet saying that, the edge to her voice was still different when it came to him. A respectful distaste perhaps.

"Still you've your uses, unlikely as they may be. I suspect he thinks you'll be of use again like you were in Calcutta," she added between spoons full of the stew.

I'd pushed my own bowl away by this point. Russian cuisine wasn't entirely to my taste, I have to say, and an empty stomach will only take your taste buds so far.

I was also playing catch up with the conversation. For a start, I couldn't think what use I'd been to anyone in Calcutta; I'd known even less then than I did now, hadn't I? Certainly, I'd had nothing useful to tell her in our cozy little conversation at my bedside, or if we call it by what it was, my interrogation. Yet what I recalled of that conversation didn't seem to add up, not if she was working for Wells all along. Unless she'd some other reason for waylaying me in my hotel room, threatening me, torturing me, and generally abusing me in ways unbefitting for the bedchamber.

Well, at least a non-consensual bedchamber…

I looked into her ever hard unforgiving eyes and saw humour in them. Dark gallows humour, but humour all the same. Clearly, she knew something I didn't. But then, of course, she knew a lot of things I didn't. She knew… and then it struck me, and that inner voice of mine started disparaging me all on its own.

'*Oh Harry, how did you miss that…?*'

"You knew…" I said to her. A statement not a question. I'd missed the obvious. I wasn't even sure why I was surprised. I was, after all, no more than a pawn, caught up in a game being played by others. It should hardly have been a revelation and if that sounds self-pitying, that's because it is. I was sick to my back teeth of being that pawn. Sick of being trapped in a game, without even been allowed to sneak a peek at the rulebook. Sick of no one being willing to tell me what was going on. I didn't know why the Ministry had chosen me to be their bloody catspaw in the first place. Come to that, old 'Not-Actually-A-Maid' was right, it made no sense for Wells to let me roam free. Even if free, in this case, was aboard an ex-Russian Airship, captained by a be-tasseled idiot like Putin. I'd tried to kill him, Wells that is, even if I hadn't been in my right mind at the time. Why the hell was I on this airship and not locked in the deepest darkest cell Wells had at his disposal?

"Of course, we knew," she said, making no attempt not to sound smug about it. "We knew The Ministry had set you as a trap for HG. We knew about that thing in your eye. We knew you were being watched. We knew everything."

"But you, I mean, all that stuff you said, you, were only concerned with Saffron in Calcutta…" replied, my mind racing back to that night and everything she'd said at the time.

A flash of anger crossed her face fleetingly. "Oh, we knew very well where The Ministry had Saffron, and what they had done to her. And it's Miss Wells to a shite like you. You haven't earned the right to be so familiar as to use her first name," she snapped and for a second that anger in her face became a look of near madness. Then, as quick as it had been lost, she recovered her composure. But I remembered how she'd had that same look in Calcutta when I mentioned Saffron's name. There was something more between them, something she wasn't telling, and of that I was sure. More between them than a man of average sensibilities might expect. Luckily for me, my sensibilities aren't entirely… average. As such I could hazard a fair guess as to what that something was. So, it struck me that I wasn't the only one who found Saffron Wells somewhat alluring.

For a fleeting second, I considered the two of them, well, together, to put it delicately. Mildly voyeuristic though the thought may be, it wasn't an unpleasant thought all told. Which led me to wondering if Saffron returned my Bad Penny's affections.

I also found myself wondering what appeal the psychopathic American could possibly hold for an Asian beauty like Miss Wells. Oddly, at the time, it didn't cross my mind how attractive I myself found Bad Penny when she smiled. Though that was perhaps because that smile which had been so winning on Justine Casey's face remained mildly terrifying on her alter-ego's.

In a moment she was smiling at me again, her anger passed over as if it had never been there, though there was still malice enough in her words.

"You know, now I think on it, I should be thanking you, Hannibal. You played your role so well that night in Calcutta…" she said, though it didn't sound entirely genuine as thanks go to me.

"My role… role… As I recall it you tied me to a bed and tortured me," I said, my own anger coming to the fore.

"Only a little, and what's a little torture between allies. Besides, Hannibal, you strike me as a man who normally enjoys that kind of thing…" she said and her smile turned impish, which was disturbing, in a couple of ways.

"What do you mean allies?" I asked, though it was more an angry snap than a question. In part, I was riled up because I didn't appreciate what she was implying, no matter how accurate those implications may be. Regardless of what a man might enjoy out of a spirit of adventurous laissez-faire, doesn't excuse what she did to me in that hotel room. But there was more to my anger than that. I may be a tad slow on occasion, but I was catching on, and I hate being played for a fool despite everything you've heard. Worse than all that, my own little Bad Penny was now looking at me with pity in her eyes. No one wants to be pitied, and least of all by an enemy. Staring back at her, my anger contained behind a quivering moustache, I looked at the pity I saw in her eyes and hated myself for it. There was no small victory to be had in those eyes, just wretched defeat.

"Haven't you worked it out yet?" she said, the pity in her voice mixed with that same nasty humour she always had.

"My, my, you're dimmer than you look, Smyth, which is quite an achievement in your case."

"I assure you that I'm not…" I retorted with venom.

Yes, I know exactly what stupid a thing to say that was, thank you. If I were trying to disprove my foolishness, I was doing a clown's job of it. But I was somewhat flustered, and all things considered I believe I can be forgiven. By myself, if not by you.

Penny, however, just laughed at me, that same oddly musical throaty laugh I remembered from the bar of that Calcutta Hotel.

She gave me a withering look.

"Really, Hannibal. Read my lips, darling, why don't you? Your masters most certainly did, bless their ridged bureaucratic stupidity. The fact is, that is exactly what we were banking on…" she said grinning at me once more.

The penny, if you will excuse the phrase, which had hanging in the air so long it had started to rust, dropped.

Quite heavily in fact.

You should take it from me, no one likes to be a pawn in someone else's game, and God knows that had been my lot of late. But finding out just how much you'd been used is far worse. Further to that, if I'm painfully honest with myself and indeed you, due to a little residual chauvinism on my part which says nothing good about me, I found the idea that I'd been used by a woman somehow all the worse.

I'd known the moment I'd come round tied to the bed in my hotel room that I was being toyed with. Set up by that oldest and most cynical of ploys 'the honey trap' as the scandal sheets of Fleet Street would have referred to it. But I'd known why, I'd been sure I knew why. Hell, I'd been tortured for that very reason… Discovering now that my torture had been no more than another ploy… That I'd been threatened and toyed with not, as I assumed, for information I didn't have but as a distraction. Just to pull the wool over The Ministry's eyes… That, in actuality, everything she'd put me through had been merely incidental… As I added it all up, I felt all the worse, all the more ill-treated, and all the more angry about it.

"It was all a show, all of it, everything you said, everything you asked me, everything you did to me. It was all for them, wasn't it? All for The Ministry's benefit…" It wasn't a question. It didn't need to be, I could see it in her face. What I couldn't see, not even in the slightest, was any hint of remorse. Instead, she just laughed once more.

"Of course, it was. What? Did you think I was some bargain basement antagonist from a dime novel? Do you think I was there blabbing all my secrets to the hero while I had him under duress? Is that who you think you are Hannibal? The hero, in some cheap pulp paperback? The man of daring-do, the man who faces down the odds, the man who saves the world?"

She laughed again, and there was more than a little sneer to her tone as she continued…

"Let me guess. I bet you even see yourself as the one who gets the girl in the end, am I right? Is that it? It is, isn't it? Really Hannibal, because if it is, you're deluding yourself. Because, my dearest darling Mr Smyth, I have to tell you, you're not so much daring-do. What you are, Hannibal, is more daring-don't."

I'd say her words were humbling, but I felt more angered than humbled.

"I would've never presumed such…" I started indignantly, but she waved off my ineffectual defense before it even got started.

"Oh, spare me, Hannibal. Of course, you did. Every man I've ever met harbors that bloody fantasy. They all believe they're the hero of their own story. All of you, men, you can't help yourselves. So, I guess I can't say you're any more to blame than the rest of them. The world is always selling you that lie, telling you that men are the heroes, the dashing protagonists, the gallant rogues, the stalwart brave defenders and all that other twaddle. You're all raised on toy soldiers and boys' own adventures. Force-fed the idiotic propaganda of the superiority of your gender from birth. Raised to believe you're all going to be the heroes you worship as children. You're buffoons, the lot of you. Sad little men, leading sad little lives, and all the while convinced us mere ladies just swoon at the thought of you. All dressed up in your neat, pressed uniforms, all gold braiding and polished brass buttons…"

I coughed. Loudly. Hoping to interrupt her bitter tirade. And it was bitter, not only in inception, but it was also bitter to swallow because it cut to the bone of things just a little too sharply.

She laughed again, which was at least a pause for breath. But then continued… "So yes, it was all a show, Smyth. All a piece of theatre for the audience behind your eye. So not even a show for you, my precious little Hannibal. You were just the medium, incidental, just a means to an end. Tormenting you was no more than a shadow play for your masters," she said, holding up her hand and pretending to inspect something on her fingernails as they slid out from under her metal skin and I found myself recalling, all too well, how sharp those nails were. "Though I'm not saying I didn't enjoy it…"

I narrowed my eyes at this last revelation. But she just smirked at me once more, though her expression did soften slightly. Perhaps she even found a momentary modicum of sympathy for yours truly, but if so, her sympathies were seldom of the lasting kind, as I've found.

She took a deliberate breath, and frowned at me for a moment, then sighed and explained some more.

"We needed a distraction. And you, well, you were what we had to work with. But I'll give you your due, you played your part perfectly," she said, and grinned, raising her forearm to her forehead and pretended to faint. "You may be no hero, Hannibal, but you do make a damn good damsel in distress. I'll give you that much. My dear Mr Smyth, my damsel, oh how you squirmed. We couldn't have planned it better; you really played the part perfectly. Your idiotic Ministry lapped it up and did exactly what we wanted them to do. Sent all their foul little Sleepmen scurrying through the night. Scurrying to defend their poor damsel against the machinations of the evil villainess…"

She curtseyed as she said the last. A nod to her performance in the role of the villain no doubt. I must vouch I saw more than a little smugness in her eye.

As for me, well, the penny which had dropped earlier was now joined by so many of its fellows. A veritable golden shower of them, and not of the kind so popular within certain quarters of the upper classes.

"Saffron, it was all about Saffron, wasn't it? That's how she got away from them. That was the plan all along, use me to free Miss Wells…" I muttered bitterly.

She shrugged at me and smiled a smile which looked for all the world to be full of innocence. In the same way a viper looks innocent just after it bites you.

"Well, Hannibal, the bastards only had so many of their pet poison apes in Calcutta. And you. Well, for reasons which frankly escape me, you were important enough to them for them to send them all. Of course, it helped that Saffron was so obviously asleep in her rooms…"

"And once they were busy 'saving' me?"

"She escaped The Ministry's clutches, yes. She just kept one eye closed and walked out of her prison. Well, the royal suite at the Benson Calcutta, if we are telling true. But prison is a prison even if it has silk sheets and silver teapots. Then she met up with our people and took to wearing a neural interlace patch like the one you're wearing now."

"How long had you been planning this?" I asked with a sneaking suspicion it had been back before I first encountered Bad Penny, masquerading as the maid she most definitely wasn't. The first time she had pistol-whipped me out cold.

Her eyes narrowed, and she had the temerity to wink at me. Then she smiled again.

"I led those foggy fuckers a merry chase through the back streets. Persistent bastards they are. I even cut one of them a few times in the process. Not that it slowed them much. Do you know they don't bleed…? Strange isn't it; most everything bleeds if you cut it but not them. Not blood anyway." The last was said with a tinge of doubt that flittered across her face.

Then for no reason that made any sense, she smiled at me again, blew me a kiss from her metal palm and said, "Still, this has been fun, but I've some real work to do. Perhaps we will finish what we started in Calcutta sometime, Harry Smith… But if not, for the moment at least you're at liberty onboard ship. Try and stay out of trouble, why don't you. You can bunk down with the crew. Keep out of the way and don't go looking where you shouldn't. We've another use for you. So it would be a shame to have to kill you and change our plans."

"And where shouldn't I go looking?"

"Oh, I'm sure we will let you know, the moment you poke your nose where you shouldn't. Or maybe just throw you overboard. Anyway, ta-ta now."

And with that last unveiled threat she turned and skipped off towards the bulkhead doors. I stared after her for a while, trying to get a handle on everything, with scant success.

Sure, somethings made a little more sense now, how Saffron Wells had freed herself of The Ministry watchmen for one. What had really happened in Calcutta for another. But where I was being taken now, what they wanted me to do and even why Wells' people had taken The Jonah's Lament, not so much. I suspected I was still being played. By Wells and his cohorts, as much as by The Ministry. I was being played by both sides. I'd been thinking of myself as a pawn in a game of chess. I'd got that all wrong. I wasn't a pawn, pawns only work for one side. Pawns are only moved by their owners until, that is, they are sacrificed or taken.

But no, I wasn't a pawn at all. I was being played by both sides at once. By two teams locked in a struggle. Locked in a bitter grudge match. Punching, scrumming and rucking away at each other. While I? What was I? I was the bloody rugby ball… And the ball gets carried into the heart of the ruck. The ball gets thrown from one side of the field to the other. Passed about, roughly handled, leapt upon and is always the focus of all the aggression on the field.

The ball, to put it bluntly, that gets kicked and kicked hard, from pillar to post.

The realisation of this weighed heavy, and I realised one thing over everything else. If I was the ball, I was going to keep being kicked about until the game was over.

If I was lucky.

Because every now and again in a rugby match, a ball gets bust, and then they just call for a new one. You see, the ball doesn't matter, the ball is just the thing the teams fight over, and they can always get another ball.

I was the ball, not the hero. Just the ball. Just a sack of air wrapped in pigskin. Nothing more.

It was hard not to feel a tad deflated about that.

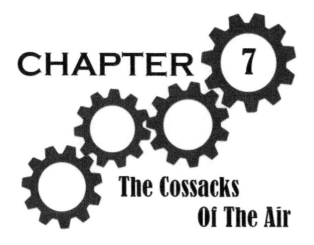

CHAPTER 7

The Cossacks Of The Air

I needed a drink. Several in fact, which was a problem because one thing that military airships tend to lack is a lounge bar. For some reason, the designers of war machines like the Sharapova seemed to believe having an airship full of munitions, guns and the occasional bomb or two dozen didn't require facilities to enable their crews to get inebriated.

I have always considered this to be a failing on the part of the designers, for a couple of reasons.

Firstly, because if there was a bar then at least you would know where all the drunks were. And secondly, because it showed a complete lack of understanding about one of the fundamental truths of the universe on the part of the designers. Also, it was clear evidence that the men with draftsmen's ink all over their fingers and Babbage contemplative engines at their disposable, never spent any time with an actual engineering crew before designing an airship. Which was foolish because the engineering crews had to keep the damn things in the air once they'd been built, so any half competent chief engineer knows more about good airship design than your average designer. You see you can learn a lot about what makes for good designs when you spend all your time fixing bad ones.

Had airship designers spent time with an engineering crew, they would've learned that using a dozen different size nut heads on the same bulkhead was a nightmare when it came to repairs, particularly when straightforward 5/8ths nuts would've been fine for almost every job, if 5/8ths bolts were used. Likewise, having seven utterly incompatible air compression valve units with dozens of different fittings on the buoyancy systems made them a nightmare to maintain. And any chief spanner would have told you any one fitting type would've worked perfectly well for all of them. As for the fussuck manipulator on the cross-bearing shaft drive... Well, I'm sure I don't need to tell you what a foolish piece of design that is, which is good because I've sod all idea what any of that means. I'm a gun-deck officer, for God's sake. I've less idea how everything goes together on an airship that I have about cross-wire corsets, and a damn sight less interest. That's what engineering crews are for. But that utter lack of understanding on my part does, I'd venture, suggest I'm fully qualified to design airships.

Had I been a military airship designer I would however definitely add a bar. Because unlike the actual designers I'd spent a good deal of time around engineering crews and I knew one, very salient fact, indeed that fundamental truth I mentioned earlier, about them. If you give any engineer access to a few yards of copper piping, a method of supplying heat, like say an engine room's boiler, and any form of cylinder, you might as well just have added a bar to begin with. With the added bonus that if you're selling the crew real gin, they are less likely to go blind.

I suspected that Russian military airship designers were probably no better at their job than British ones. So, having found a spare bunk, I decided to go in search of some Russian engineers — men who could be relied upon to be hoarding homemade vodka, even if it was made from two-parts engine coolant and one-part servo de-icing fluid. Besides engineers in my experience tend to be more welcoming of a junior office than you'd perhaps suspect. Providing, that is, he was willing to join them for a drink, and brings a pack of cards with him, along with his wallet.

I didn't have any cards, but I did still have some rupees in my wallet surprisingly. Here, aboard the Sharapova, I also wasn't an officer. But I suspected that wouldn't matter a great deal, as I knew how to drink steadily, while looking drunk and gullible, and of course I know when to lose a hand or two on purpose.

It didn't take me long to find the main engine room, where the quartet on shift unsurprisingly already had a card school going. They were playing some Russian version of poker while drinking from small dirty glasses, smeared by greasy fingers. I noticed, just as they offered me a stool and a drink, in broken English, which was a damn sight better than my Russian, that when they overfilled the shot glasses, the 'vodka' would dissolve away the grease and produce fumes that were slightly purple. So, it was definitely what my old gun crew would've called 'the good stuff' and any doctor worth their salt would've called poison. But if you can't get a single malt, while it may strip away your stomach lining, it will do the job.

It wasn't until my second glass of gut rot that I started to wonder exactly what my friend 'Never-Was-A-Maid' had meant by 'finish what we started in Calcutta'. Was she implying my torture, my murder, or a night of passionate guilt-free sex?

I wasn't sure which prospect scared me most.

Remembering why I was down in the engine room; I downed the shot. Several brain cells may have died in the process. Then I accepted the hand of cards I was offered and smiled as they poured me another.

I'd other reasons, besides a desire to marinade some brain cells out of existence, for seeking out the engineers and the almost inevitable card game in the engine room. I was, to be frank, sick of being a punching bag. Royally sick, and about as amused by the situation I'd found myself in as old Queen Brass Knockers herself famously isn't most of the time. The conversation with my Bad Penny had been the straw that broke that particular steam-camel's back. But there was one thing as sure as a Soho 'actress' isn't making a living reciting Shakespeare, I wasn't going to get anywhere by sulking about it. In short, I found a modicum of resolve and decided if I was an agent of the British Crown, I should start acting like it. If only in order to navigate my way to some semblance of safety. In short, I needed information.

Obviously, I needed to know where we were going and what the hell we would be doing when we got there? But that could wait if it had to, besides there was damn all I could do about any of that. But what I could do was find out more about those in whose company I'd found myself, and if you want to know about the captain of an airship, you don't ask the captain. Not if you really want to know about them. If you want to know all the dirty little secrets and know who the captain really is, talk to the engineers. Hence, I'd headed to the engine room, with a wallet of money I didn't mind losing and a pack of cards.

Besides, as I said, I needed a drink…

So that was why I found myself sat in the engine room contemplating a hand of Russian cards, which were close enough to a British deck that I could work out I'd a lousy hand and had been dealt two cards from the bottom of the deck.

They weren't cheating, I should say, at least not within the definition of the word for enlisted men playing cards with an officer who was drinking their hooch. Engine room rules are clear on that score. An officer has to accept he is going to be fleeced a little early on. Just because its expected, part of the unwritten charter of military life. It's all to do with the 'esprit de core'. The crewmen know they can't cheat officers too much as they could end up on a charge. But officers are obliged to lose a couple of hands at least, just for the look of the thing. Officers shouldn't mix with the ranks after all. Even if you're not really an officer, and they ain't your crew. But as long as you're drinking their hooch and losing a little cash, well, they could tell their mates they were fleecing you, and everyone was happy.

Besides which, winning wasn't the point. What I wanted was information. Not for The Ministry, not for the crown, nor for honour for that matter. I wanted information because I preferred my neck to remain attached to my shoulders and needed all the leverage I could use to keep it that way, and if there is one thing engineers like more than hooch and cards, it's gossip.

Over the next hour or two, I learned rather a lot about dear old Captain Vlad and his crew. For one thing, Vlad hadn't always been captain of The Sharapova, which confirmed my suspicions. Until recently Vladimir had been no more than a junior gunnery officer. Much like myself in fact. Though Yuri, the most talkative of my new friends, said Putin had been a gunnery officer second class. So, I reasoned with a sly smile, I'd actually outranked the idiot in back in my old RAN days.

That little snippet I filed away because you never know when you might need something to throw in someone's face. Beside, I'd been short on small victories for a while now. But there were more interesting little nuggets to learn than this.

The Sharapova's crew, for example, were mostly not actual Russians, but Ukrainian conscripts. Before his little coup, one of Vladimir's jobs aboard The Grunt, as the ship was oddly nicknamed by those who served aboard her, was the task of making real airmen out of new conscripts. You know the kind of thing, weeding out the untrustworthy and incompetent. Making sure those who remained would obey orders and flag up those best transferred to 'guard duties' at a Siberian salt mine. It was the kind of job senior officers palm off to their subordinates all the time, but in this case, doing so had proved to be a mistake.

Vladimir had indeed identified the untrustworthy. Or at least the ones who could be trusted not to care much about duty and honour if there was a better payday on the horizon. Having found the mercenary malcontents among the new recruits, he set about buying them, one way or another. As part of his job was to assign the recruits to various roles, Vlad set about stationing his bought men in prime positions. Building a core of loyalty among the crew, but loyal to himself rather than the ship's original captain. It was impressive, I have to say. He must've been planning to turn pirate for years and had the patience to see his plan through. Not that he'd call himself a pirate, neither did his crew. They were freebooters. Freedom fighters for hire. Mercenaries. Airmen of fortune or whatever they wished to claim. But it didn't matter what they called themselves; they were still pirates at the end of the day.

I found all this refreshing if I am honest. I expected a crew loyal to Wells and whatever mad plans he was setting in motion. Men of ideals, foolish, idiotic ideals, but ideals all the same. Instead, I discovered they were just a bunch of common criminals. Men only loyal to their pockets and to whoever who was filling them. Now that was something I could understand. But more importantly, that was something I could work with.

How Vladimir had bought their loyalty, I couldn't be sure but they'd plenty of vodka for a start and not just the engine room hooch variety they were pouring for me. They had a couple of cases of the real stuff half hidden under a tarp at the back of the engine room. I spotted it easily enough because one develops a nose for contraband when one engages in a little light smuggling on the royal docket. I suspect they were keeping hold of those bottles for trading, besides they had plenty of hooch and like most engineers they had long developed a taste for the homemade paint stripper they fermented. They were also playing cards with far more rubles than you'd expect to be floating around an engineering deck. So, they were bought men all.

After losing a little cash, for the form of the thing, I started to turn it around a bit and before long I was ahead. They were still cheating, but I was a better cheat, though I threw more than one winning hand. I wasn't fool enough to fleece the survivors of a crew gutted of loyalists and officers they despised. I'd no doubt, as amiable as Yuri and his compatriots appeared, if I started winning too much, they would've had little compunction against gutting me. After all, what's another dead officer to a pirate?

The threat of becoming an accident aside, the cards and the vodka were a good distraction. And I was learning more about Captain Putin, which could only be useful. He may have bought their loyalty, but he was a way off having their respect. Yuri, in particular, seemed to think little of the man. But that's engineers for you, they seldom have high opinions of those who prance about giving them orders.

Engineers tend to be practical men. Yuri was typical of the breed.

Sometime later, and reeling slightly from the vodka, I was walking back to the sleeping quarters with my new friend. Yuri was singing some bawdy song about Peter the Great, which I suspect was not entirely historically accurate. At the same time, I was learning all sorts of new Russian words which probably couldn't have been used in polite Moscow society. Then, when we stepped through a bulkhead door into another long gantry corridor, and I found myself staring into the nostrils of a large black horse.

This came as quite a shock as you can imagine. If there is one thing you don't expect to come across in a corridor on an airship, it's a horse. No matter how much vodka you've been drinking…

I staggered back into Yuri who to my surprise seemed utterly nonplussed about this turn of events. Indeed, he just smiled broadly, muttered something in Russia and started fiddling around in the pockets of his overalls.

"Aha!" he said after a few moments and pulled a small dirty looking apple from the recesses of his pocket, patted the horse with a modicum of affection, then offered up the apple from his hand. The horse for its part didn't seem to mind the oil that caked the apple skin and took it in one bite and whinnied with appreciation. Myself I clung to the side wall of the corridor. I'd never been a huge fan of horses. Not since the days of my misspent youth. The Peelers were too fond of using them for the occasional bit of riot control. I'd seen one too many people come off the worse to a horse's hoof raised in anger. To be honest, the damn things terrified me, and that was when they were out in a comparatively roomy East End street. The beast was somewhat more terrifying right then in the tight confines of an airship service gantry.

Yuri was too busy horse whispering, loudly in Russian, to notice my discomfort. So I collected myself as quickly as I could and was about to ask what I considered to be the pertinent question, '*What the holy hell is a horse doing in here?*' when a trio of crewmen ran into the corridor shouting at each other with more of those Russian words that weren't used in polite Moscow society.

Yuri laughed loudly at the three of them, shaking his head. Behaving like this was street theatre laid on for our entertainment. Then he waved me to follow him and led me back through the bulkhead door.

"We go another way, English," he said, still fighting the laughter the trio of horse wranglers had inspired. I followed quickly enough and found myself laughing along with him, though more with relief than straightforward humour.

"Why a horse?" I asked, passingly aware that wasn't the most coherent of questions. Yuri laughed again at this, probably because I was slurring my words a little. Then he took me through another hatchway and down a set of stairs into the bowels of the ship.

"Is the Captain's, he likes to go riding," he said, after a minute or so, as if that explained anything. The befuddled look I gave him must've been more coherent than any words I could manage. Smiling some more, he motioned me to sit on a convenient bit of piping that ran the length of the new corridor we were traversing. Patted me matily on the shoulder, and grinned.

"He thinks he is a great Cossack," he told me. "He rides each morning for an hour, like man of the steppes. Bare-chested, no shirt, just man on horse, 'tis a great thing, yar? To be a Cossack. So, he buys horse and ride each day. Brings horse with him whenever we travel, it is, how you say, 'his way'."

Yuri's face said much to my eyes. He was a plain and simple man. A typical salt of the earth engineer in fact. I could tell he found the whole idea ridiculous, though he didn't come straight out and say that.

I knew little about Russian history but knew enough to know the Cossacks had a great military tradition stretching back generations. They remained favourites of the Tsars, so had a certain standing in Russia. They'd stood firmly with the crown when it faced down the ill-fated Marxists a century ago, and the Tsars had long memories. But more than that, the Cossacks had a mystique about them, even for westerners like me. I guess they're somewhat akin to the Highland clans in Scotland. Warriors of a past age still harkened back to with the mist-dewed eyes of nostalgia. I've lost count of the Scottish airmen I'd met in my service years that claimed to be descended from men who stood with 'Bonnie wee Charlie' or fought alongside 'William Bloody Wallace and The Bruce'. Highland heroes romanticised even in defeat. The Russians romanticised the Cossacks in much the same way. They're the paradigms of warrior manliness to them. So, with what I know of Vladimir I could see why they held such appeal to him. It's exactly the kind of thing he would want people to think of him, and he was not a man to let reality get in the way of self-image. Of course, it was always possible he was descended from Cossack stock. But I doubted it somehow.

As an aside, if I may offer some advice to you, dear reader. When drinking with a bunch of Scotsmen who tell you their clan fought with 'The Bruce' while full of dewy-eyed, whisky inspired, nostalgia in a Soho bar at two in the morning, it is wise not to point out that Bonnie Prince Charlie was a fop from the French court, William Wallace was a brutish thug and Robert 'The Bruce' betrayed Wallace and half the clans to the English. Then later betrayed the English when he'd a chance. So he was a backstabbing turncoat twice over. Because that's a good way to end up in a cell in Charring Cross nick with two black eyes and a desire never to have a close encounter with a sporran again. But I digress.

"And is he?" I seem to remember asking my drinking companion. Who was, not unlike myself, a little worse for wear at the time or he probably wouldn't have been quite so candid with me.

"Is who what?" Yuri asked, taking a swig from the bottle of engine room vodka he was still carrying, before handing the bottle to me, having obligingly wiped its neck with an oily rag.

"Is Captain Putin a Cossack?" I asked and drank another mouthful of hooch.

Yuri laughed again, taking the bottle back and grinning. Then spat on the floor with a surprising amount of venom, and the look on his face turned to one of distaste.

"Nar, he's just another stinking Muscovite shithole like the last captain," he told me and spat again, then a thought struck him that brightened his mood. He raised a finger in the air and added with a smile, "But, he gives us good vodka."

I thought about this for a moment, while I tried to ignore the lurching feeling in my stomach and contemplated the odds of holding my stomach if I drank any more. My eyes struggled to focus on the unlabelled bottle of clear liquid which could've been used as a detergent for stripping stump oil or cleaning propeller blades. Indeed, that probably was at one time. But now masquerading as vodka due to its high alcohol content. As such I found myself considering the question this latest revelation had brought to mind.

"Then why are we drinking this shit?"

Yuri just grinned at me, tilted his head and gave me a couple of little nods of understanding, which suggested my face was as green as I felt right at that moment.

"We wanted to see how long you would last," Yuri replied. Then his grin grew broader and he handed the bottle back to me. "I've had fifteen shots, English. You have fallen behind, drink some more…"

At which point the ship lurched due to turbulence, as airships occasionally do, and that lurch was all it took.

Let's just say you can add paint stripper to the many fold uses of engineering vodka, as I left a puddle of dissolving paint sliding down the wall behind me…

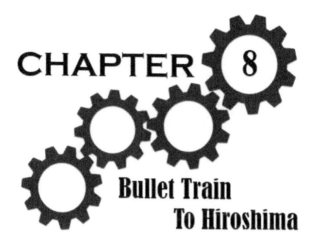

CHAPTER 8

Bullet Train To Hiroshima

In years to come, the Hiroshima bullet train would become famous for several reasons. Not least the audacity and cynical nature of the plan that put the train in motion in the first place.

It was, so students of recent Far Eastern history will doubtless inform you, the tipping point in the Nippon-Chino war, the point at which the Japanese turned the tide on the invaders and ceased retreating. It'd take three more years for the Brass Shogun to lead the Emperor's forces to final victory and drive the invaders back into the East China Sea. But it was the Hiroshima bullet train, a singular act of true belligerence, which forced China to accept just how far the Japanese would go to regain sovereignty of their islands. More to the point, it showed just how much the Japanese were prepared to sacrifice to that aim, regardless of the cost in lives. Be those lives Chinese, or their own people.

Before the war, Japan had achieved some little fame for its bullet trains. Tesla piles rather than steam to drove their locomotives, and the oddly shaped trains reached speeds unheard of elsewhere in the world, so they held a certain mystique. But it was this act, this most literal interpretation of their name, which made Japanese bullet trains infamous in the years after the Hiroshima incident.

The train followed pre-war tracks from Nagoya, a city still held by imperial forces. It passed through the Chinese-held Kyoto and Okayama provinces at full tilt and sped right into Hiroshima, and you probably know the rest.

It was an audacious plan. So much could've gone wrong. Three hundred kilometres of track, whatever that is in miles, Manchester to London I'd guess, perhaps further. All of it hostile territory but travelling so fast there was little the Chinese could have done; even had they realised the danger it represented. Had they, and had they put anything across those tracks to derail it they would've changed history.

They didn't.

In fact, they moved engines out of the way, believing this was nothing more than a runaway train. They tried to make points change, but as soon as the tracks were cleared, the points had reset by fifth columnists within the occupied zones, and the bullet train to Hiroshima had sped on.

It sped on until it met its target, the train station in Hiroshima, which was alongside the biggest aerodrome in southwestern Japan. Dozens of Chinese airships were at port. Tens of thousands of troops. God knows how many crates of munitions, fuel, who knew what else. It was the central supply port for the whole Chinese campaign and thought safe from air attack due to the sheer number of defences in place. That and a small matter of the quarter million Japanese civilians who still lived in the city itself. Besides, they knew an air attack of any note was beyond Japanese capabilities. Their fleet was in tatters, negotiations with the Russians for new craft were still falling on deaf ears.

All that changed after Hiroshima, for the Russians knew then which way the wind was blowing.

The Chinese didn't expect an attack by rail. No one would expect an attack by rail. Just as no one would expect to find themselves witnessing an ancient Japanese rite being practised by two train drivers before the Brass Shogun himself on a late spring morning. A rite also witnessed, among others, by a Russian airship pirate, a young American woman who was definitely not a maid, and an agent of a shadowy British Ministry, nursing a bad Saki inspired hangover. His third in as many days.

I look back now on said ancient Japanese rite. The solemnness with which it was practised. The way they tied the strips of cloth embossed with a large red dot representing the sun, around their heads. The way they knelt and accepted bowls of rice wine, handed to them by a Shinto priest waving fans of incense sticks around them as they drank. The way the whole thing was an act of grace and sanctity in the eyes of their countrymen. I can't help thinking I should perhaps have shown a tad more decorum. As it was, I felt ill and was fighting the urge to find a bush to vomit behind.

In fairness to myself, I'd no idea what was going on. Ancient Japanese rites were surprisingly low on the curriculum at Rudgley School For Boys. My old alma mater didn't go in for comparative culture and quasi-religious practices of the Far East. It was considered far more relevant to teach us to hold a square bat against a fast bowler and to learn to face a nasty googly when you had to.

Looking back, had I known exactly what was being planned, what indeed the bullet train to Hiroshima was, I'd like to think I'd have shown due reverence to the whole affair, no matter how much my stomach was churning from rice wine.

I'd also say this…

Had I know what was going to happen when that train arrived in Hiroshima, I'd not have, under any circumstances, set foot aboard that damn train…

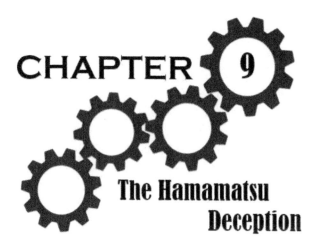

CHAPTER 9

The Hamamatsu Deception

I got ahead of myself back there, I know. I'd apologise, but one must build a little tension in the telling of a tale, don't you think? I'll get back to the bullet train incident soon enough. How I came to be aboard that infamous train heading for what had at the time been just a small Japanese city only of note due to the Chinese airbase there. A city barely heard of by the outside world until that fateful train arrived. Well, that can wait a little while.

The Iron Tsar Sharapova arrived in northern Japan a few days before that train left on its fateful journey. It set down at the old-style naval base at Hamamatsu, which had a couple of cobbled together airship masts near its main docks. One of which was a twisted nightmare of metal with the broken remains of some ill-fated craft still tethered to it.

The Sharapova was flying Russian colours, which made us welcome, if not entirely trusted, by the locals. The Nippon-Chino war was in its seventh year. Russian 'free traders' were supplying the Japanese with much of their munitions. Doubtless part of the Russian states plans to keep the war in stalemate. Russia and China had been playing this game for a long time. China supplied Afghan freedom fighters for years to keep the Russians busy in the west. So, Russia kept China busy in the east by surreptitiously supplying the Japanese.

In the meantime, of course, the British maintained a policy of non-interference as long as everyone kept their eyes off India. Of course, government policy did make sure not to preclude British trading concerns from selling to either side through proxies. War is, after all, an economic opportunity. Her Royal Brass Nipples government may insist Britain would remain neutral in local oriental wars, but it would be a cold day indeed before they stood in the way of honest commerce. All those Russian 'free traders' had to buy the munitions somewhere, didn't they? And their rubles were blood free, well as long as no one asked difficult questions in the mother of parliaments, and the arms merchants lobby saw to it that such an eventuality never came to pass.

Thanks to these quirks of foreign policy among the major powers, The Sharapova had less problem sailing into a war zone than you might otherwise imagine. The Grunt was just another Russia ship trading munitions as far as the interested parties were concerned. That this particular Russian ship was a man-o-war was neither here nor there. A Chinese gunship tailed us for a few hours the day before we sailed into port, but much as they might not like Russian traders supplying their enemies, the Chinese would not interfere with such a craft if it stayed wide of their airspace.

Besides the locals were used to such sights, Japan had been on a full war footing since the first days of China's mistaken invasion. Warships of all kinds were as common as an East End accent. The locals paid the Russian beast no thought at all. If it wasn't firing at them, it wasn't worth worrying about.

The Chinese, in my opinion, would've done well to follow the British example and leave the land of the rising sun well alone. There was a damn good reason the British never tried to do to Japan what they'd done to India. Something the Chinese hadn't counted on in their own attempts to bully themselves out an empire. Japan wasn't a place of a hundred despotic kingdoms as India had been before the Brits. A place full of local despots who mostly welcomed in the British as allies in their silly little wars against their neighbours. I imagine it came as a surprise to them to discover once the British were camped within their borders, they showed every intention of staying there. The same despots were probably even more alarmed when they realised while the British might appear to be training troops for their armies, all those officers in red coats were doing a fine job of distributing rupees among the new sepoys, men who were discovering loyalty lay best when you lay it with your paymasters.

Japan was not India. Japan was an imperial state in of itself. Loyalty to the emperor centred around the strict code of bushido honour. Authority was centralised, not dispersed. Making the land of the rising sun an entirely different prospect when it came to colonial endeavours. This fact China discovered rather too late once they'd landed troops on the southern islands.

But that's frankly enough of geopolitical rhetoric, don't you think? What I suspect you really want to know is why the Sharapova was landing in the middle of a war zone.

Certainly, it's what I really wanted to know or as I put it at the time…

"What the bloody hell are we doing in Japan?"

I'd been 'invited' to join Bad Penny, Captain Vladimir, and a half dozen or so of the crew on the mooring tower as expeditiously as was convenient. Or as my good friend Yuri had put it when he was sent to fetch me 'Now!'.

My Bad Penny looked up from examining her fingernails. A habit of hers which always put me on edge. I'd seen little of her on the voyage itself. Indeed, I'd seen little of anyone but engineering crew for the last several days. While Yuri and his chums were remarkably good company, my vain attempts to find out where we were going had fallen on deaf ears. I've never liked being kept in the dark, which is ironic considering how often this was the case in my life. Literally on some occasions. It made the back of my neck itch. Not that knowing would have made any difference, but knowledge of what we were about would've been a small victory of sorts.

There'd been damn few of those of late.

Imagine my delight, however, when I discovered we'd arrived at our destination, and it was a damn war zone. I was, it is fair to say, filled with no small measure of trepidation.

"We are here to make a delivery for the furtherance of their most noble cause," Vladimir told me. He somehow managed to sound like he believed every word he was saying. For all I know, he did. Though I later came to suspect old Vlad believed in very little beyond what was best for old Vlad. So, in hindsight, I doubt he was quite as sincere as he sounded. Not that I believed him at the time.

"Among other things," my Bad Penny added, archly, but eluded no further.

As I looked around at the port city, I wondered just how noble this cause could be. The place looked grim, and the people grimmer. But years of war will do that to a place.

"Wells sides with Japan?" I asked. It wasn't really a question, more a statement of surprise. I couldn't fathom what motives he might have in doing so.

"Of course, they are a noble people, much like my own. We too have known the horrors of invasion of our motherland. We too have known sacrifice in the face of adversity. I have great respect for the Japanese people; they like Russians do not bow to the yoke of others," Vlad said with typical pomposity, and that strange lack of self-awareness he managed to maintain. He was, after all, a man who'd abandoned his own country. What with inciting mutinies, stealing airships and recasting his lot as a pirate captain.

"I see," I said, and didn't, though behind me I could see other members of The Grunt's crew starting to move various crates and barrels through the loading bay doors. It didn't take much of a leap to figure out what was in the boxes. It seemed Wells and his cronies weren't above a bit of gun running for profit. I presumed he had to finance his efforts one way or another and doing so off the misery of others was always a popular choice with revolutionaries of any flavour. Someone is always sacrificed for the cause, one way or another.

"Yes, the Japanese and the Russian peoples have much in common. Though our oriental friends lack a certain nobility of visage, it is true. We shall lend them our aid, and in aiding them, we will rein in the excesses of Chinese imperialism," Vlad continued, clearly warming to his subject.

It struck me again that for a mutineer Vlad sounded surprisingly patriotic at times. It wouldn't be the last time that thought struck me. Which just goes to show you should listen to yourself more often, I guess, but I'm getting ahead of myself again. Besides which I attributed it all to his usual bravado. I'd noticed he was wearing even more tassels than normal that morning. Presumably in order to impress our hosts. He'd a few more medals pinned on his chest as well. One of which was a huge brass star with a multitude of points, pinned on his coat more or less where his heart would be. No doubt this was some valiant Russian order of gallantry he'd purloined from somewhere. A second set of piped ropes hung from it and around his side, then back up to his shoulder with yet more tassels. The overall impression was, to me, that he was wearing curtain retainers from a tart's boudoir. I did note, however, the one my Bad Penny had snipped off was still conspicuous by its absence…

Speaking of Bad Penny, as Vlad made his little speech, I caught sight of her rolling her eyes and felt a momentary sense of comradeship with the mad harpy. I even managed to smile slightly in her direction. Which, I add with little surprise, earned me nothing but a disparaging look in return. She may have thought little of Captain Putin, but she clearly thought a damn sight less of me.

I sighed heavily, as the lift gave a worrying judder then started to descend. There was an odd little screech, followed by a scratching sound, and for a moment I was more than a tad concerned about how sound the rudimentary box cage we were in actually was. But then the scratching sound changed to what could be described as music, at least if the one describing as such was a deaf man…

Do, be Do be DO Do Doobee…

I was struck by the odd realisation that this was the same tune that played in the lift in Cairo as me and Miss Wells had descended beneath the Sphinx. And for a second I found myself distracted, wondering just why the makers of lifts insist on adding music to the experience of being lowered to or beneath the ground… I mean, why on earth do they think anyone wants to listen to music on a two-minute ride in a lift? But perhaps, more importantly, why is it always 'The girl from Ipan-bloody-ema'?

What's worse is that the damn song gets stuck in your head all day after you hear it. So, I ask you, are all manufacturers of lifts and elevators secretly part of a grand scheme to drive the world's population to the point of utter distraction? Is it, in fact, some strange attempt at mass mind control? Or perhaps some Pavlovian nightmare experiment designed to make us all feel trapped in cages with no control over our destiny every time we hear that song?

It's strange the things that go through your mind when you're stuck in a lift having music played at you…

But let's put that on one side. As the lift slowly descended, I asked a question that actually concerned me more than Pavlovian mind control experiments. "Okay, that explains why we are in Japan, but why am I here specifically?"

I directed my question at Bad Penny rather than the pomposity with tassels, in the hope of a more illuminating reply. If Vlad took offence at this, I cared too little to notice, though I suspect he did. Vlad liked the role of captain too much to have his authority sidestepped without it prickling him. He said nothing at the time, so perhaps he was wise enough to let the slight pass, or just deafened by bad lift music, which seems more likely.

"All in good time, Hannibal, all in good time," she said dismissively. Then added, "but don't go wandering off while we are here. I wouldn't want to have to come and find you," with enough relish in her voice to suggest that actually, she would quite enjoy doing just that, but I wouldn't.

'In good time' turned out to be several hours later. Before that, there was a whole lot of talking to port officials and arranging travel documents to take care of. In which time I could've gleaned a great deal, I assume, if I'd paid even a modicum of attention. But my hangover had set in for the morning, and I spent most of the next few hours dozing on a bench in the offices of the port officials. Happily leaving the captain to organise unloading, paperwork and all the other tedious stuff that came with the position. If he was fool enough not to farm out such work to his junior officers, then good luck to him. I took it as more proof he was new to his role. My Bad Penny meanwhile spent most of the morning talking to official-looking types who seemed to be nothing to do with the port itself.

I suspect my snores irritated both of them; I cared not if that was the case. The Japanese make damn fine benches for sleeping on; I will say that for them.

It was early afternoon when Penny kicked me on the shin and forced me to wake.

"Come on," she instructed, and set off without bothering to look and see if I'd followed her. Which I did, of course, just in case she did decide to check and then came looking for me in a bad mood. Rude awakening aside, the plus side to this I found was there are worse views in the world than the one a man can get walking a few yards behind Bad Penny. It almost made following her seem a worthwhile exercise. Not that I'd a great deal of choice in the matter, of that I was sure. You'll have to forgive me if that sounds tacky, but as I have said before, as murderous psychopaths go, she was a fine looking killer, and it had been quite a while since I, well, it had been a while, let's leave it at that.

The woman whose name was almost certainly not Bad Penny led me through the outskirts of the city itself, then up a steep path that led to a hill commanding a remarkably good view of the whole port. There, by a small Shinto shrine, she stood and waited for me to catch up. By the time I got to her, I was a tad out of breath and cursing Yuri's vodka for the umpteenth time. Hiking up mountainsides hadn't been listed on my agenda for the day.

"Quite a view isn't it!" she said as I finally caught up to her. Which in fairness it was, though I'd still claim the view going up the hill had been better, but again, it had been a while. We were however now a good fifty or sixty feet above The Sharapova, looking down on her and the bay itself. Sunlight glinted off the ocean, where little fishing boats bobbed in the bay between moored warships that were mostly wreaks. The detritus of an earlier phase of the Nippon-Chino war.

"Aye, it is that," I agreed. '*Not worth the bloody climb to see it through,*' I added to myself.

"I'm sure your good friend 'M' will be delighted to get a glimpse of it too. He's probably worried about you after all…" she said with one of her trademark nasty smiles.

Pennies, as it were, fell into place and I cursed my own stupidity for not seeing it before. This was the reason they'd dragged me along to Japan with them. All the way to the middle of a damn war zone. Disinformation. Which, as I am sure you're aware, is a powerful tool. Last time I'd lifted that patch I'd been in Wells' study in Nepal. It only made sense they'd want to throw the dogs off the scent and set up a false trail, and there was one obvious way to do so…

"You want me to lift the patch?" I asked, knowing the answer, and I swear I felt something moving behind it for the first time in days. Psychosomatic, I've no doubt. But still, the reminder that 'M's little pet was still there gave me a shiver.

"It's why you're here," she told me, confirming what I'd already guessed. Then she leant her head to one side and smiled once more, which was another of her odd little habits, which just reminded me that when she wanted to, she had the cutest little ways about her. Justine Casey had that same mannerism, which I'd found delightful back in the hotel bar. At that moment however it just reminded me how quick she could switch into a coldblooded killer. Cute as a whole pocket full of buttons one second, knife at your throat the next. Which was why I wasn't about to argue with her...

"That and the other reason, but we will have to get to that one later," she added while I plucked up the courage needed to do as she asked. But she didn't have to wait long. Not wanting to dwell on what those other reason might be, I took a long breath, then edged my monocle away from my eye, allowing light to penetrate a little before I pulled it completely clear and braced myself for the inevitable...

And nothing happened.

No mad urges.

No uncontrollable rage.

No squirming spider in my eye or flashes of light burning into my retina.

Nothing...

It was very anti-climactic. Instead, I found myself just staring out over the bay. Blinking at the brightness one eye was no longer used to and as my vision settled down enjoying a much-missed sense of depth perception.

I must have stood there staring out at the bay for a good couple of minutes before I turned to look at my Bad Penny, slightly bemused but relieved all the same. I started daring to hope that the spider may even have developed a fault of some kind rendering it inert, or perhaps its enforced dormancy had shut it down, or maybe my masters had assumed I was dead and it just didn't work anymore, so they had stopped sending it any instructions. For whatever reason, nothing happened, and a wave of relief washed over me as I turned back towards my pet psychopath. I was finally free of The Ministry. Free to make my own way in the world. No longer a piece in someone else's board game. I think I even started smiling.

Then I turned and…

Well yes, of course, it was still working. Of course, it hadn't gone dormant. It was just taking a while to wake up, and when it did, it exploded into life with predictable results…

W… the pain was intense

H… burning my retina

E… like looking directly at the sun

R… each letter punctuated by a ghost of itself

E… fading for a fleeting moment

I… coronas of red flickering in afterglow

S… then another burst of light

W… angry pain inducing light

E… burning intensely for a moment

L… and each moment is a lifetime

L… and all the while

S… the spider scurried across my eyeball

As the last of the crippling light burned away, I found myself reeling on the ground, the spider clawing at me, twisting and forcing its insidious tiny claws further around my eye.

I remember anger and rage welling up within me. Partly this was the spider, controlling my emotions, controlling my id, directing my thoughts to those that served its master's will. Partly I was just plain angry…

I remember scrambling to my feet. I don't remember making any conscious decision to do so, but then I don't believe I was in full control of my faculties.

Or any level of control come to that…

Someone was angry; someone needed to vent their frustrations. My own rage burned underneath it all, perhaps making it easier to push me towards violence, but whatever control I had over my emotions was systematically stripped away, and I rounded on the nearest person on whom I could vent that anger…

Which of course was my dear sweet, lovable Bad Penny, who was standing only a few yards away.

I remember myself howling in anger as I charged her down. A primal howl, a howl of frustration, rage, hatred and not all of it my own, but not all of it external either.

So I leapt at her, with murder in my eyes, vengeance in my heart, my blood boiling with rage.

I leapt…

And…

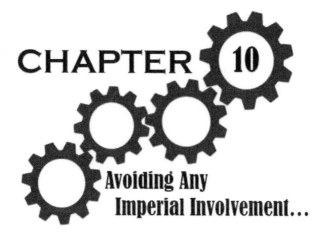

CHAPTER 10

Avoiding Any Imperial Involvement...

I've noticed, over the course of time, that when you're taken over by the shadowy government ministry's mind-eating mechanical spider, you develop a tendency to wake up with fresh wounds and inevitably in pain, normally several hours later. Strangely I find the knowledge of this intelligence no compensation whatsoever.

On this particular occasion I woke strapped down to a bed of some kind, and not in a good way, another thing that seems to happen a lot in these circumstances. This was also something I'd concluded seldom bode well for me. Indeed, it had also occurred to me that it had been a long time since anyone tied me to a bed for reasons of mildly deviant sexual appetites. I'd grown to look back on such things with a misty-eyed sense of reflection on more innocent times.

It took a while for my head to become clear of the cobwebs, though as the veil started to lift, I at least avoided the urge to panic. You can get used to many things given enough exposure to them. Awaking tied to a bed with a concussion and a head full of drugs is one of them, I'd discovered. Indeed, I was becoming an old hand at such awakenings, to such an extent I'd started my own mental checklist for such occasions.

Still alive?

Check.

Tied down?

Check.

Still in one piece?

It would appear so.

Threatening presence in the shadows of the room intent on sticking mechanical spiders in my eyes or visiting some other vile depravations upon me?

Not that I could see.

Okay, so just mild panic with a certain degree of good old British reserve is what's needed then…

I took a few slow deep breaths, collecting myself as my vision started to clear, and the woozy feeling of whatever had been pumped into my system faded away. Though the latter took a while.

The bed I was strapped down to was more a low pallet, with a thin mattress that barely deserved the name. In all, it raised me no more than half a foot above the floor, which made for a strange perspective from which to gather my surroundings. Apparently, such contraptions are much the norm in Japan, I'm not sure what that says about the Japanese, but it certainly felt strange to me, but wherever I was, it was very Japanese. So, whatever had happened on that hillside I hadn't been returned to The Sharapova.

This struck me as odd.

The walls of the room were mostly wood and paper screens, and I remember thinking if I'd not been strapped down to the bed, I could've escaped through the walls themselves. Which I supposed was the point of the odd metal manacles that held my wrists. For all the relative freedom I'd enjoyed in the Tibetan monastery, and aboard the Russian airship, I was still a prisoner of Mr Wells little conclave. So, I suspected they weren't about to let me just wander off any time soon. This irked me somewhat as I'm sure you can imagine. However, as I lay tied to the futon, I considered some of the alternatives they could have chosen when it came to dealing with a troublesome British spy in their midst, willing or otherwise. On the whole, I was against them disposing of the problem by the most obvious means. I rather liked my throat uncut, call me mindlessly sentimental but I've always been fond of maintaining my continued existence over other options. Indeed, I'd come to consider remaining on this mortal plain when I wake each morning to be a small victory of sorts over a collective universe that seemed determined that I should wake to discover otherwise. Well, not wake at all to be more exact… And one has learned to revel in these small victories somewhat as you're no doubt aware by now.

Though, when just still being alive is considered a victory, small or otherwise, then I humbly suggest to you that wisdom would dictate you reconsider your life choices…

I was considering mine that morning in Japan. I was also considering the precarious nature of my position. It was clear to me that Wells had set me aboard The Sharapova with a definite aim in mind. I was sent with the odious Vladimir and the terrifying Bad Penny to Japan to draw off the imperial hounds. Even for one as dim as myself when it comes to matters of technology, it was obvious that Wells suspected The Ministry could track that insidious spider in my eye. It made a horrible kind of sense. They could use it to look through my eyes, and they could use it to exert some control over my emotions. That implied they could communicate with the device as easily as it could communicate with them, though god only knows how that was achieved. I doubted even my old friend 'Spanners' Clarkhurst could've explained that, not that I ever understood Hettie's explanations it has to be said. But, the how of it all hardly mattered. However, it was, I suspected not the how that concerned Wells and his band of revolutionaries, but the how much. Specifically, how much The Ministry could track the device.

When I'd removed the monocle that blocked its signals in Wells' presence there had been a delay of some moments before it had exerted control over me and sent me into a murderous rage. Here in Japan, it had taken a moment or so longer before it did the same. But what you could derive from that was hard to quantify. I'd attacked Bad Penny, ever a far from a wise action, but that could've been purely a matter of whoever operated the device in front of one of Mr Gates' viewing screens taking a while to decide to set me on her. Or else further away from the Empire's power base, as I was here in Japan, the signals took longer to communicate… I doubted that mattered much to anyone other than myself. That hadn't been the point of the exercise.

The point of the exercise, I'd little doubt, was to send the Empire scurrying in the wrong direction. Letting them see Wells in Nepal, or Tibet or wherever his hidden little valley was located, had been a calculated risk no doubt. Sending me to Japan to repeat the exercise was the result of a similar calculation.

But as I lay there, strapped to a futon, somewhere in war-torn Japan, it occurred to me that there was a final calculation Wells should've made. One I would've made if I was him. Having used me to send the Empire's agencies scurrying towards Hamamatsu in the land of the rising sun, I was now surplus to requirements. And, willing or otherwise, I remained an agent of the British Empire, and a ticking time bomb as far as Wells himself was concerned. A weapon pointed directly at him. I was, in essence, an enemy and a clear and present danger both to himself and his organisation. So were I Wells, well let's just say the final calculation seemed obvious. It's not like I hadn't done it before, as Hardacre's inglorious demise testified. Hannibal Smyth was no longer of use to Wells, but remained a threat, and threats of that nature were best disposed of...

Permanently.

The realisation of that obvious conclusion made the small victory of my continued existence, seem a sallow one. One likely to be short-lived.

Indeed, the only remarkable thing, it seemed to me, was that I remained alive at all.

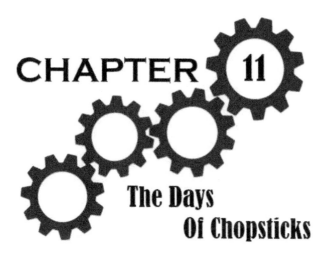

CHAPTER 11

The Days Of Chopsticks

I never took piano lessons as a child. This probably comes of little surprise to you if you have been paying a modicum of attention. For reasons that should be obvious, learning to tickle the ivories in a delightful manner for those after dinner gatherings around the cocktail cabinet, is not considered an important life skill when you're scraping a living out of the gutters of the East End. Practising skills of light-fingered discounts, ignoring an empty stomach and agile evasion of pursuers was considered of far more importance in my childhood years than developing flair with a keyboard and an application for the classics. In later years I did learn to hammer out a sort of tune from between the ebonies. The kind of drunken carousing music that relies greatly on big cords and knowing how to throw in 'Ave a banana' at random. To say I'm no virtuoso is a statement of the obvious to rival 'Queen Victoria is not a virgin...' and just like a statement on the old crotch-less Brass Knickers' chastity, it is equally redundant. I have therefore never learned to play chopsticks. Which is a horrendous little ditty taught to all true students of the white and black keys, because while simple in construction, it requires, and builds up, a certain deftness of fingers which serves a pianist well in later years. A deftness I've never acquired, as hammering your hands on a keyboard for a couple or three cockney standards requires very little in the way of deftness, though a little deafness in the audience is generally a benefit.

It was however during my confinement in Japan I learned just how apt the name of that piece I'd never played was. For like their musical namesake, chopsticks require a certain amount of deftness with your digits to employ them for the task for which they are frankly not very well designed. Also, like their namesake, it was a deftness I never learned.

But I digress, for a change, so I'll leave this particular side-track there and jolly along...

Several terminally dull hours passed before the restraints holding me to the futon suddenly snapped open. This came as a welcome relief to my cramping muscles and aching joints. Bravely ignoring the painful cramp I struggled to sit up.

Well, I struggle on at any rate.

Soon however I was sat nursing my aching wrists and resisting the urge to pull off the bandage that covered an area below my left shoulder. It was blood spotted and ached both front and back. Luckily, if that's the right term, I'd a reasonable idea why. I'd attacked Bad Penny after all. Something experience had taught me, even by that early juncture in our association, was mildly equitable to the act of suicide. Oh, I'm sure she knew it was the spider, not myself, that originated that attack, but doubtless, she'd been more than happy to defend herself with her usual degree of excessive violence. I had a few little flashes of memory that starting to fill in some of the blanks. Memories that involved sudden pain, the bite of flashing steel, my being thrown to the ground, being held there by a grip of steel and razor-sharp fingernails hovering close to my jugular. It wasn't, as you might imagine, a pleasant memory.

In all honesty, I was probably lucky to be alive. Whatever she had stuck me with, a few inches lower and it could have pierced my heart or some other vital organ.

I remembered something else as well. The look of glee on Bad Penny's face when I had leapt at her. I don't doubt she'd known what would happen when I removed my monocle. She'd been anticipating it, her blades were out before I'd even turned to look at her, and she'd damn well enjoyed it.

In a moment of reflection, I wondered just what I'd done that so offended her. But Bad Penny was a psychopath, she didn't need a reason to enjoy maiming me or even killing me come to that, with impunity… So that moment passed quickly. I was sure no action of mine had caused such venom. She was just a crazy woman who enjoyed inflicting pain. Me? I was just a readily available victim for her wanton visceral desires.

It also occurred to me then that it said much about Wells that he would set such a murderess harpy as my watchdog… It also said I was disposable, much as I'd already guessed. So once again, I wondered just why I was still alive, and became all the more determined to free myself of all sides of this bloody affair.

My mind set, I struggled to my feet and surveyed my surroundings some more. The room was small, with a single sliding door that remained firmly shut. I'd little doubt that was I to open that door, someone would object to me doing so. As I suspected any objections would be expressed by people with little compunction against expressing those objections violently upon my person. So, I chose to ignore it for now.

Instead, it was the unglazed window that drew my attention. I sauntered over to it in order to 'admire the view', I guess you could say. Not to mention find out where in hells name I was. The view itself turned out to be breath-taking, a little terrifying, and neatly ruled out any hasty escape via the window.

It looked out over the town, the same town to which I'd originally arrived yesterday. Though I say yesterday, that was at best a guess, as I'd no idea how long I'd been unconscious save for the ever-familiar growl of an empty stomach. But judging by the light and the angle of the sun, it was sometime around midmorning, and it had been late in the afternoon when I'd climbed that hill with little Miss Knife-fingers. So at least a night had passed me by while I was out.

The town itself was maybe a mile away and a couple or three hundred feet below my vantage point. Wherever I was, I was high up, and the drop from below the window was near as damn sheer and led to jagged rocks and an invitation to a sudden death by splatter, if you get my meaning.

I trawled my memory for all I'd seen on our arrival, but soon realised I'd not paid anything like half the attention I should've done. The cliffs had risen quickly from the shoreline, that much I remembered. I recalled vaguely that on the western side of the bay they were steeper still, though I'd paid no attention to them at all at the time. It was, however, there I currently resided. In what, for want of a better word, was a castle.

Castle is perhaps a misleading term. Castles are those lovely picturesque ruins that dot the English countryside after all. Generally ruinous piles falling down around the aristocratic ears of this lord or that baronet. This, however, wasn't that kind of castle, this was a fortress, as I was later to find out. A living bastion built at a time when Japan was still a feudal nation of samurai, shoguns and warlords.

So, it was probably constructed a week last Thursday.

This castle clung to the cliff tops overlooking Hamamatsu like a vulture waiting to strike. It was also I later discovered the residence of the most powerful man in this quarter of Japan, but more of him in a while.

Down in the bay, I could see The Sharapova still moored to one of the harbour towers, which, I found to my surprise, came as a relief. Little desire as I may have had to spend more time with Russian pirates, it was preferable to being abandoned in the middle of a war zone in a country where they didn't speak a civilised language like the Queen's own. Though it did occur to me, such a fate wouldn't be without advantage. War zones make good hiding places, if that is, you can avoid being killed. This is because people really have to want to find you if they're going to willingly come looking somewhere where bombs are flying about. On the other hand, however, I was starting to miss dear old London. I'd have cheerfully killed for a hearty full English, with its artery thickening sausages, burnt to a crisp bacon, fried eggs oozing chip fat oil into the yoke and enough grease to lubricate the gears of a steam engine.

Give me overpriced watered down ale in a Soho pub, over the best Russian vodka and the finest Indian gin any day. Give me lung-eating smog over crisp mountain air and Pacific breezes. Give me the honest thuggery of an East End villain, over the smiling assassins of the inscrutable east. Give me a… oh, you probably get the point.

One never misses London quite so much as when one is certain you'll never return there, which as the Crown's noose still lay about my neck, figuratively speaking, it seemed likely to me that I never would…

However, before I drown myself in melancholy, I heard the screen door slide open behind me. And so in the finest tradition of brazening things out, I straightened myself up, ran my hand over my beard to smooth it out and said to whoever entered, without turning to greet them., "Finally, I was starting to think you had forgotten about me…"

There was an odd whirring noise, followed by several clunks and more whirring, where I'd expected footsteps. Though like footsteps the strange noise was moving towards me.

Paranoia that most basic, and so often in my experience correct, of instincts, took hold. I felt a sudden chill, as the thought of some clockwork death machine closing in behind me took hold. So, I spun around rather too quickly to preserve my dignity. Half stumbled. And my hand unconsciously reached down towards the hidden sleeve in the top of my boot where my trusty cutthroat still resided.

The sight that befell my eyes, as I righted myself, couldn't have been further from my paranoid expectations, however. Instead of some wrought iron death machine, a delicate contraption, in a pink and white lotus blossom kimono, greeted my eyes. Indeed, had it not been for the strange mechanical sounds, I would have thought a woman had walked in carrying a small tray of food.

Well, I say, woman, for that, was my first impression. That impression didn't last long as I realised what I was seeing was something else entirely.

The kimono covered a body of moving metal parts. While what I took for a fleeting moment to be a face in traditional Japanese make-up, was, in fact, a delicate ceramic mask of white porcelain, locked in a lifeless hollow stare. She, or more exactly it, even had hair, though as it came closer, I could clearly see this was a wig of some kind. It was indeed every inch a perfect simile of a Japanese serving woman, rendered in brass and porcelain. Except that it moved in little fits and starts that lacked fluidity, making it a tad unnerving. I've never felt entirely comfortable around automata. Call me a Luddite by all means, but soulless machines mimicking humans give me the creeps.

The clockwork Geisha moved to the centre of the room, its blank, lifeless stare never straying towards me. A hiss of steam was released from pistons hidden beneath the kimono, and the device actually kneeled to place the tray it was carrying on the floor. Little legs on springs popped out beneath the tray itself, so it came to rest a few inches above the polished wooden floorboards.

I watched all this with a strange horrified fascination. I'd seen automatons before, but they were generally built for more obvious purposes. The heavy lifting drones we used in the Royal Air Navy, closely controlled by operators to move heavy loads about. Or similar devices used by civilians for similar tasks. But seldom had they seemed so independent, or so fragile. Unlike those devices, this one had no obvious control cables for receiving instructions. Clearly it could not be entirely independent, it had to be following instructions of some kind, but still, I found it unnerving.

Having placed the tray on the floor, it paused for a moment before its arms withdrew and it shuffled back a couple of steps before it slowly stood once more, accompanied by a sucking sound as air was drawn back into pistons. Then, once it was again upright, it did the oddest thing of all, and its head turned perceivably in my direction, before executing a perfect if minuscule bow of respect. Then it turned back towards the sliding door and retreated the way it had come, whirring, clicking and with the occasional clung as it went.

It was that bow that undid me. It had turned towards me first. It knew I was there, not just in the room but exactly where I was. This machine bowed to me, not to the room in general but to me. It didn't just mimic human movement, it mimicked humanity itself. This I found utterly chilling. A machine that could think, or at least interpret the world around it. A machine that didn't need a human intelligence to guide it… If that doesn't scare you, you're a braver man than I. Which I'll admit doesn't say a great deal, but all the same if that doesn't scare you, then you're a fool. But then perhaps for me, it was worse. Think for a moment, imagine, if only for a second, that you have something in your eye. A little machine, a little machine that both could and had overrode your reason… Imagine then, for a moment, that you come across another machine, something bigger, and in visage far less terrifying perhaps, but still. It may have been just some quirky device in domestic servitude but it was a device that shows all the signs of rudimentary self-awareness… Imagine that, and think upon that spider in your eye, and what it could be if it too had a rudimentary intellect of its own. If it didn't just report back to its masters at all, if it wasn't they that took control of you but the spider itself…Perhaps then, as you think on all that, you will realise exactly why this automaton scared the hell out of me.

That wasn't all, her, it, whatever the pronoun is for a machine that acts like a Geisha… And I'll settle for 'it' if you don't mind… It reminded me of other mask-wearing monstrosities that didn't seem quite human. Why I'm not entirely sure, but there was something about the way it moved in not quite human ways. The way its countenance was blank and lifeless. Sure, in all other ways it was utterly different, it was a delicate device, a fragile thing, and for all it scared me on an intellectual level, physically it didn't appear threatening at all. Which was exactly the opposite of those hulking things in gasmask-covered faces and heavy black coats. Yet still, there was something terribly similar about them both. I was struck with a horrible feeling that something I'd dared not contemplate before was in fact true. My mind went back to a Calcutta hotel room, a momentary glimpse of the face behind a Sleepman's mask, a bloodless white face that looked dead in its visage after Bad Penny had shredded its mask.

The more I stood there staring at the door through which it had retreated, the more it dawned upon me that this automaton was in so many ways just like The Ministry's hulking enforcers. That this machine was perhaps merely a more refined artistic version of those dreadful creatures, which made the Sleepmen even more terrifying if that was possible.

Eventually, hunger won out, and I knelt to eat the bowl of noodles 'it' had set before me. Only to discover 'it' had supplied me with nothing but damn chopsticks. A fact which made a bad day just a little worse. As I said, when it comes to chopsticks, be they on the piano or as eating implements, I lacked the deftness that comes with practice. Given that, and the way my hand was shaking after witnessing the Geisha and my epiphany on the probable nature of Sleepmen, I'm surprised I managed to eat at all.

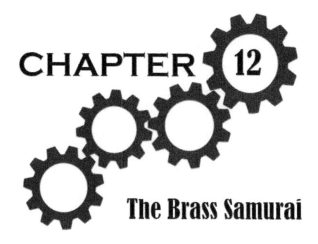

CHAPTER 12

The Brass Samurai

The Geisha automaton visited me several more times over the next couple of days or so, indeed, was my only visitor. It brought me food, water, a bowl to wash in, a bowl for other necessaries. In and out it would trundle. And each time, no matter where I placed myself in the room, it would turn and bow to me before it left. And each time I found it no less unnerving.

You can get used to anything, or so I have been told, but if that's so, it was going to take more than a couple of days to rid me of my sense of unease about that shuffling imitation of life. But then two days in a single room albeit one that was reasonably pleasant, does grind on your nerves a little. Besides which I've spent, as I'm sure you're aware, more than my fair share of time in cells. And it was clear to me that for all its pleasantness this was indeed a cell. As such, my only real question was what kind of cell it was. Did I, to be blunt about it, need to add a new entry to my 'Best Death Cell Guide'…

The Upper Rooms of Hamamatsu Castle

A pleasant place to spend your final hours on this earth. A distinct shortage of rats and cockroaches, comfortable if minimalist sleeping arrangements and the onsite staff polite and deferral to a fault, provided you can manage to put their utterly terrifying nature to one side.

A solid eight out of ten, (point deducted for lack of proper cutlery). Highly recommended if you happen to offend the empire of the rising sun…

In short, I've been in worse places, and whatever they were keeping me here for, I was mostly sure it wasn't just to wait for a noose to become free. So, I tried not to dwell on the countenance of my maid and did my best to wait things out in the relative comfort provided.

By the third day, of course, waiting it out in the relative comfort provided was swift turning to boredom. I'd even shaved that morning with a small mirror the Geisha provided. Though it required a degree of extra care once I discovered my faithful old cutthroat was in desperate need of a good stropping. I'd planned to keep it hidden on the off chance I needed a weapon at some point. But boredom and vanity got the better of me. However, as I've often found, boredom is generally far preferable to other options which present themselves shortly after the boredom ends…

It was the afternoon of the third day when the screen door slid open, and the Geisha shuffled in, carrying a larger tray than normal. This alone gave me a twinge of apprehension. One which only amplified when she turned to one side and knelt to set down the tray, and then stayed knelt before it.

In case you're wondering, by the third day I'd given up all pretensions with pronouns and settled on calling it, her. If only because it helped to think of it as a her, as it stopped me thinking of it as a soulless death machine.

Not sure what to do, I settled on doing nothing because I could see there were two small round bowls on the tray, a jug of steaming water, and a teapot. I knew enough about Japan to be aware the natives had such a thing as a tea ceremony. Though of course, I'd bugger all idea what said ceremony entailed, how it was performed, whether they used tea bags, and if by chance there would be any scones in the offing. Sadly, I strongly suspected the latter was unlikely to be the case.

What I did know, at least vaguely, was that the tea ceremony was a traditional way of greeting a guest, which suggested I was going to be joined by someone important. This wasn't necessarily good news as it suggested that my 'friends', for want of another word, weren't the ones in charge of my captivity. Not that I'd any faith in my 'friends' at all, but they were at least a known quantity.

I stood by the window, on the wisdom that at worst not kneeling at one side of the tray to await my 'host' would be seen as simply foolish western ignorance if it was a faux pas to do so, rather than risk being insulting by taking a seat before he arrived.

A few moments passed before two men in ancient-looking laminated armour, entered and took up a position at either side of the doorway. Each of these was armed with somewhat less ancient-looking rifles, with wicked bayonets attached. They bore that time-honoured serious expression adopted by guards everywhere. That blank visage that stares forward, and pays you no heed at all, while giving you the distinct impression if they were to start paying you any heed you weren't going to enjoy that one bit.

I let my eyes rest on each in turn, but otherwise continued to stand silently watching the doorway, and another long moment passed before a remarkably unassuming young man in an unassuming uniform stepped into view. He was not much older than me and reed thin. The kind of reed thin that doesn't get described as wiry. Were he a few years younger and had this been good old Rudgley school, then this man would've had victim written right through him to any prospective bully. Let's just say there are those who are good at sports and there are those who are the victims of those who are good at sports. This was a man whom I suspected had never been good at sports, and he looked way too young to have any real authority. But as he entered and stood before me, meeting my gaze with an iron one of his own, I realised something, any bully who picked on this victim would regret it in a heartbeat. He was young, but his gaze was old and made of stern stuff. Old eyes framed by small horn-rimmed spectacles.

I felt a momentary cold breeze across my neck and knew in an instant that I didn't want to upset this man. He reminded me a little too much of 'M' my old 'friend' from The Ministry. Yet I suspected he'd a grasp on power of which 'M' could only dream, which made him far more dangerous.

The small bespectacled man stood examining me for a while, his gaze questioning and considered, though damn little expression crossed his face and I'd no inkling what he may be thinking. I wondered if perhaps that was because I was unused to Japanese mannerisms, but even as I considered this, I ruled it out as folly. This man was the very definition of inscrutable, because he chose to be inscrutable. Which he'd remain until he chose otherwise, something he seemed in no hurry to do so.

Eventually, with a small nod of the head and a smile that said less than nothing, he motioned towards the tea service before me. "Please, Mr Smyth, sit," he said, his voice soft yet holding enough steel in it that there was no pretence this was anything less than a command.

After he spoke, a strange grinding noise started up, which could only be some hidden gear works, and the central portion of the floor descended into itself, dropping just less than a foot. When the floor ceased to descend, the tone of the gear noise changed and a second smaller square, a couple of foot wide, rose up from the middle of the first. It was on this smaller section of the floor that the tea service resided. So, when the gears stopped turning, a recessed seating area complete with table had been revealed.

As you may imagine, I was surprised by all this, though not so much by the party trick with the floor, no doubt designed to show his full command of the room, in a most literal sense, but because despite having spent three days in this room I hadn't detected even the trace of a square pattern on the floor that would've suggested such a thing was possible.

I wondered for a moment what other secrets the room might hold and found myself mildly worried that I may yet find out. But all that on one side, I did as instructed and perched myself down. Once I was settled upon the step, he joined me on the other side, sitting with carefully controlled movement, met my gaze once more, then proffering a delicate bow of the head, which I returned rather than risk insulting him by error.

"What's going on, and who are you?" I asked, quite reasonably in the circumstances I thought. But my questions were welcomed with a flash of anger across the faces of both guards. Though my host merely raised one eyebrow momentarily. Then tilted his head to one side for a fraction of a second, enough to look like a mannerism and not a signal to his two guards, instructing them to stand easy. Yet I'd swear that is exactly what it was, as the guards' faces resume passive disinterest immediately. This left me in no doubt who was in charge here, if that was in doubt, for that was more respectful deference than any mere functionary could ever command.

"All in good time, Mr Smyth. There are forms that must be upheld. This is Japan, we do things in our own way. First, we must share tea, and do so following those forms, then we may speak, and some of your questions may be answered," he said, a thin, far from reassuring smile crossing his lips.

Despite the amiable tone his words and that smile made me shiver in a way I couldn't explain. Another 'friend' of mine would have explained this as a Pavlovian reaction on my part. On account of the number of times that people smiled at me a few moments before they caused me to lose consciousness, normally due to violence of some kind on their part.

I don't know much about this Pavlov bloke, beyond he was cruel to his pets in the name of science. 'Never trust a man who is cruel to his dog' as my old mum would say, bless her gin-soaked heart. But while I could follow the logic of what he claimed to have discovered, anyone who'd ever actually trained a dog - shepherds, for example - could've told you much the same as he. But mere animal trainers and working men aren't scientists so you can't just put credence in what they say now can you. After all, Pavlov wore a white lab coat so he must be cleverer than the average shepherd...

Still, not to get side-tracked on the relative merits of experimental psychology. The man before me had the same kind of smile I'd seen on too many faces of late, but for once I decided the greater wisdom lay in not antagonising the man who was smiling at me, as he was clearly in charge here. So, how's that for personal growth.

Explain that, Pavlov, you old fraud.

Yes, I know, don't labour the point…

Smiler clapped his hands once and the automaton Geisha raised her head, performed a nodding bow to each of us and then preceded to go through overly elaborate motions, in my opinion, while pouring two cups of tea.

The milk first or last debate that runs so hot in the drawing rooms of the Empire is as nothing compared to the Japanese tea ceremony, let me just say that. Well, that and that I could've boiled, stewed and poured two cups of Earl Grey, and drunk both of them, by the time all her faffing on was completed and two small bowl-like cups lay before us with a dribble of thin-looking tea in each of them.

I suspected it should've been more than a dribble. But for all the brilliance of her design, the Geisha of gears wasn't quick or dexterous enough to perform the ancient tea ceremony without spilling a little tea on the floor. Which caused my host's visage of self-assured control to slip momentarily with a wince of apology and a hint of anger, making me suspect some engineer or other was going to be in for a tough conversation later.

My host leaned forward slightly and gestured towards the cup in front of me. Then raised his hands, saying, "Drink."

I nodded in reply and followed his directions and raised the cup to my mouth with both hands then sipped at the tea, which I will admit could've tasted worse. Though that said, the only reason I know this is I've tasted tea made with the leaves that have been dried out on the mantel after use and returned to the caddy several times, in the days of my youth. Dear old mum was not a woman to waste money or tea if she could help it.

"It's good," I said, trying to hide my grimace.

"That is kind of you to say, Mr Smyth," my host replied, which made me suspect he knew I was lying. All the same, he drank the last of his, and I drank the last of my own. Then he sat back once more and peered at me over his spectacles for a long moment, in a way which I found slightly unnerving. Until finally, he spoke again.

"Tell me, Mr Smyth, why did my niece bring you with her to Japan?" he asked.

If I'd been drinking the tea at that moment, I would've probably sprayed it everywhere.

"Your niece?" I asked while thinking to myself that he surely couldn't be talking about…

"Yes, Mr Smyth, I am told you've taken to calling her Penny, which is not her name, Bad Penny to be exact, some joke or other based on an English colloquialism, I'm given to understand." He replied, his tone serious, even a tad scolding, he might even have found the pet name offensive, which I found a tad worrying.

I coughed, wondering if I should explain. I mean, I knew it wasn't her actual name. I'm sure you, dear reader, know it wasn't her actual name. Did, I wondered, 'Turns up like a bad penny' even translate into Japanese?

"It's, erm, it's a private joke…" I told him, feeling compelled by his silence to say something.

"Not so private I would say, as others have taken to using it also, I am told." He replied, sternly.

I suspect I gulped slightly at this. Another of those Pavlovian reactions perhaps. I realised something as well. I could not remember ever using that name when conversing with her. I couldn't remember ever using it out loud in fact, except when discussing her a couple of times with Yuri and his comrades, who wanted to know what I knew about 'The American woman, she crazy yar?' But what were the chances they mentioned that little nickname I had for her to anyone…? I was suddenly a tad worried and tried to mask my discomfort with humour.

"Engineers, they gossip in ways that makes fishwives seem tight lipped…" I said with a sigh.

"Ah yes, ha, ha, most amusing, I'm sure," he said in a way that suggested he didn't find it, or me, overly amusing. Then he continued, "That is however not any of my concern. I believe my niece also finds the name amusing and so chooses not to correct you at this time, which is, of course, her right. Though I would advise you take care it continues to amuse her. She appears fond of you for some reason. It would, I believe, disappoint her, were she required by honour to have you beheaded."

I coughed again, choked is perhaps a better word. And if you're asking what made me choke during that exchange, frankly, take your pick.

"We are talking about the same woman here, right? Petite girl, short hair, metal arm, razors for fingernails… Aggressive approach to problem-solving?" I asked and found myself regretting doing so immediately. My retreat to humour was doing me few favours.

His smile somewhat lessened. He nodded curtly and continued, "I assure you, Mr Smyth, I know my own niece. But you have not answered my question. So please, if you don't mind, tell me why my niece brought you with her to Japan? I find your presence here to be quite unusual, and I would know the reason, one way or another, but hospitality demands I first merely ask."

"She is not Japanese though, she's American," I said, unable to shunt her out of my mind. I'm not sure if it was the 'beheading' or the 'quite fond of you' part, but I was a tad shaken by what I'd heard. Sadly, too shaken to pay enough attention to what else I was being told, which would have spared me some pain had I listened more carefully.

"Her father married my sister, Mr Smyth. She is my niece by marriage, though she is no more American than you are. All that is of little consequence, however. Now please answer my question."

"Not American… but she is definitely American…" I replied. Which was a stupid part of the conversation to focusing on, all things considered. Very damn foolish as I didn't see the signs of irritation on my host's inscrutable face.

Sighing, he stood, and had I known a little more about Japanese culture the absence of a bow towards me before doing so would have put me more on guard. As it was, I was still trying to square the circle on these strange revelations I barely registered this ill-fated insult.

Without a further word, he and his automaton Geisha left the room, but as he did so he gave some minor signal or other to the guards as he passed them.

This was the point things became a little unpleasant for me. Shortly afterwards everything went black…

I know, I was surprised by this too…

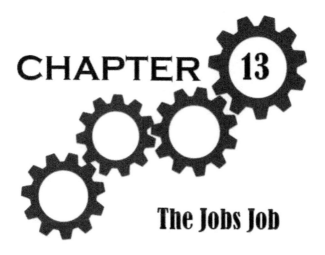

CHAPTER 13

The Jobs Job

The Lower Rooms of Hamamatsu Castle

An utterly unpleasant place to spend your final hours on this earth. A definite surplus of rats and cockroaches, uncomfortable sleeping arrangements on straw that may or may not be only wet due to the water dripping from the ceiling. The onsite staff impolite and more than willing to spit on you on your food for your convenience, will make you miss automatons dressed in kimonos in no time.

A regretful two out of ten, (point deducted for lack of fresh air). Highly unrecommended if you're foolish enough to offend the empire of the rising sun…

"Hannibal, you bloody idiot. What did you have to offend Yamamoto for?" asked an American voice which apparently didn't belong to an American. As it asked this only a few moments after its owner had chucked a bucket of cold water over me, I wasn't feeling overly compelled to give a coherent answer.

"Who the hell is Yamamoto?" I blurted belligerently, which earned me a second bucket of cold water.

"Yep okay, okay, small guy, glasses, big bodyguards," I said, spluttering a little, though I was somewhat more with it after the second drenching.

"Well?" she asked, impatiently, which is almost the default emotive position for my dearest own sweet Bad Penny, as you may have noticed – impatience which was generally followed by violence being perpetrated upon my person. As I was already nursing a throbbing head from my pounding at the hands of this Yamamoto's guards, I felt disinclined to antagonise her further.

All the same, I took the time to wipe the water from my eyes and look up to meet hers properly. You see, making and maintaining eye contact with a cobra is the best way to keep them at bay. Or so I was once told by a Swami of my acquaintance. This seemed like sage advice, though I will admit to being a little dubious at the time. Not least because it was advice from Ken Swami, a rear gunner on HMAS Beckham on which I served on for a short time early in my career in the RAN. Ken was a man full of sage bits of advice like that, which didn't always ring true. For example, I suspected at the time and still do that Ken had never seen a cobra in his life.

Still, I reasoned, in regard to my own little spitting cobra, Bad Penny, looking her in the eyes would at least give me half a chance of seeing the inevitable blow coming…

I was, however, in for a surprise when I looked up. Though I should've known better than to be surprised by anything in Penny's case. She was, after all, as I'm sure you remember, quite the chameleon when it came to her sartorial choices. Clearly, as we were in Japan, she had decided to dress the part, and so she was wearing a dark red silk kimono, with wide sleeves that hung low from her arms and a red silk sash that pulled the outfit in tight at the waist. Her hair was up in traditional Japanese fashion, held in place with two crossing hairpins, which, I'd no doubt, could be employed as weapons at a moment's notice. She was even wearing traditional Japanese makeup, pale with dark shadows over her eyes and an oddly bright red lipstick, which made her mouth look smaller and even perter than it actually was. Indeed, she looked every inch the imperial courtesan.

Her kimono wasn't entirely traditional, however, what with the long split up one side that ran, somewhat scandalously, to just below her hip. A split which revealed more than just her ankle when she walked. I've no doubt this was for practical reasons, my Bad Penny was always one to be prepared to fight after all, and letting her choice of garments constrict her movement, say with a tight-fitting skirt, would've been foolishness. All the same, her choice of outfit reminded me that there was more to Bad Penny than just a vengeful compassionless killing machine.

She was a very attractive vengeful compassionless killing machine…

"When you have quite finished looking at my legs…" Penny chided me. Which helped to remind me of what old Ken had said about cobras. As such, I snapped my gaze back to her eye level.

"Sorry, still a little light-headed, I'm afraid. What did you ask me?" I said, though I could tell from her eyes I'd failed utterly to cover myself with that line.

"What did you say to offend Yamamoto?"

"I've no idea. He asked me some questions, and then the blighter just walked off and set his guards on me."

"What questions?" she asked, a worried expression crossing her face. At least I think it did, it was hard to tell with all the white face makeup.

"He wanted to know why you brought me to Japan with you," I replied honestly, and found myself also wondering what had caused him to join the 'knock Hannibal out club'. A club whose growing membership was becoming something of a menace, in my opinion.

She laughed, more at me than with, which did little to placate my mood. Then she asked the somewhat loaded question, "And, what did you tell him?"

"I didn't tell him anything. I was a bit distracted by something he said to tell the truth," I replied with more honesty than I'd intended. Looking into her eyes, as I was at that moment, I wondered why the thought of her being 'quite fond of you' had distracted me so much, though the 'have you beheaded' part made perfect sense to me. It wasn't as if I liked the damn woman. I mean, sure she was very attractive as psychotics with one arm made of steel and cog, and a temper they'd no compunctions about on taking out on me, go. But I'd rather get into bed with a pit viper and would vastly prefer to not see her one waking day to the next.

No matter how nice her legs were…

Or, as we are on the subject, how clad in tight-fitting leather, she'd make a wonderful dominatrix, of the kind that brings some men to tears in some of the clubs I know in Soho.

Why the bloody hell, for that matter, would I care if she was American or not, or anything else about her come to that. Even with that cute smile of hers and that way, when she wasn't actually being homicidal, she would occasionally twirl her hair through her fingers in an oddly endearing absentminded way.

Sure, she had fingernails like razors, literally, which could flay a man's back with a single raking swipe. And yes, in certain other circumstances the feel of fingernails gouging at your skin isn't an entirely an unwelcome or even unpleasant sensation. So, in all honesty, I am sure you can see that it is only natural for a man to wonder what it might be like to have those razor nails of hers scraping down your back in the height of passion…

But no, really no, not even in the slightest did I think of Bad Penny in that kind of way. I certainly wasn't dwelling on thoughts like these right at that moment. My eyes were certainly not focused on the way her pert little chest rose and fell as she breathed in that tight-fitting red silk kimono that followed her womanly curves so almost like a second skin…

"I said, Hannibal, what the bloody hell distracted you?" she asked me, for the third time apparently.

I forced myself to focus on the conversation at hand and blamed the multiple bangs on the head I'd recently received for my lack of an attention span. But before I could reply, and to my relief, all things considered, she waved her own question away. Turning her back on me, she walked around the room beyond my cell. Affording me, I hesitate to mention, a different but equally distracting view before she turned back to me with a less angry, more thoughtful look on her face.

"Oh, I guess it is of no consequence. What does matter is you didn't tell him the truth of it - that would only make things more complicated. If he asks you again, just tell him it was because of that spider thing in your eye. I've no doubt that will fascinate him, which may be useful to us and it's close enough to the truth that it will set him at ease when I ask about Jobs," She told me.

I listened to all this, confused once more. Was she after employment of some kind in Japan? If so, it seemed to me, she was going a bloody strange way about it. *'And, just who in their right mind would want a job in Japan in the middle of a war?'* I wondered to myself, then remembered who was saying this to me and realised it was a fool's question. Besides I had other concerns I wished to express right at that moment.

"I didn't tell him because I've no bloody idea why I'm here," I said, with a tad more snap than I intended, my groggy awakenings were giving way to anger. I had, after all, just found myself in yet another cell and once more in the dark both figuratively and in actuality.

"Yes, well, of course, you don't. We can hardly trust you now, can we, Hannibal? You are a bloody spy after all," she replied with venom equal to my own.

I sat down on a convenient pile of rags in the corner. I did so with feeling, the feelings of a petulant child who has just been told there is no candy to be had, but with feeling all the same. I took a couple of deep breaths, only to regret the putrid taste of the air, and tried to push the anger from my voice. Instead, I tried to sound calm and reasonable. Neither of which I felt. So, I took another deep breath before saying…

"Look, for the sake of Queen V's frilly barbwire knickers, Penny, I'm…"

"That's not my name…" she interrupted. Though she did so with a hint of a smile in her voice, which struck me as odd, but I went with it.

"I know," I said and took another deep, unpleasant breath. "Look, 'Penny'… Clearly I'm been kept in the dark here, and I understand why, but if you're trying to pull a fast one over your uncle, well I can be a damn sight more helpful if you tell me some little details like why we're here, why I'm here, and what the bloody hell Wells has us up to. That way perhaps I won't go upsetting your dear uncle, Yan-ka-mo… or whatever his blasted name is."

"Yamamoto, who I should add is the Brass Samurai and the default leader of Japanese forces in this region."

"You're kidding me?" I said, I'd some vague recollection of hearing the name Brass Samurai before. I'd read the odd newspaper piece about the Nippon-China war in the Times. After a glance at the ankles on page three of course, and the sports pages and the funnies, and whatever celebrity interviews took my attention. You know, when I'd read all the interesting stuff and resort to the actual news. But of what little I'd read; I was damned if I could remember much of it right then. Not that this mattered, let's just say his early victories in the war were but footnotes in history compared to what came next, but let's not get ahead of ourselves.

"As it happens, no. Yamamoto is the de facto warlord of this region. As such he is a man used to people answering his questions directly, which given your inability to answer anything in a straight forward fashion may explain the beating you just took at the hands of his guards," she told me, then after a heavy sigh added, "But I guess you're right, you need to know more. If only so you know what we don't want you to tell him."

"So, tell me then," I said, frustrated yet intrigued. Not least because if I actually knew something for once, then maybe I'd have a hand to play. You can't betray a cause you know nothing about after all, and I can't say I cared a great deal for any of the sides involved but my own sweet self. But then I had to because no one cared a damn about my side but me.

"Before I do, I should ask your word that you will play your part and not betray the trust I'm putting in you."

"Of course." I smiled and nodded.

"Oh please…" she said, giving me a withering look. "I said I should ask your word, not that I would. I know your word's worth less than a confederate dollar in New York.

I'm not going to waste my breath. Luckily the one thing I do trust is your entitled self-interest. That I trust."

I did my best to look wounded by this accusation. Which was a pointless pretence I'm sure, but one must try to keep up appearances. I didn't bother to try and correct her, however. You can only take a pointless pretence so far, I feel.

"As it happens, self-interest should be enough, as the reason we're here in Japan is to locate a scientist by the name of Jobs. Professor Steffen Jobs to be exact. He is an old friend of both my uncle and the Wells family."

"Jobs, I've heard that name before…" I said, trying to remember where it had come up. Perhaps the most recent blow to the head had shaken me up more than usual because at that moment I couldn't place it. Though there was something about eyes. What was it now? '*Eye this, eye that, eye, eye, everything bloody thing…*' Who'd said that to me?

"I'm sure you have, Hannibal. He designed that monocle you're wearing. Though he didn't design it specifically for you. He's the reason The Ministry doesn't know your every damn move. Yours and more importantly Saffron's."

"Gates…" I swore as I pieced my memory together.

"Precisely, they're old friends, or rivals at any rate, and enemies on occasion but that's the egg-heads for you. They share some common interests in certain technologies."

"Well then, I'm grateful to him for designing this. But why are we trying to find him?" I asked, conscious my hand had gone straight to my monocle as she alluded to it and the damn spider Gates had put in my eye. The spider I was convinced would be the death of me.

"I'm sure you are, but then you wouldn't be here if it wasn't for his device," she said with a smile on her lips. That special kind of Bad Penny smile that suggested the reason I wouldn't have been there was because I would no longer be of use to Wells and his cronies, thus would be lying in a shallow grave somewhere, if, that is, they had bothered to bury me at all.

I swallowed hard, trying to remove the lump in my throat if you will. Though all this still didn't tell me why they'd dragged me all the way to Japan. Or indeed what they hoped to gain by doing so. Luckily, I was about to be illuminated on the subject.

"Wells hopes Jobs will be able to remove that little spider of yours permanently. Aside from Gates, he is probably the only one who can. So, as I said, I trust the enlightened self-interest on your part. Jobs can free you of our friend 'M's little pet, which I am sure is up there near the top of your list of desires," she said. Which was true, it was right up there on my list of desires alongside the fountain of youth, the contents of the vaults of the bank of England and dying in bed, at a ripe old age, with a smile on my face as a girl a third of that age put it there. So, if there was even a remote possibility of being free from The Ministry's grip, I'd was certainly willing to play along with whatever scheme was afoot. She wasn't wrong about that whole enlightened self-interest thing she had in her favour.

"Well?" she asked.

"Well, indeed, I am of course at your disposal, whatever you need me to do," I replied all too hastily I'm sure. Nothing was ever going to be that simple after all.

"Good, that's that settled then. My uncle can be told why we brought you here, why we need to see Jobs. I've no doubt he will be reasonable about that, intrigued, knowing him. He has a boyish enthusiasm when it comes to technology. He believes the future of Japan rests upon it."

"Okay… In that case, I don't see the problem," I said, because I am a tad slow at times.

"Oh, that's simple. We mean to take Jobs with us when we leave. And that Yamamoto will never allow. So, we are going to steal the Brass Samurai's lead scientist out from under him, in the middle of his dirty little war."

At which point, well, I could see exactly what the problem was going to be. I suddenly had a sinking feeling; one I knew only too well. None of this was going to be simple, and I was utterly sure it wouldn't go to plan.

You'll be surprised to learn, I'm sure, that I was bloody right about that…

CHAPTER 14

Curiosity Killed the Shogun

"Show me this spider…" Yamamoto said, his voice soft and even, as he peered at me closely from no more than a foot away, which, as you might imagine, was slightly disconcerting.

"I can't," I said, and a shadow of anger passed over the warlord's otherwise implacable visage. Luckily my old faithful Bad Penny came to my defence before my refusal could cause irreparable offence.

"If he raises up the eyepatch, it will most likely take control of him, uncle. I know this is hard to believe, but he becomes quite dangerous at that point…" she told him.

I decided to let that 'hard to believe' slide by. There are some battles not worth fighting.

"I see," the warlord said and clapped his hands once which brought forward two of his guards, who obeyed with their normal stoic reserve. The pair grabbed an arm apiece and pulled them firmly behind my back. Which, it has to be said, was far from pleasant from my perspective, and did rather immobilise me. Unless that was, I wished to tear my arms from their sockets, which if the spider took hold was entirely possible. Needless to say, I was far from happy with this arrangement. Unsurprisingly no one asked me my opinion on the matter.

Yamamoto, however, was satisfied that I was firmly restrained, trusting in his guards, no doubt because in typical Japanese fashion they would sooner kill themselves than fail their master, or at least be expected to do so soon shortly afterwards if they did. Say what you like about the mad buggers, but their loyalty was never something you could question. Even their criminals consider personal honour an absolute and they make the East End mafia look like a bunch of schoolkids taping each other up for lunch money in comparison.

The soon to be Shogun nodded almost imperceptibly to his guards, whose collective grips on my arms tightened a little more, straining my shoulders, which were already starting to burn by this point. Then, once I could do nothing but watch him, the little bastard reached up and pushed my eyepatch device up and away from my eye.

A moment passed, that usual tension-filled moment that always hung there like a spring, coiled on a hair trigger. Then I felt the thing in my eye move slightly, an overwhelming urge to scratch at it and the blurring from the influx of light cleared then came back as my eye watered, and tiny metal legs began to swim in my optical fluid. Which, on the off chance you're wondering, is not a pleasant experience.

I blinked a lot.

It didn't help.

"Kare no hiza no ue ni," Yamamoto ordered, and I felt the guards simultaneously kick out at the back of my legs sending me, somewhat painfully, to my knees. As I said, he was a little guy, and he wanted a closer look at my eye and the thing inside it. So he wanted me down on his level, as he took out a small mechanical, optical device of his own, and peered down it into my eye.

It made an odd whirring sound as the optics focused in and out in response to him pressing buttons. The lens moved in smooth fluid movements, extending like a tiny telescope.

"Omoshiroi," he said, which given my firm British grasp on all foreign languages meant sod all to me but I assume was him telling me to keep my eye open, which was something of a challenge, but I tried all the same as he nodded slightly and peered in ever closer with his device. Which, in hindsight, he really shouldn't have done…

Neither Penny nor I had seen fit to warn him about one of the things that was likely to happen.

"Hai… Omoshiroi," he said again. But I was too distracted to care what this meant by this point. I could feel a tingle of pressure building up behind my eyelids, and I knew what was coming. I'd never really noticed that pressure building up before, I'd generally been focused on other things every time. But right then I was more than half expecting what was about to happened next. And that knowledge made me more aware of the process. So I was at least prepared a little this time round.

Just a little bit of pressure build-up, followed by…

W

H

Y

"Tawagoto," the little warlord screamed, a word I suspected wasn't the kind of Japanese word that gets used in pleasant company…

I

S

Yamamoto reeled backwards and had to catch himself to avoid losing more of his precious dignity, his optical device scattered to the corner of the room.

W

E

L

L

S

Not that I gave a damn about his plight right at that moment. What with the accompanying agony of The Ministry's method of communication burning my iris.

I

N

Besides I also was a tad distracted because on top of the burning pain in my eye, I had the added pain caused by my involuntarily bucking against the hold that Yamamoto's guards had on me. Remember what I said about it being entirely possible the spider would cause me to wrench my arms from my sockets the way they were holding me? Well, be it possible or not, I was doing damnedest to try, with accompanying agony.

J

A

P

A

N

I was screaming by this juncture. Screaming enough to drown out Yamamoto's angry shouts. I could feel myself tensing up. The rage was hitting me, rage and frustration.

Looking back on all this, I wonder if that rage was induced by the spider this time, or was purely my own. I couldn't tell you which, truth be told. I wasn't in a happy place full of fluffy bunnies at the time, and if I'd had the chance to strangle someone right then and blame it on The Ministry's spider, I dare say I would've done. But the blinding light from my oppressors was not quite complete. There followed a final three bursts.

?

?

?

If I may add here a minor observation of my own. It takes a certain type of individual, with a certain depravity of mind to end any sentence with three question marks. Particularly, I'm of the opinion, when it is a sentence written in eye-burning, head-splitting flashes of light…

But with that, it was over.

Bad Penny in an act of compassion quite at odds with her normal character, reached over and pulled the eyepatch back into place. And just like that, the spider fell dormant once again, leaving the ghosting afterglow of question marks still burning in my eye.

I could've kissed her for that. Though I suspect that would've earned me a punch in the mouth.

After a moment, Yamamoto's guards, under Penny's direction for the warlord was still a tad incapacitated, released me from their grip. At that point, I fell face first upon the nightingale floor.

My head was splitting, a migraine starting in vengeance, pain wracking my body, I suspect for a moment I even passed out…

But then, what else is new?

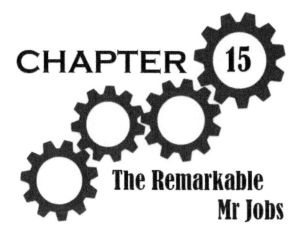

CHAPTER 15

The Remarkable Mr Jobs

Several days later, I was watching that damned ceremony at the railway sidings in Nagoya. Which was several hundred miles north of Yamamoto's castle. A lot had happened in the meantime. Not least of which had been several more examinations of my little friend. The Brass Warlord wasn't a man to baulk at the first unpleasant experience. As such, he insisted I remove my eye patch in his presence several more times as we journeyed north aboard The Sharapova, which the warlord had chartered for his purposes. Well, I say chartered, but only because 'pressganged' is such an ugly word.

It seemed this Jobs character that Wells and my ever-adorable Bad Penny were so interested in was busy working for Yamamoto on a secret project in the north, so if we wished to speak with him then we must sail to Nagoya. Thus as Yamamoto was heading north himself, he politely, with irrefutable manners requested Vlad offer up his ship in temporary service to the Japanese cause. While his manners were as I said irrefutable, and his request quite the most polite pressganging I've ever witnessed, the fifty heavily armed troops he brought with him to the dock did suggest that the polite nature of the request was, well, only a matter of politeness, not to put too fine a point on it.

Captain Putin had understandably bristled somewhat at this, much as you would doubtless expect. Vlad was never a man who liked taking orders from others. But there were other considerations. Not least the compensation that Yamamoto offered for this service. So, in the end, Vlad agreed to the 'request' as the combination of avarice and self-preservation outweighed any reservations he might have. Not that I was much privy to negotiations. What I knew of them came second or third hand from my old friend Yuri in the engine rooms of The Sharapova, which had once again become my retreat. Short of those times, I was required to subject myself to more demonstrations of The Ministry's pet spider.

For an engine room rat, Yuri always seemed to know far more you'd expected. He told me there'd been a few harsh words between the 'Psycho killer bitch with the nice legs, yar' and the captain, for example. But when Yamamoto had several crates of the local 'funny-vodka made from rice' and no small amount of bound boxes of 'stuff', delivered to The Sharapova's loading bay to serve as payment, the matter was quickly settled. Yuri and the rest of The Grunt's crew were happy enough with their Cossack want-to-be captain all things considered. Particularly as Vlad had been wise enough to share the bottles of rice-wine among them liberally. Old Vlad had many failings but being a miser with the crew's share wasn't one of them. If nothing else Putin seemed a firm believer in the value of bought loyalty.

I can't say I developed much of a taste for saki, but along with Yuri's company and cards, I tried my best to do so. Which is to say I spent much of the voyage north losing a little at cards but drinking a lot of saki. Which accounted for me suffering from my third rice wine hangover in a row that morning in Nagoya. It was also one of the worst post binge mornings I've ever suffered, which is up against some stiff opposition, I can tell you that for nothing.

Still, in my defence, it was something to take my mind off Yamamoto's taking every opportunity presented to him to examine my spider. It has to be said, the anticipation of eye-burning light and fits of rage were wearing on me a little. Remarkably however I was sent no messages from my friends at The Ministry after that first time, which was in my opinion a blessing at least. But the trepidation was there every time Yamamoto had my patch lifted. There were no sudden induced rages either. I would've almost thought the damn thing was broken if I hadn't felt it moving about my eye every time.

I'm not given much to reflection on the motives of my imperial masters. They never made much effort to keep me informed of their plans after all, but even I got to wonder about this. I started to suspect they were studying whatever images they were receiving from their insidious little friend in my eye, and were, I hoped, a tad puzzled by them. If only because it was nice for the shoe was on the other foot for once. They knew where I was, and they knew I'd been in contact with Wells, what with them forcing me to attack him back in Nepal. Judging by their messages, they'd surmised, wrongly, that Wells was also now in Japan.

A turn of events which I had no doubt would please Wells himself no end. I also suspected I wasn't the only one assuming this was the case, my 'friend' 'Not-Actually-An-

American-And-Never-Was-A-Maid' Penny had doubtless surmised much the same. Hence, she was all too keen to encourage her 'uncle' Yamamoto to continue indulging his inquiring mind. It played nicely into her hands as the whole reason I'd been dragged to Japan in the first place was to sow the seeds of disinformation. She'd told me as much that first day on the hillside overlooking Hamamatsu, as I'm sure you recall.

So by the time we set down at Nagoya, I'd an odd sense of both dread and ennui settling upon me. I'd half considered the possibility of taking Yamamoto himself into my confidence. Not least because he was being played by Wells and Penny, to advance whatever scheme she'd come up with to get this Jobs character out of Japan. It wasn't like I owed her any kind of loyalty after all, or Wells for that matter. By rights, I should've been trying to find a way to contact my actual masters back in Whitehall, to warn them what Wells was up to and where they might actually find him. But to my mind, I owed them, indeed the whole of Queen Rusted Cogs' bloody Empire, damn all of my allegiance either thanks to the damn spider.

Some other man might draw a line in the sand and decided which side of it they wish to stand upon. But as far as I could tell, no one was about to stand alongside me no matter which side of any hypothetical line I chose to stand. So sod that for a game of soldiers. Better, I'd decided, to take the side of whoever was least likely to kill me or get me killed at any given moment. Principled stands are damn all good to a corpse, and no one would be raising any statues after my demise, I was damn sure of that. Hannibal's column wasn't going to adorn Trafalgar square. There would be no state funeral. No weeping housewives and stiff uppers while men raised a glass in my honour. Indeed, if I got a bloody gravestone, it would be a minor miracle.

England, in short, may well expect each man to do his duty. But it was going to be damn well disappointed in me. Or, I suspected, not, as I doubt it had high hopes in regards to me to begin with.

But I digress once more. So let me take you back to that crisp spring day at a railway yard in central Japan, and a hungover, not particularly patriotic Englishman watching a group of four train drivers with white cloth strips tied around their heads, kneeling before rice paper sheets spread out on the ground, while a Shinto priest murmured prayer over them.

Our erstwhile host Yamamoto was watching the ceremony, all solemn, inscrutable and determined. As indeed was everyone else present. Even Penny, still dressed in that odd red kimono, looked moved by all this. Though she didn't look quite the elegant woman of the tea garden she might otherwise have been. Kimonos, I believe, don't normally have a leather harness strapped over the top of them. A harness with two guns in holsters and pouches full of spare shells.

I found Penny's get up slightly worrying, mainly because I wasn't armed myself, except for the cutthroat in my boot. She was clearly dressed for trouble, which considering we were in a war zone made plenty of sense, even surrounded as we were by Yamamoto's troops. Though of course with Bad Penny it wasn't so much a question of is she expecting trouble, more was she planning to start any? It hadn't quite escaped my mind that we were here for a reason, and part of that reason was to steal Yamamoto's pet scientist away from him. Whether he was her uncle or not, I suspected if he got in her way she'd waste damn all time worrying about killing a few of his men on the off chance it might upset him.

Or a whole lot of them if it came to that.

The ceremony dragged on, the way these things do, and I was finding it hard to stand still and keep my eyes open. I'd really pounded the saki the night before as I'd gotten into a drinking competition with Yuri. Which was probably why I'd little recollection of how I'd made it back to my bunk. It seemed I'd forgotten that old proverb. You know the one, *'Don't get into drinking competitions with Russian airship engineers unless you want to end up with a hangover reminiscent of a Russian engineer pounding your head with a spanner the following morning'*. Okay that's not so much of an old saying, as one I'd made up that morning, but trust me when I say it holds water. I'll admit it could be snappier, but I wasn't really feeling up to snappy right at that moment.

I think I must've dozed off while still standing, which is something of a feat I'll admit because I didn't realise the ceremony was wrapping up until my Bad Penny gave me a dig in the ribs.

"Time to go, lunk-head," she said, and half dragged me in her wake as she headed for the train. I'd only the vaguest idea what I'd just witnessed at the time, and if I fully understood the ceremony I would've probably asked why we were going towards the damn thing. Or at least argued vociferously against doing so. True, there was little need to worry. The train wasn't due to set off for another hour, and that was only if the man we were going to see had finished his work. But I wasn't to know that. Though had I done so I'd still have thought twice before trusting fate not to throw a spanner in the works at an inopportune moment. But as I barely understood what was being undertaken at that station in Nagoya, I wasn't worrying myself sick at the time about the twenty carriages of highly volatile, super compacted, weapons-grade TNT that comprised most of that damn train. Instead, I was just feeling sick from a saki hangover, which is possibly much the same thing.

BP lead me towards a carriage in the middle of this impossibly long train which stood out from the others because it had a whole array of odd-looking antennae sticking out of it. There was also an odd dome-shaped device on the roof, which at first I took to be some kind of turret, though it lacked anything resembling a gun. Instead, it was studded with valves of some kind which were going through a strange slow dance of colours. Each lighting up for a few seconds before it dimmed and another took its place. I can't say I cared enough to ask what it was, but it did strike me there was something familiar about it.

There was something familiar about Professor Steffen Jobs as well. Both his name and the manic grin on his face when we entered the carriage, which was jammed full of equipment of one kind or another. Most of which I didn't recognise, though it brought to mind another lab I'd stood in only a few months before. A lab hidden below the sands of Egypt at the foot of the Sphinx itself. I found myself unsurprised by this, or by the itchy feeling seeing Jobs gave me. That same itchy feeling I'd got when I'd met William Gates for the first time. It was the way each looked at you, like you were another species, one of little worth in terms of their attention. People, I came to believe, were less real to them than their work. That's what Gates and Jobs had in common. Indeed, I suspect everything was less real to them than their work. I could see that from the glint of obsession both their eyes shared. As such, on meeting him, I was less than keen to let a man who struck me as another mad scientist try and remove the Ministry's insidious little pet from my eye. Call me a coward if you will, but I don't have much faith in men in white lab coats who look at you as a prospective science experiment...

"Oh, what do we have here?" the scientist in question asked us as we entered the carriage. Then he proceeded to look us up and down several times before he strode over to me, reached out, and started tapping the glass fount of my monocle. "Still working, I see. Good, good, would be most inconvenient if it stopped, but never fear it is entirely reliable and will be until I design 'The Eye-patch Three'."

It was disconcerting to have the man tapping the device while it was still strapped to my head. But I resisted the urge to thumb the blighter. Mainly because despite myself I was curious at this point. Which was, of course, a mistake on my part.

"And what happens when you do that?" I asked as it seemed the obvious question.

"Well, then 'The Eye-patch Two' will be entirely redundant. So it will slowly start to fail over the course of a couple of months or so, develop a few glitches here and there, that sort of thing. It's built into the design you see, has to be." the professor said, smiling the same mildly vacant smile that was favoured by his rival Gates. A smile that said, '*I am smiling at you because that is the human thing to do, and I want to you to know I am human.*' Indeed, the resemblance between the two men was quite uncanny, despite them looking nothing alike.

"Why would redundancy be built in?" I asked with a degree of confusion, and no little worry on my part. As I had no desire to find out what would happen when it failed.

"Why? Because well, no one would need 'The Eye-patch Three' if 'The Eye-patch Two' still worked fine clearly. I would have thought that obvious." He looked surprised I'd needed to ask such a question.

"Well yes exactly," I said, still confused. But Jobs didn't seem to follow my logic any more than I followed his.

"Good, you understand," he said and I didn't. "Excellent, now I suppose you want that contraption of Gates' out of you, yes? Of course, well I can't do it here, but I am sure once I have 'Little MAC' here fully operational, we can sort that out for you."

I didn't ask what 'Little MAC' was, not least because I didn't really care. But as it happened, I was going to get an explanation anyway. Jobs, more so than Gates, was a bit of a showman, which is to say he loved to have an audience to explain his contraptions to. Unfortunately, that was as much of a showman as he got, for he'd sod all idea how to entertain an audience when he had one. But as we were there, and as captive an audience as he could ask for, Jobs turned and started to narrate what he was doing with the odd collection of devices crammed into the centre of the carriage. I'll not bore you with the details, not least because I stopped listening to him after the first minute or so. Right after he started explaining it all, if I am honest. About all, I bothered to grasp was the name of the main device. The Multiplying Asymmetrical Cylinder. It was some special new kind of Babbage that Jobs had designed himself.

As I understood later this particular difference engine was vital to Yamamoto's plan. It had something to do with fixing signals and points on the route and calculating the Tesla charge that would be thrown through all the carriages at once to boost the impact of the TNT when the train hit its destination. Apparently, the Tesla charge had to be exact to ultra-excite the electrons which would, in turn, cause them… oh, let's just say it was going to make the boom bigger, much, much bigger, and leave it at that, shall we? I can't say I entirely followed the explanations I heard afterwards any more than I followed what Jobs told me at the time. Though, to no regret on my part at all, the professor only got about halfway through his explanation when the carriage doors slammed shut. What I did regret, however, was that the doors shut in a very final, these will not be opening again any time soon, kind of way.

Which, if I am honest I should've expected, because, let's face it, it was bound to happen. If you happily walk into a train that is ostensibly nothing more than a mile long super bomb about to hurtle across Japan at speeds of up to a couple of hundred miles an hour, what do you expect to happen apart from you getting trapped on board the bloody thing?

Well, perhaps if it was anyone else, they'd probably not get trapped on board. I, however, almost certainly trod on the wrong ant in a former life, if my understanding of basic Buddhism is anything to go by, and, 'Karma is,' or so I'm often told, 'a bitch'.

Oddly enough, I once knew a club girl in Soho who worked under the name Karma. I suspect she thought it made her sound exotic, and in fairness, she looked the part as she was half Indian. What I suspect no one ever told her however was that pale brown skin and a name like Karma doesn't make you exotic when you open your mouth and have a Croydon accent. I'm not entirely sure what, if anything, I ever did to wrong her. Though I sure as hell never told her about the problem with her accent because when she wasn't speaking she did things with her hips that... Well, that's not important right now. Let's just say she was a girl with many talents and leave it at that. However, while I don't recall offending Karma from Croydon, but her namesake, seemed to have had it in for me for a long time.

A moment or two later, while two of us were still staring at the doors, we heard sirens starting up outside. The kind you sirens people sound when a fleet of airships you didn't order appears on the horizon.

Jobs, oblivious to all this, was still working away and explaining something about 'Multiplex Trans Diodes' or whatever. I'm not even sure he noticed the carriage shunted beneath our feet, which sent me reaching for something to hold on to, and grabbing whatever was the closest thing I could get a hold of, which proved to be a mistake when Bad Penny batted me away.

I doubt Jobs even noticed when the train started to pull out of the station and started picking up speed at an alarming rate. But whether he noticed or not the bullet train to Hiroshima was underway. And underway with three more people aboard than had ever been intended. Not that I cared a great deal about it being three people. What I cared about was that one of those three was me.

"So how far is Hiroshima?" I heard myself asking in what was a surprisingly cool tone of voice, if a little edged with panic, even if I say so myself.

"Give or take? Four hundred kilometres," Penny replied, with none of her normal passion.

"I see, and how long will that take?"

"About three and a half hours before the war. What with all the stops in between," she said.

"But we won't be stopping at any stations, will we?"

"I would imagine not, no."

"So how long?"

"Two and a half, three at the most I'd guess."

"Three hours, I see, and say we manage to open the doors, how fast will this thing be travelling?"

"Fast enough," she said.

"Fast enough that?"

"That you'd probably die if you tried to jump out of the carriage because the suction caused by the air displacement caused by the speed of the train would drag you straight under the wheels," I was told. This last was put to me by Jobs, who it seemed had finished tinkering long enough to realise the predicament we were in.

"Thanks for that…" I said, wondering just how in the hell we, by which I meant I, was going to get out of this one…

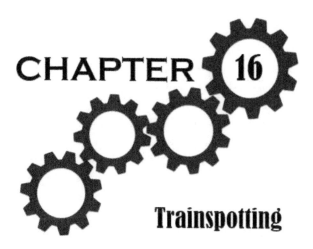

CHAPTER 16

Trainspotting

You might be wondering, what the hell was going on. Why had the train doors slammed shut? Why were the air raid sirens sounding in the train yard? Why had the 10:30 to Hiroshima set off early, without any warning? You may be thinking all that. I was a bit busy at the time thinking '*How the hell do I get off this thing?*'.

The whys mattered to me not at all, that 'how' was the only important question as far as I was concerned. Which was why I didn't get the full story of what happened in that train yard until a lot of other things had happened. It was months later in fact, and in the end, the events were explained to me by no one.

Be that as it may, I'm aware that much of this narrative has always been somewhat 'Hannibal' centric.

I've told you only of events as they happened to me and merely alluded to some I didn't witnessed directly. However, as I was locked rather abruptly in a train with a scientist I suspected of being at least a little on the mad side, and a psychotic woman whom as we have established by now is 'Not-A-Maid-But-A-Bloodthirsty-Killer-With-A-Cute-Smile', I didn't have a clue what events were unfolding outside. Or indeed whose fault it was that all Yamamoto's careful plans had to be set in motion somewhat earlier than he had originally envisioned.

Surprisingly, I'm sure you'll agree, it wasn't my fault. Well, not exactly my fault at any rate, not directly.

The first sign of trouble occurred just as we'd entered the train carriage. The newly blessed drivers were in the cab, running through a series of safety checks, ironic as that may seem on what was ostensibly a couple of thousand tons of rail mounted bomb. But safety checks were important. Apparently, it wouldn't do to have an accident before you devastate a whole city. Somewhere in the middle of this ultimately pointless exercise, undertaken out of a strict adherence to a rule book, in this case presumably the Nagoya to Hiroshima express drivers' safety handbook, a tome which strangely makes no mention of exceptions to the standard checklist which may be made if you are pulling something equivalent to a million ton of primed and ready TNT, one of the drivers spotted something in the sky heading towards Nagoya from the mountains to the north.

It quickly became apparent to the kamikaze train drivers that the rail yard was about to come under attack by several Chinese airships. A logical conclusion and as utterly understandable as it was utterly incorrect. As such, they started to follow a different rulebook, this one based on the orders of the Brass Warlord himself. Those orders were that at the first sign of anything that could prevent their mission going ahead, they were to take all possible steps to pursue it to its natural, somewhat explosive, conclusion. To wit, they hit the emergency button that sealed all the doors, threw out the rest of the checklist they'd been carefully following and started the engine. Setting off exactly like, well, exactly like a bullet train sets off, which was remarkably slowly all things considered, for the first minute or so.

This unfortunate circumstance, for yours truly, could've been averted even then had not others in Yamamoto's forces, those set to watch for such things, having heard the thrum of the bullet's main engine started scanning the sky and saw that same small fleet of airships moving quickly towards their positions. As it was clear to the guards that the only force in Japan who had enough airships to be even called a fleet was the Chinese, they leapt to the same utterly understandable though erroneous assumption as the train drivers had and thus sirens started to wail.

The sounding of the siren no doubt only reinforced the decisions of our Kamikaze train drivers that it was time to get underway, so they engaged the lockouts that would keep the train moving and hand direct control over to 'Little MAC', and so all chance of recall was gone. It was at this point professor Steffen Jobs, Bad Penny and I realised we were locked inside the biggest bomb the world had ever seen and were in the process of being fired at a city. Which on a personal note, I considered to be rather lamentable.

Other things were happening at the train yard while the train got underway. Things which I pieced together much later.

Yamamoto doubtlessly was quietly issuing orders to men who then shouted them at other men. Yamamoto wasn't an officer to do his own shouting after all. I doubt he spared much of a thought for his niece and the British officer she had in tow, at the time.

My old 'friend' Vladimir meanwhile was shouting at his own people and getting The Sharapova ready to depart in a hurry. While he had a fine Russian Steel Tsar at his disposable, there looked to be five or more Chinese ships heading towards the train yard, and The Sharapova was sitting like the proverbial duck. He later lamented that he was torn between rescuing his comrades, or as I like to call them us, and making sure his ship and crew were safe from the oncoming fleet. I suspected when he told me this he was lying through his teeth as I'm sure rescuing 'us' never occurred to him for a moment. Not with his own skin on the line.

Yamamoto's troops quickly manned gun emplacements and prepared to open fire on the incoming fleet. Yet they never did, luckily for them, I suspect, as Yamamoto's force was grossly outnumbered. Though that wouldn't have stopped the Brass Warlord, I'm sure. His resolve was as steadfast as you would imagine for the man who later became the Brass Shogun and led the Japanese drive to rid their nation of the Chinese once and for all. But someone, probably some lowly gunner officer, as they tend to be the smart ones in my experience, took a closer look at the oncoming craft through binoculars and noted that while it was true the Chinese air fleet was the only sizable force he knew of in Japan, the Chinese were not in the habit of painting Union Jacks on the nose cones of their craft.

So, you see, the intervention that led to us being locked into a speeding bomb on its way to Hiroshima wasn't, as I said, my fault, not directly.

Oh no, not my fault at all.

It was, in my opinion at least, the fault of one of my charming companions. The one who has a habit of being charming right up to the point she isn't, in a blunt object to the back of the head, razor-like claws, iron fast grip, inflicting maximum damage on whoever is available, kind of way, generally me. Or as I like to call her Bad Penny, whose influence on my luck, namely to the bad, never ceases to astound me.

She was after all the one who had purposely used me to distract the British, namely The Ministry away from Nepal, India and importantly from her point of view, Wells. Though I suspect it was the more attractive Wells with the long legs, light brown skin and a shared passion for sharp objects, rather than the grandfather that Bad Penny agreed to misdirect the British for.

Penny was also the one that positively encouraged Yamamoto to keep having me lift my eye patch so he could examine the spider. Knowing full well, I've no doubt, that she was leaving a trail of breadcrumbs for The Ministry to follow.

Of course, I'm sure that she didn't for one moment suspect that the British would go so far as to mount a raid into the heart of a war zone, and in doing so risk unbalancing the conflict. British foreign policy was always very firmly of the opinion that if two sides were at war, the best thing to do was to stay out of it and sell guns to either side. But we were not dealing with the foreign office. This was The Ministry, and for them, the usual rules of careful diplomacy and profiteering didn't apply.

I've no doubt that in the view of the Foreign Office, this kind of incursion was damnably un-British. No doubt there would be harsh words and condemnations in the gentleman's clubs of Whitehall. But that was all beside the point. The point was after all that, Penny's manipulations had landed her, and more importantly me, in hot water.

Somehow, no doubt to the delight of the Foreign Office, this incursion never led to much. Not a single shot was fired, Yamamoto being too astute a general to start firing at British airships. Vladimir, while 'regretting that we were moving swifter than any airship could travel in the direction of Hiroshima and a date with destiny,' as he told us later, met with a delegation of British officers and swiftly claimed he was a commercial ship on a trade mission. Something the British ships claimed was also the case. So, Yamamoto played host to an impromptu three-way trade delegation of liars who all pretended to be simple merchant captains despite having enough ordinance between them to level a small town. He too, I am told, regretted that we had got trapped aboard his death express, in particular as one of us was his niece by marriage. However, with the exception of that one regret, he was pleased with how his day turned out, not least as he managed to 'convince' the British delegation, now on the ground surrounded by armed Japanese army, to sell him a large quantity of munitions at a very reasonable price.

All while the 10.30 to Hiroshima sped on, with its unfortunate, unexpected passengers on board.

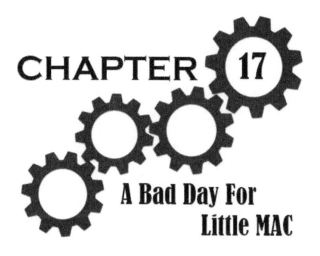

CHAPTER 17

A Bad Day For Little MAC

Aboard the bullet train, things weren't going too well, I'm sure you'll be shocked to learn. Despite the insistence of my companions that jumping through the doors would be a short trip to a swift death beneath iron wheels, I was trying my damnedest to open the bloody things. The Japanese, however, take safety on the railways, like almost everything else, very seriously. So, once the doors had been remotely shut by the crew in order to release the main breaks, they weren't going to be opened again now the train was in motion.

I felt this odd obsession with safety to be ridiculous. Underground trains in dear old London had no such safety locking systems on them, and passengers hardly ever jumped through the door of a speeding train to their death.

Suicidality inclined British commuters considered it far less of a fuss to wait patiently on the platform then just jump in front of a train.

I wasted a good twenty minutes utterly failing to get the doors to open. All the while cursing loudly the whys and wherefores of being trapped in the only compartment on the whole train that didn't have windows. While I did this, my own dear Bad Penny was trying to open the connecting door, which presumably should've led through to the next compartment. She was doing so with an equal lack of success, which says something as she was for, all her diminutive size, somewhat stronger than I. Thanks to that mechanical arm of hers.

Now, you may be asking, what Professor Jobs, the genius we had come all this way for, only to get trapped with, was up to at this time? Well, to my complete lack of surprise, he just continued messing with that baby Babbage machine of his and didn't seem particularly concerned about anything that was going on around him. Indeed, he seemed entirely oblivious to the danger we were in, and utterly engrossed in whirring cogwheels and flashing valves.

"Hell's bloody teeth," Penny shouted at some point, then as if her vocal exasperations weren't enough, she punched the door she'd failed to open in a fit of rage. Which, I may add, left a sizable dent in the damn thing, one I suspected would by no means make opening it any easier, given she buckled the housing completely. In fairness, this matched my own frustration, and it was at this point I stopped pointlessly struggling with the doors and kicked them into the bargain to underline my annoyance. Which only succeeded in hurting my toes, typically.

Our violent exclamations did however stir Jobs from his tinkering long enough to look over his shoulder. Then, in a voice that was calmer than it had any right to be, he chose to lecture Penny, with ill-chosen words. "There really is no need for such language from a lady, I'm sure."

I must've been close to hysterics by then unless it was the after-effects of all the saki I'd been drinking, but this struck me as not only an utterly absurd thing to say in the circumstances, but a piece of comedy fit for the music hall stage. So perversely, I found myself laughing loudly despite the growing fears I had in regard to our situation. My doing so, it must be said, didn't amuse Penny one iota.

"Stow it, Hannibal," the lady in question snarled in my direction. Her gaze, however, narrowed on Jobs, which had our current predicament not been quite so life threatening was something I might've taken solace in.

What's that saying about a wise man knowing when to say nothing? Jobs had never heard that saying.

"Really there is no need to become uncivilised about all this. We are perfectly safe for now," he told her and met her gaze surprisingly well, I thought. Which to me just confirmed my opinion that he was as barking mad as his rival Gates. Though he did seem a little more attuned to the world around him and people in general. Jobs could almost pass as normal, I suspected, on the right occasion, in a dim light, with a following wind.

"It's the 'for now' bit that worries me," Penny snarled, putting voice to my own opinion as well.

"We have two and a quarter hours left to us to find a means of safely extricating ourselves. It really should be no more than a simple matter of applying some logic to proceedings and thinking everything through," Jobs replied in a voice that would've seemed condescending if it condescended to be condescending towards you. And with that nugget of advice, he just turned back to his machine and started making some more minor adjustments and taking notes in a pocketbook.

Penny vented her frustration again, this time on the wall, in typically volatile fashion. I, meanwhile, was trying to reconcile how half an hour had slipped by so quickly, my eyes slightly wild as I looked around for solutions to the mess we were in. Let's just say Professor Jobs' lack of urgency wasn't universally felt, shall we? So, as the professor fiddled with his machinery, I cracked a little.

Now I'd like to think I've a fine sense of self-preservation. But I also have little time for boffins who tinker about with machinery, lost in a world of their own, while my life is in danger. Oh, I'd love to report I kept my upper stiff and faced down the problem with good old British decorum. But frankly, I was well past all that.

"What is wrong with you, man? What the buggering hell are you doing? Sticky Vicky's inbred heirs have more sense than you. Are you quite bloody mad," I shouted suddenly, feeling the need to vent my own frustrations on a somewhat softer target than the walls. Jobs' prematurely balding head for example…

"This is vital data from an unparalleled opportunity. Do you realise how extraordinary it is to have the chance to observe how Little MAC's design copes with this situation? With all these extra stresses and strains from our journey. It like Newton and the apple to you, see?" Job said in that same irritatingly calm, passive voice, turning to look at me over the rim of jeweller's lenses that were clipped on to his spectacles. As if he was giving a lecture in some well-lit lecture hall at a collage, rather than in a cramped compartment on what was effectively a speeding bomb. This niggled me somewhat.

"What?" I asked in a tone that was far less even, and no steadier than the mattress in Old Brass Nipples' bedchamber must've been when randy old Albert was still alive.

"Sir Isaac Newton and the apple. Surely you know the story. He was sitting in an orchard when…"

"Yes, Steffen, we all know that bloody story. What's that got to do with anything?" Penny interrupted sharply, clearly as frustrated as I.

"Serendipity. Don't you see? Those little things that make all the difference. This is a perfect opportunity to monitor the Little MAC in action. Dozens of calculations a minute, all the cogs turning perfectly despite our speed, the G-forces on the carriage, and all the other pressures upon it. Why had we not been locked in here, I would've never had this chance. Just like Newton's apple… Apple… Hum…Something about that word, don't you think… Apple… Sorry, where was I…? Oh yes, you see I can't waste this opportunity. The chance for scientific advances is too valuable to miss. Why that should be obvious to even the most dedicated luddite…"

Bad Penny turned to me, her face a veritable picture of disbelief. Then she nodded her head in Jobs' direction and said. "Hit him,"

"What?" I asked her, still in the grip of red misted terror and playing catch up after Jobs' little lecture.

"Well if you don't, I will, and right now I would probably kill him if I did," she replied, giving me no indication she was anything less than serious.

I let out a little chortle of nervous laughter, and the look she gave me was enough to confirm just how serious she was. So, smiling, I pretended to tip my hat to her wisdom, took a step forward and cracked the professor a good one right on the chin.

The punch sent him sprawling backwards into his own machine, bouncing off it and dropping to the carriage floor.

As punches go, I was quite proud of it. It was also quite absurdly satisfying and vitriolic in many ways. The pain it left throbbing in my knuckles made me feel I'd struck a small victory for common sense. Though that particular small victory wasn't one I got to revel in for long. Indeed, as small victories go it turned out to be a somewhat bitter one, considering what happened next.

The 'Little MAC' Babbage, which Jobs had fallen on to, started to let out weird little whining noises, which grew in pitch alarmingly. Worse from our perspective, however, was that as the whine grew louder, we were thrown forward by a sudden burst of acceleration. I stumbled but managed to right myself, and Penny grabbed for one of the many straps that hung about the place to prevent herself from clattering into the professor.

The train was very definitely going faster with every passing second. Which was saying something as we had been clattering along at a fair lick in the first place.

Then the new whine switched to a loud thrumming the whole carriage started to shake and this time I was sent sprawling to the floor. Penny still gripping the strapping tightly, swung into the air and had she been anyone else would doubtless have lost her grip entirely. As it was, when her feet swung up, she would've all but taken my head off had I not already been sent sprawling. Luckily, I just took a glancing blow for once, but my head was ringing as I struggled back to my feet, just as the train started going round some long curving corner, the G-force sent me reeling into the opposite wall, and the floor of the carriage started to tilt alarmingly.

"Oh, my dear lord," the Prof exclaimed as he struggled to get back to his feet and tried to get back to the Babbage which was still making alarming noises. He then started searching around the floor of the carriage for something. It wasn't till he found it, I realised it was his notebook and pencil.

"What's going on," I shouted at him above alarming screeching noises.

Jobs, recovering more manfully than I would've given him credit for, took a breath, tried to write something down, snapped his already broken pencil and threw it down in frustration. Then looked up at Penny and me with disgust on his face.

"Well, it would appear your Neanderthal histrionics have damaged 'Little MAC' here, and it's trying to run all its calculations at double speed, which by extension means the train is also trying to go twice as fast," the professor said, with more urgency and far less of the lecture hall to his tone than previously. Clearly what it took to get him to take the danger of a situation seriously was to make it twice as bloody dangerous. Which is not a course of action that has much to recommend it, let me tell you.

"Is that even possible?" Penny shouted above the racket. There was a familiar cold-blooded calm about her now, of the kind I'd come to dread. She'd found her feet again but still clung to the ceiling strap tightly, which made her wiser than me as the train started leaning again as it hit another bend in the track, sending me crashing back against the wall and cracking my head for the second time in short succession. At this Jobs had the gall to let out a little chortle. Though why he chose then of all times to develop a sense of humour escaped me.

"No, it's not possible. I could tell you just how not possible it is if your pet thug here hadn't just broken my pencil," he snapped back.

"I'm not her pet thug," I retorted, with a certain degree of venom, ridiculous though that was given the turn of events. I'd other things to worry about than personal affronts, after all.

"Never mind all that, how do we slow it back down?" Penny said calmly.

"That, I am afraid, escapes me entirely at this time, unless we can take the Babbage offline completely and leave it purely to the engineers to run the train," Jobs told her.

"Well, let's do that then!" I said, as it seemed the obvious solution. The drivers were never going to let the damn thing get derailed if they could help it, after all. I mean it's not like they were suicidal…

Yes, I know, let it pass, will you? It's not quite the same thing, you know…

"It's not that simple. The connecting cables would have to be cut," Jobs insisted.

"Then cut the damn things," I shouted above the noise of the train, which suddenly got louder still and there was a booming noise that sounded like an explosion. Which I may add did little for my nerves as I was flung back against the wall once more.

And then, everything went black…

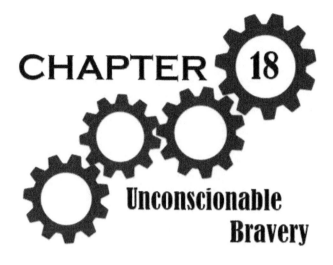

CHAPTER 18

Unconscionable Bravery

Now I know what you're thinking. Isn't that just typical. A little action and then suddenly Hannibal get knocked out again. Does he ever manage to get through a situation without blacking out for one reason or another? Well, as it happens, this time I did. The booming sound and the sudden blackness were caused by the train entering a tunnel passing through a range of hills by which the train entered Chinese territory. This was not merely a lucky coincidence but part of Yamamoto's grand plan. The mouth of the tunnel we had entered was some two miles inside Japanese territory; once we fully exited the chain of half a dozen tunnels through the hills of the Hyogo region, we'd be deep in Chinese-held territory. This was how the train was to cross over the front lines. Indeed, the Japanese forces had fallen back twenty miles or more over the last few days just so those tunnels spanned no man's land.

Of course, I was unaware of this at the time, so the sudden darkness and the noise from the train which doubled in volume within the tunnel was a tad disconcerting. And sure, I can hear you saying, 'It's just a damn tunnel, man. You've been on trains before surely?' But there is a difference between sipping tea on a GWR heading down to Devon for a weekend's liaison with a young lady called Glenis and riding in the windowless carriage of a high-speed bomb on rails in Japan. Not least of which is that Glenis was particularly entertaining company in the tunnels... Oh, and GWR trains don't rely on fifth columnists within the Chinese controlled regions to make sure the tunnels don't get sealed, which is a minor, but somewhat important difference.

Yamamoto had gambled on his fifth columnists doing their job right. Though he reasoned that if the worst happened and they failed then the train would explode on impact and the resulting explosion would at least take out a large proportion of a Chinese division in those hills. So, while those troops may not have been the main target, a win would be a win, either way.

I'll admit I'm thankful I was unaware of all this at the time, not that I could've been any more terrified than I was already, but I think had I had knowledge of 'Plan B' that may have sent me over the edge into utter despair. Keeping a stiff upper is all well and good in principle, but I defy anyone to find themselves enclosed on a moving bomb hurtling down a track at twice the design speed, to just keep bloody calm and think of England.

As I gathered my wits about me, I became aware the professor was shouting something, though I could hear sod all due to the noise of the tunnel. Penny was arguing back at him and after a minute or so I saw a couple of sets of glowing eyes looking in my direction. They'd an eerie green glow to them that suggested some kind of chemical light like the glow sticks so popular with the last night of the prom's crowd. My wits were a little shot, and my head was killing me, so this creeped me out for a moment until I realised one set were small valve bulbs on either side of Gates glasses. The other set was Penny's, though where she had gotten her goggles from, I've no idea, as her kimono lacked pockets as far as I could see, or any unsightly protrusions that could be hidden items. All her protrusions were indeed of the slightly kind, but not to digress…

Unable to make out anything being said, I huddled against the wall and thanked God that the track at this point seemed to be straight at least. A minute or so later we erupted into the open air once more, and the sheer volume of noise abated. Which wasn't as encouraging as you might think, as the first thing I heard was Penny shouting. "Are you off your bloody rocker?"

"It's the only way," Jobs insisted in return.

"How long till the next tunnel?"

"Minutes maybe. We'll need to get this done before the last tunnel. The track curves there for several miles, and at this speed we'll be lucky to stay on the tracks."

At this point in the exchange Penny scrambled across the floor of the carriage and start doing something with her back to me. Having missed most of the exchange, I didn't have a clue what was going on. Then she turned to me and shouted at me to come over and give her a hand. As I gingerly crossed over to her I discovered she was trying to unscrew bolts holding down a long metal plate that ran down the centre of the carriage.

"You're not serious?" I asked, oblivious to what she hoped to achieve. But serious or not, anything was better than just waiting for inevitable death. I mean, it wasn't as if I'd a bottle of scotch to keep me company while I waited.

She was unscrewing bolts with her fingernails. Which was quite a sight, but then she did have fingernails of surgical steel. I suspected my own would not fare as well.

"Do you have tools?" I asked the professor, more in hope than expectation, but as I looked up towards him, he held out a piston screwdriver, which I took willingly, happy to be doing something.

I've found, you see, when faced with imminent death, doing something, no matter how futile it may seem, is a vast improvement on doing nothing and waiting for a guy in the black cowl with a healthy interest in medieval farm equipment to turn up. Though my preference remains doing something with a good bottle of scotch.

I set about unscrewing the long bolts on the opposite side of the plate to Penny. While the professor kept looking back at the whirring cogs of the Babbage, making tutting noises and occasionally pressing buttons that didn't seem to have any effect.

Adrenaline must have been coursing through our veins, well, mine at any rate, your guess is as good as mine about what courses through the augmented veins of 'Psychopathic-Not-In-Anyway-A-Maid', two-stroke oil for all I knew, but we got the bolts out in double quick time. The whole plate was six foot by two foot, and was bound to weigh a figurative, if not a literal ton. But despite this, we each grabbed one of the recessed ring handles and faced off at each other and our eyes locked with a weird form of intensity passing between us.

Have I ever spoken about Penny's eyes? Well… okay, perhaps this isn't the time…

I closed my own eyes for a second and took a deep breath before opening them again, nodded to Penny, and said, "On three… One… Two…Thr…"

We dragged the plate up and out. Or to be more exact Penny dragged up the plate while I struggled to get my end to move at all, which led me lurching forward towards her, completely off balance.

Timing, as 'they' are want to say, whoever they are, is everything. I've always suspected whoever 'they' are, they are a bunch of patronising bastards who revel in being wise after the event. The kind of smug-faced swine that make your hands twitch and your knuckles ache to be relocated in the direction of the smug face in question.

But timing, as 'they' say, is everything…

Everything in this particular case was the train hitting another tunnel, with a loud boom followed by us being pitched into darkness just as I was pulled forwards headlong over a six by two hole in the floor, thanks to the ridiculous strength of a petite blonde woman. Thus, as I found myself clinging to one end of the bulkhead cover while I stared down into darkness, I discovered the bullet train had small maintenance lights running at intervals down its underside. A fact I would've found more interesting were they not illuminating the underside of a train speeding down a track a few feet below me, at a speed far in excess of its design parameters.

I opened my mouth to scream, but that scream was lost in the howling gale that was now blowing up into the carriage through the hole in the floor. I was still screaming several minutes later when the train boomed out of the tunnel and light flooded back in through the skylights. Oddly enough being able to see even more of the underside of the train in daylight and the blur that was the wheels, did nothing at all to make me feel any more relaxed about dangling down the hole.

"Help him up," Penny shouted, though I barely registered her words at the time. If she said anything more salient, I've no idea, but I suspect the odd swear word was flying about the carriage.

The professor clearly thought it wise to drag himself away from the Babbage at last and pulled me none too softly back into the carriage proper. My relief at no longer staring at certain death was to be short-lived, but I embraced it all the same. Breathing hard and fast, I fought to get the panic out of my system as Penny pulled the cover fully out of the way and revealed the whole inspection hatch.

"Now what?" she asked the professor, her voice lacking any emotion. I will say this for Bad Penny, when action is called for, she doesn't waste any time with complexities like human feeling. Which when she is working with you rather than against you is actually quite reassuring.

"Now I believe you should dangle your acquaintance down the hatch and cling on to his legs while I instruct him what to disconnect," Jobs said in such a matter of fact way it sounded like he was ordering tea and scones at a small brasserie on the English Rivera.

My response to this suggestion rhymed with a common type of waterfowl, and fashionable headgear.

"Really, sir, there is no need for all this constant profanity!" Jobs insisted, which garnered a response from yours truly which, which raised the question of his parentage and a repetition of the waterfowl rhyming word.

"Regardless of your opinion of me, sir, the lady is clearly stronger than you, and to be frank, I'd reason she would feel safer holding you than trust you to hold her. Furthermore, I'm too valuable to risk. If this plan fails, someone will have to formulate an alternative plan, and you sir don't strike me, sir, as much of a thinker…" Jobs retorted, and I caught sight of my dearest Bad Penny nodding along with his reasoning.

The damnedest thing was I couldn't fault that reasoning either, more's the pity, and while you, dear reader, would probably now claim to know me well enough to know I'm not one to put my own life on the line if there is some alternative, time and indeed the train was rattling on, so to speak. Consequently, one thing there wasn't any of was time to argue. Sometimes, frankly, needs must. No matter how much you might want it otherwise.

I looked up at Penny who returned my gaze with a look which defied any argument. So, shrugging my shoulders, I did my best to look heroic and manly, smoothed down my moustache with one hand, set myself, and then gingerly made my way around the hole in the floor. Which probably ruined the effect.

I knelt beside it and looked down into the hole while Jobs pointed out a set of three connectors looping up below the place where his confounded Babbage stood whirring. They were a good four foot across from the inspection hatch so I'd need to hang completely under the train and hold myself in place with one hand while Penny held on to my legs, hopefully ready to pull me back if I needed her to, while I pulled the connectors free.

"You're kidding me?" I said, looking at the drop to the tracks speeding below which was less than a yard. At full stretch, if I lost my grip, my head would be bouncing off sleepers. Well, bounce was perhaps the wrong word for what happens when something is obliterated on impact, but I'm sure you see my point.

"Of course, normally you would never do this while the train is in motion." Jobs said, as the obvious needed to be stated apparently…

"Let me guess, we don't have a safety harness either, do we?" I asked, hopelessly.

"Not as such, I suppose you could hook a belt over one of the conduits and lash up something rudimentary with what he have available, if we had the time, but sadly I suspect we do not, so you will just have to risk it," came the professor's overly considered response to my question.

There was a rash of waterfowl rhymes once more. Followed by me wishing I'd a half bottle of gin to steady my nerves, or bloody saki come to that. But in the absence of strong drink, and after a warning glance from Penny, I steeled my nerve with as much rusty iron as I could muster, leant out over the abyss once more and found myself a reasonably firm grip on one of the main conduits. I looked back over my shoulder at the woman about to hold my life in her hands, not for the first time, and risked a moment of bravado, with a wink and smiled as much as one can when one is about to face almost certain death.

"When you speak of this in days to come, speak well of me!" I said.

"I wouldn't hold your breath on that," Penny replied, with no humour at all.

I sighed, let her take hold of my legs, and I pulled myself under the carriage, trying to ignore the noise of the tracks we were racing along under me only a few feet below me.

I inched my way along, holding the conduits, hoping they would not break loose and feeling sick to my stomach. Luckily for me, I was at least looking up at the underside of the carriage, though I could think of other things I could be looking up at from underneath, and all of them were more inviting.

It was another of those times when you would think some might begin to question their life choices. But I can tell you from my own experience, at times like these what you actually do is find religion and then in short order start to curse the Almighty under your breath. '*Oh God, oh God, don't slip, Harry old boy, oh God…*' and what not.

I inched my way under the train till I was just about close enough to reach the three cable connectors plugged into a small bulkhead that hung down from the carriage floor. Stretching one arm, I could just touch them, just, but they were all individually latched in place, and I was damned if I'd the purchase to push free those latches.

"I need a hammer or a bar or something," I yelled above the noise of the wheels, trying to look back the way I'd come. My left arm was already burning with the effort of holding myself up. Even if Penny had hold of my legs, I was still struggling to hold the rest of me in place. I adjusted as much as I could, managing to wedge my arm through the small gap above one conduit and grasp a second, which made things a little easier but not by much.

"Take this," Jobs shouted and reached under the carriage towards me with a screwdriver in hand. After two flailing attempts, I managed to grab it off him without losing my grip on the conduits. I looked at it; it was far from ideal, a claw hammer or a jimmy bar would've been a damn sight easier to work with. But needs must when the consumptive is coughing all over you.

"Which one first?" I yelled back. Last thing I wanted to do was make things worse.

"The left hand one," came the reply, so I set to work with the screwdriver. After three tries at it, I finally managed to jerk free the latch mechanism and then putting the screwdriver in my teeth, I wrenched the first of the plugs free.

There was a sudden jolt, and I could feel the train straining to go faster once more. The vibrations almost shook me loose. I clung on with both hands for dear life. Biting down on the screwdriver so hard I'm surprised I didn't break a tooth. The taste of metal in my mouth was making me want to retch. A moment or two passed before

I dared to release one hand to take the screwdriver back out of my mouth.

"I said the left," yelled Jobs above the racket.

"That was the damn left," I yelled back after spiting to get the taste of iron out of my mouth.

"The other left, my left…" came the inevitable reply.

"Oh, for the love of Lady Mountbatten's arse," I screamed back at him. And set to work on the other left, because what else could I do. But try as I might I couldn't get purchase on it. Unlike, if the rumours were true, Lady Mountbatten's arse, the old buzzard's current lady wife, as I'm sure you know, is a former bare ankle model and firm favourite on page three of The London Times. The current fashion for bustles made it hard to be sure, but from the pictures that appeared in the society pages, I suspect there was a lot of purchase to be had there.

I digress I know, but when you're facing impending death hanging below a train, your mind will sometimes wander for a few seconds to happier thoughts.

Finally, I managed to wedge the screwdriver into the latch tightly and get my weight behind it. With a shove, the latch came free and I managed to catch myself before I broke my arm in the process. Unfortunately, what I didn't catch was the screwdriver which skittered onto the track below and made a shower of sparks as it was crushed below one of the wheels.

Someone of poor hearing may have confused my next few words for those of someone counting a lot of ducks.

The latch gone, I pulled free the second plug and the train jolted once more, but not as badly as the first time, perhaps it might even have started to slow. All I knew for sure was that I couldn't stay down there much longer, and of course I'd now lost my damn screwdriver. The only way I'd get the last latch free was if I could get closer to it.

I dragged myself a few inches further forward and reached out, but the latch was utterly jammed in place. With nothing to free it but my fingers, I could do nothing but wrap my arm around the cable itself and try to pull it free of the plug. Some hope of that, I thought, but I had to try.

I strained at it one-handed, the other clinging on for dear life, muscles burning. But dragging at the cable didn't seem to be getting me anywhere. If I pulled any harder on the damn thing, I would be wrenching my arm out of my socket.

Then suddenly, with an explosion of noise the world went black, as the train plunged into another tunnel, while still hurtling along at breakneck speed, though break everything speed would be a more apt description.

All pretence of trying to free the last cable went out of my mind as I just clung on with both arms in the hope the tunnel was a short one and I might be able to hold on long enough to see daylight again.

An age seemed to pass, that in actuality less than a minute, before light erupted around me once more.

In desperation, I grabbed hold of the last cable and pulled down hard as I could, and somehow this time it came free. Which nearly saw me fall to the tracks below in shock.

The train bucked, losing speed fast but in erratic bursts. I screamed for Penny to pull me back out of the hole. Or perhaps I just screamed. Screaming seemed the thing to do in all honesty. Brave heroics, well, you can keep them, utter terror has little to recommend it.

Somehow, I'm far from sure how, I found myself back on the carriage floor, blackened, bloody, hyper-ventilating and not quite in my right mind. My arms burned, my head was pounding, and I could hardly hear a thing. After the deafening roar in the undercarriage my ears were still ringing. When the train plunged into yet another tunnel, and darkness consumed us, I may even have screamed at that point, or blacked out for a few moments, my memories of those events are shattered. All I know is sometime later I found myself staring across the carriage floor at Bad Penny and Professor Jobs, not quite being able to take anything in. The next thing I remember with any clarity was Penny saying the first thing she has ever said to which I was in full agreement.

"We need to get off this damn train."

I found out later almost half an hour had passed since my wildly out of character heroics beneath the train. The train had decelerated to something closer to its normal cruising speed, despite all odds was still on target for Hiroshima, and was now deep in Chinese territory. The fifth columnists had done their jobs well, and the Chinese were either blissfully unaware of the approaching calamity or at least had no idea just how big a problem they had headed towards their central command.

"You're right about that," I muttered and started struggling to my feet. Which after the strains I'd put my body through in the last hour was harder than you might imagine. Every muscle screamed its own private complaints. I felt utterly bone weary, but in the circumstances, I put on my best impression of plucky British grit and ignored the pain as best I could. "But I still don't see how?" I added.

"You could just open the door," Jobs said, the smugness of his tone almost inviting another good thumping.

"What?" both Penny and I said in unison. Oddly on the same page for once.

"The doors were keyed into the automatic controls through Little MAC. Now we've cut the link, they will open quite easily, I'm sure," the professor told us, speaking to us like poor students, confronted by the obvious but failing to grasp it. The look this new intelligence brought to Penny's face matched my own, I suspect.

As I said, Jobs was a man always at the cusp of inviting a good thumping on himself, and like all science obsessed types, he seemed utterly oblivious to the feelings, violent or otherwise, he inspired in others.

Penny rolled her eyes and stalked towards the main passenger doors. Taking hold of the handle, she as good as ripped it off its hinges.

I looked at Jobs, who seemed his usual oblivious self. Then made my way over to join her in the opening, the wind howling as the train sped through the Japanese countryside like a, well like a speeding bullet, which explains where they came up with the name.

"What about all that stuff about getting blown back under the wheels by the slipstream?" I asked as I stared out through the doors, the wind whipping at my hair.

"Well in theory, now we are travelling at a more sedate speed, provided you jump far enough you should break past the slipstream and be fine," the professor said, with just enough uncertainty in his voice to worry me.

"In theory?" I asked

"Well yes…"

"In bloody theory?" I pressed, with a mild level of hysteria.

"Yes."

"For the love of Victoria's brass nipples!" I said, turning to face the professor and considering my options. I could shove him out first, of course, test the theory. He was a pointless egg head after all. A simpering boffin who no one much would miss.

The more I thought about that, the more the thought appealed. After all, if you want to find out if it is safe to jump from a train hurtling along the tracks, you might as well test the theory with someone worthless in the grand scheme of things after all.

My mind made up; I reached out to grab the irritating pigeon-faced brainiac with every intention of throwing him out into the void.

Which was exactly the point in time when Bad Penny shoved me hard in the back and sent me hurtling through the doorway into the gale-like wind.

Apparently, she had made much the same calculation herself...

CHAPTER 19

Land Of The Rising Sun

"Well, it seems safe enough…" Penny said, or may have said. Whatever she said, it was probably something witty, nasty, cynical, or all three. Whatever she said was also lost in the howling wind, the crash of the landing and the general disorientation one gets from being shoved with rib-crushing force from a speeding train.

I was, it has to be said, a tad peeved by this.

All things considered though, when I found myself alive, and not crushed under the wheels of a speeding train, I wasn't as put out as I may have been.

I landed in a field some ten feet below an embankment. Rolled hard across the stony ground and came to rest on my back staring up at the sky.

By the time I'd found my feet and stumbled gingerly after the speeding train now disappearing into the distance, I'd discovered I was none the worse for the experience. Admittedly I was battered and bruised, my clothes had rips and tears in them, my head was ringing, I'd been half-deafened and felt like I'd been dragged through a hedge backwards. But I'd felt much the same before Penny shoved me out of the train.

I did think to myself, for a fleeting moment, that I could take this opportunity to put as much distance as possible between myself and her, Wells, The Ministry and everyone else that seemed so intent on finding new and interesting ways to end my existence. It was a perfect opportunity after all, out here in the countryside, miles from anywhere.

Except of course it was miles from anywhere, in a country where I didn't speak the language, I didn't even look like the locals, also happened to be a war zone, and I still had The Ministry's damn spider in my eye. So yes, apart from those little quibbles it was the perfect opportunity to exit stage left as it were.

As it was, I just starting walking in the direction of the train had taken, until I stumbled over Professor Jobs who was also looking somewhat worse for wear. Though he did seem to be taking all this in his stride, more than I was at any rate. A little further on we found my sweet dearest one and only Bad Penny, unsurprisingly looking perfectly fine.

"What now?" I asked, rather than start an argument I wasn't going to win about being thrown from the train. There are some arguments you're just going to lose.

"We make for high ground," she said and just started marching towards the hills before us, which lay in the direction the train had been going.

It took a half an hour or so to climb to the top of the nearest hillside. Which gave us a good long view down the valleys of the Hiroshima lowlands, right down to the city itself, nestled around the bay that bore the same name. We didn't have long to enjoy the view, however. Within a few moments of us cresting the hillside, a second sun seemed to rise in the west of Japan. The flash would've been blinding had we been closer than the twenty miles or so that stood between us. The sound of the blast and a great rush of wind passed over us almost three minutes later. I have in my life never seen a more terrifying sight that the great bulging cloud rising above that city.

The bullet train to Hiroshima had reached its final destination and as I watched from that hillside, I found myself wishing I could've done something to avoid it ever arriving there. Though not so much that I wasn't glad I'd alighted the train when I did. I was even grateful for the punch in the back that that old Bad Penny of mine had given me that had sent me clear of that damn death train, though I was loath to tell her that.

I have read of survivors of that dreadful event talking of the firestorms, the burning bodies, the ash and dust that drowned your lungs that dark day and for days afterwards as they picked their way through the rubble. The screams of the dying, the smell of the dead. The horror felt by the Chinese as they realised just how far the Japanese would go to reclaim their nation. The strange acceptance of their fate among the Japanese who survived. From that hillside twenty miles away, it looked like a door to hell itself had been opened.

We watched in shocked silence. A sense of awe upon us. At some point, Professor Jobs slumped to the ground and said something that, had I listened, may have been profound. Something about becoming death and destroying worlds, or something. I was too numb to care, too numb to comment. Amid such tragedy, such death, such destruction wrought by human hands, a holocaust of fire the likes of which the ancient gods of Greece and Babylon could only dream, such fury unleashed of biblical proportions, Sodom and Gomorrah laid out by the hand of man. Amid all that it was hard to know what to say or think. Hard to even contemplate an age when humanity could wreak such destruction upon the world and upon itself. In that one act, that one moment of utter destruction, that single moment of annihilation, that single blast that wiped Hiroshima off the face of the world, man had surpassed god, and in doing so left all morality in its wake.

In the midst of all that, I was numb and could think of nothing to say, nothing I could do. Yet felt there must be something, something profound, some insight I could express, some solace I could find within it all.

I looked at Bad Penny, at her face, normally so carefully cold, so careful under control and not betraying any of her emotions, so calculated. I looked in her eyes and glimpsed something which may have been a reflection of what I felt, this enormous weight of grief and guilt, for she, indeed we, had survived the bullet train but done nothing to prevent the ending of so many lives, so intent had we been on saving our own precious skins.

I'd never claim to be a philosopher, but there are moments in everyone's life. Moments when you recognise the grief and horror in another's eyes. Moments when even the most cynical self-satisfied, self-obsessed narcissist might realise they needed to move beyond their own selfishness. Realise that their own survival is not perhaps more important than the survival of others. In the face of something like that, there comes a moment when a true hero realises that they owe a debt to the dead. How could one not in the face of Hiroshima, in the face of all that horror, realise there were more important things in this world than you. That some sacrifices should be made, that the needs of the many outweigh the needs of the few or even the one. It was clear to me there on that hillside that my sweetest Bad Penny was coming to such a realisation as we watched Hiroshima burn.

As for myself, well, I was pondering more important matters…

"Don't suppose anyone has anything to drink?" I asked.

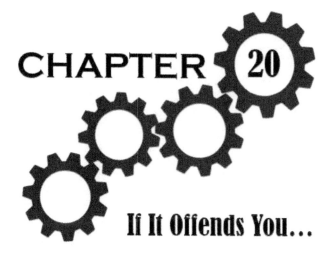

CHAPTER 20

If It Offends You...

We were two days on that hillside, watching the fires still burning on the horizon before The Sharapova showed up and airlifted the three of us out of there. The view of the devastation from the air made me feel sick as the big airship's flight skirted the edge of the city and headed out over the Sea of Japan. I turned away before long, hunger and thirst driving me down to the galley. I wanted nothing more than to put the whole sorry incident behind me.

During the long journey back to Nepal, I saw little of anyone other than Yuri and the rest of the engineering crew. If it's possible to drink yourself blind on engine room vodka, then I tried my best to do so. In my defense, I'd just witnessed, nay taken part in, one of the most cataclysmic events in human history. If there is ever a time to retreat into the bottle, then when you have the blood of four hundred thousand on your soul is probably as good a time as any.

From what little I managed to glean between games of cards, drinking from shot glasses and fitful sleep full of haunted dreams of burning cities, we were lucky The Sharapova arrived when it did. Not least because our erstwhile Captain Vladimir had been in his element at Yamamoto's impromptu trade conference, drinking, smoking cigars, and exchanging pleasantries with British Captains. Playing the dashing Russian aristocrat. According to Yuri, the British officers had lapped up his compliments and warmed to Putin's stiff authoritative personality like the lapdogs they were. Though Yuri's view on British officers was somewhat... tainted. Personally, I suspect this was because they didn't have enough tassels on their uniforms for his Slavic tastes.

In any event, once news of the death train's successful arrival at Hiroshima filtered through, the British Fleet took no time in making its excuses and turning tail. Even the most hidebound RAN captain knows a political mess when he sees one. They may have been ordered to execute a raid into Japanese territory by missives from The Ministry, but as all hell had broken loose, they wanted to distance themselves from the whole bullet train incident as fast as possible. The foreign office was going to be livid, and if for a moment there was any suspicion that the British had been in any way involved the Chinese Ambassador was going to be inscrutable.

Putin, however, for reasons that made no sense at the time, sailed north in tandem with the British fleet that evening, and that night put in at Komatsu, a small town on the north coast where Britain had a trading compound. Apparently, he'd been invited to dine with the British that evening and enjoyed a five-course meal while I sat on a hillside watching a city burn, starving and thirsty.

In all, when Yuri told me this, I was rather annoyed. But I was also rather drunk at the time so paid it less heed than I may have done in other circumstances. In light of subsequent events, this was an error on my part... But I will come to the whys and wherefores of that later.

Most of that journey back to Nepal was a bit of a blur, full of vodka and haunted dreams. It wasn't until we got back to Wells' hidden valley that I really sobered up at all. At some point during that journey, I agreed to let professor Jobs examine The Ministry's spider and see if he could remove it from my eye. Though I drew the line at him attempting this operation on the damn airship, no matter how keen he seemed to be of the idea.

I could blame the vodka. I was doubtless either hungover or drunk when I agreed or at one of the stages in between.

I could also blame the whole Hiroshima mess. I swore I could still smell the stink of hot ash, melted concrete and burning flesh on my clothes, and the nights when the vodka failed to blank them out completely were full of bad dreams.

I could blame a lot of things, but the simple truth was I wanted out of this whole mess, and as far away from Wells, The Ministry, and the whole of bloody Brass Buns Empire as I could right then. So, agreeing to let him extract that damn spider wasn't a decision made with much forethought. Mad swine though Jobs might be, he seemed at least as skilled as his bloody rival Gates. He also, which struck me as important at the time, seemed a tad saner than Gates. Though that wasn't saying a great deal.

All things considered, I decided I'd take my chances if only to be rid of the damn spider. Even if it meant being a guinea pig for surgery, which I was sure was the main reason I was still alive. Wells' granddaughter had the same device in her eye after all. I didn't doubt that the bastard thought it better to let them attempt to remove mine first than take any risks with his darling Saffron. And in truth had I been more the gentleman I pretended to be, I would've been expected to volunteer for that reason alone, I've no doubt. I suspect; however, my hosts weren't under any delusions about the nobility of my spirit. But all the same, I played up to the expectation which wasn't there, as I recall.

"Of course, better to take the risk with me than dearest Saffron," I remember telling them, putting on a show of a stiff upper, with considered undertones of the stoic hero.

Penny, who was there at the time of this conversation, merely raised an eyebrow in my direction, snorted, gave a little shake of her head and stalked off. So, I suspect I got off lightly, rather than be subjected to the full weight of her opinion.

Professor Jobs, on the other hand, didn't seem to pick up on Bad Penny's derision, any more than he saw through my own faked heroism, but was delighted. More I suspect for the chance to pick apart William Gates' device than out of any genuine interest in my wellbeing. But one takes what one can get when the devil vomits on your primroses.

"Mr Smyth, how are you today?" the professor asked me in an excited tone as he entered the ad-hoc surgery, which lay in a shed behind the main monastery buildings. He sounded like a child with a new toy. Which did little to inspire confidence. I had the feeling that to him I was the packaging, you know, the stuff that kids rip apart to get to the toy.

"A little tied down," I replied, retreating to humour defensively, an old habit of mine when I feel scared, and right at the moment, given the somewhat wild look in the man's eyes, I was edging towards terrified. It didn't help that I was strapped down and at the mercy of a mad egghead. I was regretting agreeing to all this when drunk and regretting more being sober right at that moment.

"Ha," Jobs said in response, and I mean said. It was not a laugh, more a statement from someone who didn't actually know how to laugh. One who only knew that occasionally laughter was required of him and filled in the otherwise blank space with words.

"Is there any chance you could untie me for a minute? I could do with scratching my nose," I added, though I knew why I was strapped down. Indeed, I'd agreed to it.

The shed we were in had been built to Jobs' specifications, and strange wires ran to odd devices from each of the walls. It was, Jobs had told me the day before, shielded against the radiographic aether wave assimilations, not that I've the slightest clue what that meant. But, in essence, it had been built to block signals between my spider and The Ministry, in order that Jobs could operate on me without the spider taking me over and causing me to fight back.

Jobs was, he told me, "Ninety-eight percent certain," the precautions he'd taken would be effective at blocking the signals. He still recommended I was tied down for the whole process though. As well as insisting on the presence of guards with tesla batons in the operating room, just in case I got out of hand.

So clearly, he trusted his own work absolutely.

"Ha," he said again. Leaning over me, with absolutely no concept of personal space. His eyes bulging through jam jar glasses that had an extra set of lenses clamped to one side again. These he swung down at this point with a nervous hand, as he leant in to examine me in finer detail.

His breath, I should add, could've laid low a dung beetle.

"I am afraid not, Mr Smyth, we must get on," he said, while playing with the strap on my eyepiece.

"I guess so. Time to be rid of the damn spider," I replied, trying to keep my reservations from my voice. Making him more nervous than he already was didn't seem wise for some reason.

"Spider…" he said as if trying the word for size. "Spider, ha, yes very droll. Spider, a spider in your eye. Oh, my yes, a spider indeed, and what a bite it has, quite poisonous I can assure you. Spider… yes, that is a good one… Ha…"

"I wasn't making a joke," I said.

"You weren't? Hum… how odd… I could have sworn you were. Spider indeed. But it needs to be out, I am told, so you'll have to wave goodbye to it. I must warn you however that you may feel a little discomfort when I remove it. My good friend William's toys can be most persistent once triggered."

"You consider Gates a friend?" I said, not entirely surprised by this nugget. This was, however, the first time we'd really discussed Gates himself, not that I'd spent much time with Jobs. After the whole Hiroshima debacle, I'd tried to avoid him for the most part. I was still unsure how I felt about trusting a man who'd thought it a good idea to become involved in something like the bullet train in the first place. Though Jobs had only ever been interested in the science and what he could make his 'Little MAC' Babbage do. Well, that was until he was confronted with the human cost of his experiments. To his credit, that weighed heavily on him on that hillside in Japan. It seemed swiftly forgotten though once we were picked up by The Sharapova. By the time we returned to Nepal what little I'd seen of him had suggested he'd put the whole incident behind him. He was in the end too much the scientist to worry himself over the human cost of his designs. Much like Gates, I suspect, he believed he was striving to create a better tomorrow, and as such he didn't worry himself overly the events of today.

"Of course, why would he not be? His methods are a little mundane, of course, really, he should stick to playing with the Babbage. His formulas for the engines are his real strength. He shouldn't be messing about with optics. He should leave the eyes to me. They take a delicate touch, after all. Really it is the precision that matters and the elegance of the design. A thing has to look right first and foremost, that is my motto. Working right will come afterwards…"

I'd no idea what he was talking about if I'm honest. I tuned most of this out, as at the time he had commenced peeling my monticule away from my head. As he did so, I felt the spider moving on my eyeball. I may have been imagining it, but it felt like all those legs were clamping tighter around my eye.

A surge of adrenaline flushed through me and a burst of rage tugged at my soul. Whether it was my imagination or otherwise, I don't know. But I felt anger all the same. Yet it wasn't quite that surge of uncontrolled rage I'd experienced before. Whatever was blocking the signals seemed to be doing its job and just my own innate anger lay in my soul.

"Now this will sting a bit, Mr Smyth. But I am afraid I have little choice," he told me. Which was all the warning he gave as he brought up a strange looking device, pushed a button and sprayed something into my eye.

'Sting a little' it turned out was the understatement of the century. It felt like he was burning my eye out. He may as well have shoved a red-hot poker in my eye. I think I screamed. In fact, I'm sure I screamed. Screamed like it was the last thing I was ever going to do. Then I suspect I blacked out, but for once, at least, that was short lived.

The next thing I remember is the chink of a burnt-up piece of metal being dropped into the kidney dish on the small table beside me. Then Jobs began undoing the straps that held me down.

My vision seemed a little blurred, I felt light-headed, not quite with it at all, then I passed out for a second time. But again, I wasn't out very long. Just long enough to be untied, I suspect. Though it took me a few moments to find my bearings again. I managed to force myself to sit up and found myself staring down at the kidney dish and the metallic remains of the spider, which were curled up around something I didn't recognise at first.

It was such a tiny thing, so small and innocuous. Curled up with its legs and some long trailing tendrils of some kind. Curled up around a white ball of gooeyness.

It looked wrong, everything looked wrong. The perspective was all screwed up. It was hard to tell how far away it was. I presumed it was my left eye still feeling much abused and a little cloudy. I'd been living with odd vision from that eye for so long now, between the spider and the monocle, and my mind was still fuzzy, so it was hard to put my finger on what was strange about it now.

"Ah, Mr Smyth, you're back with us. All sorted, the little device is out. Really, it is quite primitive. I am almost embarrassed for Gates. How are you feeling? There will be a little residual pain, I suspect," the scientist said as he turned and walked back towards me.

"It's so small," I said, still looking down at the Aracno-Oculus, and the odd ball of mush it was clamped around.

"Small? No, really it is far too large. It could be smaller if he had just reduced the power needs. Dragging heat is a clever method of getting power, I will grant him that, but really tapping into the blood supply would have been better. You would gain heat directly from inside the body, you see?" he told me.

The offhand nature of the way he said all this was chilling. There was also a horrible note of glee to his voice as well.

The glee of the scientist who is too wrapped up in what he could do to spare much thought for what he should do.

My vision still seemed bizarre, and whatever he had used to numb the left side of my face starting to wear off and it tingled in an itchy irritated way, I brought my hand up to massage the pain a little and suddenly realised what was wrong, at the same moment I realised what the squidgy white thing the spider was coiled around was.

I rubbed at the place where the spider had sat so long. Where The Ministry had stared out at the world and controlled my emotions. The place where my left eye used to be and was no longer.

Instead, my questing fingers found only the bloody hole where the eye in the kidney dish used to be.

CHAPTER 21

None So Blind As Those That Cannot See

The little shed was in an uproar. Those baton-wielding guards tried to drag me away from Jobs before I succeeded in beating him to a bloody pulp. Which, as I'm sure you can imagine, was something I felt a strong desire to do. As such, I was somewhat resistant to their remonstrations, for all my groggy post-op state. They, however, wasted no time in subduing me at all.

In fairness, I can understand why they hit me with the clubs. I was way past raving, I was incandescent in my anger, and I'd every intention of killing the man. I could claim this was due to residual effects from the device so recently removed from my eye. I could claim that maddening rage it induced still flowed through my veins. I could claim that, and as a defense it might even have some merit. The truth, however, was I just wanted to beat the hell out of the swine.

He had, after all just burned out my eye.

As such, I took a fair amount of restraining. This once I shan't even claim the guards were overzealous in their attentions, because I was frankly beyond reason. All the pain, all the humiliations, all the utter crap I'd gone through. It was all focused-on Professor Steffen Jobs right at that moment. All I wanted right then, at that moment, was to kill the swine, whether he truly deserved my rage or not.

In the end, I was dragged away, battered, bruised and beaten senseless. This, as you're aware, was not an unfamiliar state of being for me of late…

Unsurprisingly, I awoke to find myself restrained once more. For once, however, I'd happy memories of what had occurred in those last few moments before I blacked out. To wit, getting one well-aimed kick in before they finally brought me down. Not that I was particularly happy about my situation, but the memory of the anguish on the face of Jobs as my boot made contact with his nether regions did at least bring me some minor solace.

My mother had a saying… she doubtless picked it up from somewhere or other over the years, and while I've long forgotten most of the wisdom my dear mum imparted to me in the days of my youth, this particular turn of phrase had seldom seemed so apt than in the case of that Professor Steffen Jobs. For he was a man whom, to quote my Mam, 'I'd break my toes before I tired of kicking him in the gonads…'

My mother had a tender heart, or so I've been told. The kind of heart that has been made tender in a similar way to which you tenderise a steak… By the constant, relentless pounding of life upon her. Her bitterness had a sharp edge to it, and I'd learned young to avoid that edge whenever possible.

And so, battered, beaten and bruised I'd once more found myself in a small cell of some kind. This time strapped to an iron-framed bed, albeit one with a mattress. In all honesty, it made a pleasant change from some of the cells I'd found myself in. Though, that I've reached a point in my life in which I spent time comparing the different cells in which I've found myself incarcerated, still struck me as a worrying development.

This particular time I consoled myself with the thought that this one at least probably wouldn't need to be an addition in my 'Good Death Cells Guide.'

Small victories and all that.

A couple of hours passed, quite dull ones, I may add. Once again, I found myself wishing there was a book or a magazine lying around with which I could pass the time. Though having my arms tied down would've made it something of a challenge to hold up a book and turn its pages, I will admit.

Despite my situation, or perhaps just to distract myself from it, I found myself wondering about the latest 'Holmes' stories in the Strand. The old standards were ever being reprinted, and I must admit to having some small passion for the great detective. Perhaps it was his own roguish streak that appealed to me, the difference between Holmes and his arch-foe Moriarty was always little more than which side of the line each chose to stand. Hero, or villain, reduced to a moral choice. Simplistic, I know, but one sees reflections of your own nature in fiction. One always wishes to be the hero, one is so often the villain. For the line in real life is seldom quite so well defined. Of course, it helps to lie to yourself about which side of the line you chose to stand on, from time to time...

Frankly, cells of any kind always seem devoid of literature in my experience. Generally, to stave off boredom I'd have been happy to read the back of a cigarette packet. The joke health warnings may be wearing thin these days, but they still tend to raise a smile. If only because there are still some people taken in by them.

After an indeterminable period of time, the shutter on the door dropped down momentarily, and I caught a brief glimpse of a face peering in at me through it before it clanged back in place. Which at least meant I hadn't been forgotten about. Something that has been known to happen to prisoners of all kinds.

At Rudgley school they used to punish us for underperforming in the cross-country trials by locking us in the changing rooms for hours at a time. The Physical Education teacher, a Mr B Clough was, I always suspected, a man unhappy with his lot in life. He'd long dreamed of the dizzy heights of housemaster and long been disappointed at being passed over in favour of someone who was at least vaguely qualified for the post. Brian, therefore, was known to nip off for a beer or two after turning the key. Leaving us, his poor charges, to half freeze to death in the unheated changing rooms after the obligatory cold showers.

Once on a particularly dismal Friday afternoon, Clough, after being rejected for a post as a junior math teacher, probably due to his inablity to add up without using his fingers, started out on a three-day bender. It was only when the following Monday's PE class came in that my fellow 'prisoners' and I were discovered, with various degrees of minor frostbite and exposure.

It wasn't the best weekend I'd ever spent. Not least because the only way to keep warm had been to take turns beating up the plebs. Or taking turns at being the plebs in order to stave off the boredom. It is remarkable how your social standing can change in a few short hours when the pack starts looking for its the next victim. But as with many things within British public-school life, if you could take the first beating or two without blubbing, you graduated to dishing out the beatings yourself for a while. It may not be pleasant, but there is something strangely character-building about it. Though the characters it builds have a habit of being unpleasant ones…

More time passed.

I wasn't sure how long. The one window was frosted green glass, the light beyond may have been daylight or just a lit corridor, for all I knew. As such, it didn't offer much of a guide as to the passage of time. I slept for a while, and had fitful dreams of giant spiders, Sleepmen, crazed women with razors for fingernails and Hardacre falling… The same dreams I always have. As unpleasant as they ever were.

Finally, sometime after I woke, the door opened.

It didn't come entirely as a surprise when HG Wells stepped through the portal. Equally not much to my surprise, he was flanked by two guards. Their strange uniforms as vaguely familiar as ever. Though I still couldn't place the octopus-like insignias on their sleeves. I knew they formed his central cadre of guards as they always hung around the man himself, but I was again struck by the nagging thought that they weren't exactly his. It was another of those things that niggled me about the whole situation. Though I'd be damned at the time if I could've told you why.

The professor was with him too and looking a little disheveled. His glasses, for one thing, were twisted out of shape, and one of the lenses was cracked. He was also, and I mention this purely incidentally, nursing a black eye. I must admit that shiner pleased me more than it perhaps should have. Beyond that however, I didn't feel quite as vindictive as I had. In the time I'd spent strapped down to the bedframe, I'd managed to rationalise losing my eye. Jobs might have been the butcher who removed my eye, but it was 'M' and his pet boffin Gates that had put the damn spider there in the first place. Jobs probably had little choice but remove it in the way he had.

All the same I would be lying were I to claim I no longer felt the urge to smack him in the face, my old mum's infamous dictum on broken toes not far from my mind, bless her badly knitted socks. But I could push down that urge to mere background malice; besides I had felt that way since the moment I'd met him.

Lastly, behind the scientist came Saffron Wells. Looking angry and beautiful, a combination which was both flattering and not unfamiliar on her. She was still wearing one of the eye patch devices. I suspected, not unreasonably, she'd hoped that the removal of my own spider had gone better. Not out of concern for yours truly of course, though I wish it had been, but because she'd one of the damn things in her own eye. Considering I knew what that was like, I can't say that I blamed her overly. Lose an eye or be condemned to be The Ministry's pet, is hardly a winning set of options. All in all, at that moment I was still unsure that I hadn't got the better of the deal.

"Ah, my dear Mr Smyth, how are you feeling now?" Wells asked me, interrupting my chain of thought.

"Somewhat less than I was," I replied bitterly, making no real attempt to hide my emotions behind stiff-lipped British pragmatism. I'm sure the masters of Rudgley School would've been apoplectic with me for such a display.

"Yes, it's unfortunate. A lamentable business all round, I assure you. And one for which I deeply regret the necessity. Professor Jobs informs me it was the only way to remove the spider, as you called it. The device had started to embed itself fully around your eyeball. Its tendrils ran too deep, you see, right into the optic nerve itself. In time they could have reached clean through to your brain or so he tells me. Gods only know what would've happened to you then, but I am led to believe The Ministry would've gained full control of your mind. As such rendering you little better than a puppet. God knows I wouldn't put it past them. As you know you've already experienced an aspect of that control. I am sure you see the necessity of removing it when we did, even with the regrettable consequences involved."

I found myself just staring back at him, taking all this news in, it left me no less resentful but did focus that bitterness on 'M' and his damn Ministry, where it belonged. And given all I knew of that organisation I'd no reason to doubt Wells' word. I could still remember the hate, the rage, the loss of control and being taken over by some outside force. That memory, and its echo was still there like the afterglow of a migraine. So, I'd no difficulty believing what Wells was telling me and no difficulty focusing my anger on those who deserved it most. I guess you could consider it a moment of revelation, of the kind you read of in pulp paperbacks. The moment the hero realises who his real enemies are and vows his revenge upon them. The moment heroes are forged, focusing their anger on their desire to put things right. To rise up against the true villains and fight for liberty, for justice, and all that.

I felt mildly sick, wanted a stiff drink and to get as far away from the lot of them as I could. Indeed, right at that moment anywhere with a bar, no extradition treaty and a bevy of ladies who would exchange the pleasures of the flesh for negotiable currency would've done. But then I never claimed to be a hero…

"Go on," I said to Wells.

"Well, yes, removing it was the only option, and unfortunately it became clear that there was only one way to do that. The loss of your eye was, I have to say, a most regrettable outcome." In his defense, he sounded sincere in this regret. I was, regardless, far from mollified. Lose an eye and see how forgiving you feel. If you're anything like me, I'm guessing not in the slightest.

"Regrettable, bloody regrettable? Is that the best you can offer? Your bloody regrets?" I snapped back at him but found myself regretting my outburst as soon as I'd said it.

I closed my eyes and took a couple of deep breaths, fighting for calm, but my reward was a sharp stab of pain where one of my eyes should've been. Muscle memory is a swine when you lose a body part. The bits that are left just carry on regardless. Right then the hole was still naked and had not been sewn shut. Something to do with me trying to beat the hell out of my surgeon. The stitches that were there were temporary ones holding the eyelids open.

It was, in a word, unpleasant.

It took me more than a moment to find my calm, taking more long breaths. Feeling it was wise to try and project the more considered, thoughtful side of my nature.

And I'll thank you not to laugh at that…

You see, for all my ire at that actual moment, I was also all too aware that Wells no longer needed me. My value as a test case for the removal of Aracno-Oculi had run its course. He now had no reason not to dispense with the troublesome British spy. Also, there was still that great sodding cliff edge to drop me off if I proved intractable. Besides, as you may recall I'd made a career out of acting the gentleman even if I wasn't and a certain grace under vexation was expected of men of rank. Even those who have fallen from that grace. As such, I measured my next words carefully, deciding to play the put upon good solider, which all considered wasn't that far from the truth, well apart from the 'good' part.

"Please, forgive me my temper. My words were… ill-considered… I'm afraid I've found myself sorely vexed of late as I am sure you know, but that is no excuse for ill-manners," I said, in as calm a voice as I could manage.

"That is perfectly understandable, old boy, perfectly understandable. But please tell me, are you certain you're not still suffering from the urges the device brought about earlier? We have to be sure you see," Wells asked me.

"Right at this moment, I could cheerfully strangle a few people," I said, in a poorly chosen attempt at humour that held a tad more edge than I intended. I tried a weak smile, which turned into a grimace as a shot of pain ran from my eye socket. But I hoped they could see it was a good-natured jest on my part rather than a threat of any kind.

"I'm sure you could, old boy, I'm sure, but we can forgive you your sharpness all things considered. Such things would try the patience of a saint, I've no doubt, and I'm aware you are, well, let's just say you are unlikely to be canonised any time soon. But my question stands all the same, and I find I must insist upon an answer," Wells said still smiling at me.

I looked up at him, deep into those odd world-weary eyes of his and felt little, if truth be told. Certainly not the hate I'd felt the last time I'd laid eyes upon him, weeks ago, before Japan, before Hiroshima. Pity, perhaps, that most hateful of emotions. Yes, pity, I realised, for there was something desperately sad about Mr Wells. I couldn't tell you, even now, why I felt such pity for him right at that moment. But pity him I did.

I took another painful breath and calmed myself some more. Letting the rage within burn cold for a moment or two. I was all too certain that shouting the odds would get me nowhere. I was, after all, still very much in the thrall of this man and his friends. Not a situation much to my liking, it's true, but that said, a few hours before I had been in the thrall of The Ministry and unlike them, Wells at least seemed disposed to ask after my wellbeing. There seemed no gain for me in antagonising the situation further. Indeed, pushing my remarkably bad luck seemed nothing but a step towards suicide, albeit by proxy, at that point.

"No urges as you put it, sir, none at all. Whatever was taking hold of me, it's gone. Gone with that damnable spider," I told Wells plainly. Which was the truth as far as it went.

"Well then, we must be thankful for some small mercy there. While I am loath to admit it, I suspect I would've regretted many things had it become an act of necessity to kill you," Wells replied, without even a slither of a smile below his moustache.

There was a chilliness about the way he said the last. It made me feel ill just hearing him. There is a difference between thinking a thing and hearing it stated to in a bland everyday tone. I found that a lot with Wells. He managed somehow to look at the world in a cold utilitarian way, easily letting emotion slip off to the side of an argument. Too easily to my mind. Eventually, I came to believe this was due to his insane belief that time was… Well, yes, we are coming to that…

"Well, I certainly approve of the not killing me part," I joked, which raised a cynical smile on his part.

"No doubt, Mr Smyth, no doubt," he replied with that same cold self-assurance. He turned away from me for a moment and nodded to one of the guards who set about loosening the straps holding me down. Clearly, Wells, having reached a decision on my fate, now saw little reason to keep me restrained. For which I was grateful because, well, small mercies, smaller victories and all that.

No more was said until I was sitting up, trying vainly to rub some feeling back into wrists which were a nasty shade of red and painfully bruised. Whoever had strapped me down had done so fully intending me to stay that way. I could feel my fingers cramping as blood started to flow properly through them. Even unshackled, I was in a poor state to do anything much if even now I was under the control of my former masters in London. But even so, the guards were still close at hand, their own thick mitts very obviously on their shock batons. I was in short, left in no doubt who was in charge.

Despite this, Wells waited patiently for me to gather whatever wits I could before he spoke further. Leaning on his walking stick as he waited and looking for all the world like a gentleman taking the air in Regent's Park. As opposed to a rebel leader standing in a cell beneath an ancient Himalayan monastery. Which is to say, a man in complete control of the world around him. But finally, when I was at least on the way to some semblance of recovery, he spoke again.

"Well now, as we have established your lack of homicidal drives towards me, I believe Professor Jobs has an offer for you. He is willing to try and repair the damage Gates did. If you are in turn willing. You see, he really is very good with optics. Eyes are his thing in many ways."

That penny dropped into place again. Gates disparaging remarks about Jobs. 'Eye this, eye that, eye everything...' or something along those lines. But their scientific enmities aside, I had a sinking feeling in the pit of my stomach.

"Hang on... You want me to be a guinea pig, again?" I asked, my voice no doubt betraying a little of the shock and reservations I felt. Particularly considering I'd only recently tried to beat the living hell out of the man. Yet, despite that, Wells was suggesting I let him back at me with a scalpel and god only knew what weird device of his design. The whole idea seemed absurd. Not to mention as a rule I've found dishing out a sound thrashing to someone is a sure way to ensure they feel resentful towards you. Up to that point in my life, I'd made it something of a rule, not to let a man harbouring resentful feelings towards me have at me with a scalpel. Well no, if truth is fully told, not a rule as such, as it had never come up before, but it seemed in my view to be a good rule to adopt going forward.

"That would be one way to look it, I guess, but it's entirely up to you, and an eye patch can look quite the dash I am told," the professor pitched in, though he noticeably kept a safe distance between myself and him. Which was uncharacteristically wise of him because if I could've got away with giving him another swift right hand or two, I probably would've.

In all honesty, my attitude towards him wasn't helped by the absurd positivity he always seemed to have about everything. Professor Jobs was a man who could put a positive spin on anything and smile that annoyingly self-assured smile of his. He was the kind of man who would fall in a pile of shit and come up talking about its qualities as a fertiliser, and still have that damn smile on his face. In that sense he shared more in common with Gates than he would willingly admit. They both managed to be optimistic despite any weight of evidence that suggested everything was going to crap.

That to my mind was the problem with both of them, they were so enthralled by what they could do, they never gave much consideration to whether they should do it, and even less consideration to the more important question of if anyone actually wanted them to do it in the first place. It was hardly surprising a shadowy organisation like The Ministry or whatever Wells' building in that damnable valley chose to make use of them. All Gates could see was the wonder of his spiders weaving a web around the world. A world he could then look out on through his damnable port hole windows in his lab beneath the sphinx. Not giving thought to the uses his masters put to his toys. While Professor Jobs, I suspect, would happily involve himself with anyone willing to fund his pet projects, as long as they let him get the cosmetics of the thing right before he worried about it actually working as intended.

In a way, I envied that. Optimism is not a trait common to the gutters of the East End. Realism certainly, but never optimism. But then look where optimism had gotten them, tied to various shadowy forces striving to control the world, littler more than toymakers for tyrants.

Well, I guess they don't call them mad scientists because they get angry a lot, is all I can say...

CHAPTER 22

Vison Thing...

It may surprise you to learn, if you have a certain bent of mind, that monasteries in the hidden valleys of the Himalayas, are dull places.

Very dull.

I realise this probably doesn't surprise to the majority of people, but there are always some hopeless romantics who have strange ideas and, if you pardon the phase, romanticise about visiting tranquil Shangri-La's. To them, it's all mystic temples, lotus blossom ponds and bald men in orange robes who sit with their legs crossed while hovering six inches above the ground. You know the kind of thing, all inner peace, seeking of ancient wisdom, while a gentle breeze blows a lone leaf from a cherry tree that dances in the air in some meaningful way that explains the inner working of the universe more profoundly than a Cambridge professor in a wheelchair ever could.

It never seems to occur to those kinds of people just how terminally dull that all is.

Of course, after all that had happened to me of late, a bit of dullness should've come as a relief. Yet in truth after a few days of just hanging around with nothing to do, I was bored within an inch of my life, despite this particular Shangri-La being about as far from that romanticised vision as it was possible to get. For, while I laboured with idleness, the crews of the growing fleet of stolen airships were busying themselves with a hundred and one different tasks. All to prepare the fleet for whatever they were preparing it for, something about which I remained utterly clueless. A fact that didn't sit entirely well with me, though I suspected if I did find out, I wasn't going to like the answer.

Along with the airships, there was a growing shanty town below the monastery built to cater for the aircrews, while at the far end of the complex a rudimentary manufactory spewed out black smoke day and night, as they smelted, forged, hammered and did all those other things that they do in manufactories.

The truth was I'd no idea what the manufactory was building. One was discouraged from close investigation by the men with the octopus insignias on their uniforms, for while it was true I was no longer a prisoner as such, I wasn't entirely at liberty either. But if I were to make a guess at what was happening inside those grim dark buildings, I'd say they were making parts and ordinance for that ever-growing fleet of airships I mentioned.

From the upper walls of the monastery, the valley looked not unlike an upturned ants nest. I know this because I climbed up the two hundred and eighty-three steps to the top of the damn thing one day and spent a dull half hour watching said ants nest. In truth, I was both watching it and wondering just how bored I must have become to climb all those steps, for what was, it has to be said, an inferior view. Yet it served as a reasonable bit of exercise, so I was inclined to make a habit out of the climb each morning thereafter. My general fitness was still far from recovered after the months of incarceration at Old Iron Knickers' pleasure. Besides which it was something to do, other than watching the local monks sparing in their training square. I had previously undertaken to practise my sword work for a while in that square, but that was an endeavour that ended... badly. It also added a new scar to add to my growing disfigurements.

The story of that particular scar I see little need to go into. Besides it sheds little in the way of favourable light on me... Suffice to say I wouldn't be setting foot in that training square again and had developed an aversion to small monks in black robes of late...

A week had passed since we returned from Japan and my daily sojourn to the top of the monastery made me witness to the remarkable speed with which Wells fleet was growing. Saffron's personal little band of cutthroats had, it seemed, been busy while I was riding bullet trains and being entertained by clockwork geisha. Three more airships had been crowded into the valley by the time we had returned, and a fourth, another large liner, had arrived since. All of which were in the process of being refitted for Wells' great purpose. Whatever that was. Though I could hazard a guess that as this involved lots of armour plating, guns and ordinance, no matter what that purpose was, peaceful wasn't going to be an apt description.

As a consequence, the common areas below the monastery had taken on an increasingly bizarre appearance. Opulent chairs and tables, looted from the dining halls of liners, were set up alongside rough cut wooden trestles. Fine wall hangings and linen bedding had been cut up for tablecloths and rags. While more than one of the natives was walking round in a purser's uniform, or clothing which had once clearly belonged to first class passengers. I've seen many a strange sight in my life, but few stranger than a yak herder going about his daily chores in a white tuxedo, sporting a hat which wouldn't have been out of place on ladies' day at Ascot, peacock feathers and all…

The crews of the various craft were mixing awkwardly down there too. Dutchmen, Russians, British, a few French, Indians, a crew of Kenyans or Zambians, I was never quite sure which, all mixed in with a smattering of Irishmen and Americans. This strange league of many nationalities were united in their open distaste for each other. If they shared a common cause under Wells' flag, it didn't lend itself to any commonality between them. Old rivalries, rooted in centuries of colonial enmities, boiled below the surface, and the occasional brawl would turn ugly before the octopus insignia wearing guards, acting as provosts, broke them up. The valley was a powder keg in other words and growing more volatile with each passing day.

Whatever Wells was up to, I could see only too clearly there was a limit to how long he could hold all this together. More crews meant more friction, not to mention more chance of word getting out beyond the mountains. Years of planning had gone into whatever he was doing all this for, of that much I was sure. At the rate his fleet was growing, new ships would soon be arriving daily. Yet the anchorage to the west of the valley was near enough full. All this suggested to me things were moving at pace towards a tipping point. Something my former masters at The Ministry would no doubt be very interested in. Perhaps even enough to forgive me my trespasses. Though somehow I doubted that.

And yet amongst all this, I still managed to be bored.

I'd not seen my proverbial Bad Penny since returning from Japan. Saffron Wells was busy with her own crew of cutthroats and I saw her only in passing and received a curt nod of recognition at best when I did. The Russian crew of The Sharapova were being worked hard on The Grunt, so even card games with Yuri and his comrades were few and far between, and the vodka, in short, was no longer flowing as it had been. Things were getting serious clearly, so serious even the Russians were going about sober, which worried me as much as anything.

When I got word that the professor was ready for me, After I begrudgingly agreed to the surgery, I remember wondering just how large this fleet actually was. Were there other ships lying at anchor elsewhere in the mountains? I couldn't discount the possibility. And if there were, well, with a fleet this big, Wells couldn't just threaten to destabilise India but would have the ships and manpower to strike at the heart of the Empire itself. This struck me as an insane idea.

At least, it seemed so at the time…

A few days after the surgery they told me Wells wanted to speak to me. I was up at the top of the monastery again at the time, having taken my constitutional climb up the steps earlier that morning. I was passing the time watching the training square from a safe distance and wondering once more at the way the monks moved in combat. Buddhism, I had come to believe, wasn't the religion of peace and harmony I'd always been told about. It was more peace, harmony, kicks that could shatter spines and fists that could be used to chop firewood. I found it strangely fascinating, but I was in no hurry to return to the Black Robes' tender mercies by getting too close, so the viewpoint from the top of the monastery walls was close enough for me. Besides, the scar on my cheek still stung when the wind blew, and in the mountains, the wind blew all the time.

Did I tell you how I got the scar on my cheek? No? Another time over a drink perhaps. As I said earlier, it was unimportant and paints me in no good light. But the sword that hung from a prayer gate by the square was at the centre of it and I still remembered how good it had felt in my hands. Even now, watching from the walls, it made my palms itch with a longing to hold it once more. But nothing was going to tempt me to go down there and pick it up. Beware of wizen old monks in black robes, is all the advice I will elude at this point. Be bloody ware of them.

Watching the training did at least pass an hour after the climb up the steps. I was still bored of course, but I was a tad less bored than I could've been had I not been watching them, or at least trying to do so when my vision wasn't swimming. That was another reason I'd resisted the call of the blade. My new eye, courtesy of Professor Jobs, had a mind of its own. As such, the last thing I wanted to do was start waving a sword around. I wasn't entirely sure I wouldn't cut myself.

My new eye.

Oh yes, my new eye.

Well as I said, it had a mind of its own. Its focus swam from one extreme to the other. Paying little, if any, regard to whatever I was trying to focus on. It was disturbing, to say the least, and not at all easy to get used to. Since the operation, I spent half my days with my left eye shut or wearing an eye patch just to avoid nausea. Even just walking about was difficult. It's hard to walk when one of your eyes suddenly zooms in on an ant on the path. I do mean zooms in. On some occasions, my new eye was akin to looking through a microscope. A telescope on others. Imagine, if you will, suddenly through your left eye seeing an ant's head at the size of a football when all you did was look down at the path you're walking on. It's disturbing, let me tell you. Almost as disturbing as looking up and seeing a yak on the mountainside half a mile away, turning away for a second and then when you look back up being able to count the yak's nostril hairs. Which wouldn't be so bad if it didn't do all this with no guidance from myself and, importantly I feel, no bloody warning whatsoever.

At other times my vision was perfectly normal and balanced, though these seemed to be precious moments. Indeed, to an extent, these moments were the most disconcerting of all because I knew full well it was bound to change at the most inconvenient moment. Yet after the first day or so, minutes, or even hours could pass with everything being normal. But then I would have another bout of wild focus shifts, that made the simplest of tasks a disconcerting knife-edge of anxiety.

Take, for example, walking down a staircase, an everyday occurrence you doubtless barely think about. But imagine while you're walking down that staircase you happen, out of the corner of your eye, to notice a silk moth fluttering by. Then suddenly, with no warning, one of your eyes is focused on its mandibles at one hundred magnitudes of magnification.

Disconcerting is perhaps not the word, come to think of it, terrifying that the word I should use.

I've never been afraid of insects, spiders, beetles or any such thing. Creepy crawlies, it is safe to say, didn't bother me at all. Growing up in an East End gutter had left me all too acquainted with roaches and the like. Thus I never developed a phobia about them. That was until I found myself getting acquainted with them on a whole new scale. The day you suddenly see the jaws of a millipede the size of an elephant coming at you along a wall… It's a whole new perspective, no pun intended, on insects, let me tell you.

Aside from that issue, there was a worse one to my mind. My reflection had an alien quality. There was a strangeness to it I hadn't felt with The Ministry's spider, or even in all the weeks I had spent wearing those damn one-sided goggles. Even, come to that, when there'd been nothing there, just a hole where my eye had been. All those iterations had seemed less wrong, less alien, than what I now saw in the mirror each morning. All those reflections had still been entirely me. This was no longer the case.

Now an alien eye sat in the left side of my face, looking back at me. Wey and silver, as if made of mercury. No iris, no flecks of colour, no pupil I could observe. Just a molten silver thing staring right back at me. Sometimes it observed my reflection in sharp focus, the tiniest of details in the glass, other times I looked to be far away. It did things to my peripheral vision as well; it went from normal, to tunnel, to seeing sideways. All without warning when it switched between states.

I hated it.

I hated it with a passion I'd seldom felt before.

Hating something that way, something that has become part of you, well it's hard to accept. You'd think such feelings would pass, but they weren't, not as far as I could see, so hate it I did.

The professor had informed me that getting used to it would take time; he was right on that score. Though his cryptic advice that, "Your new eye needs to get to know you," didn't help a great deal, and the implication it was a thing that could get to know me didn't help me accept it at all. Apparently, according to Jobs, it would learn over time to work with my other eye, and after a while, its capabilities would become normal to me, something I could even learn to control. I wasn't sure I believed him. As I said, it showed all the traits of having a mind of its own. A stubborn obstreperous mind at that. A mind which seemed to delight in making me bang into things and made me utterly terrified of shaving.

In my more paranoid moments, I was starting to believe that what with the spider, ambushes at the sink by 'Not-really-A-Maid-At-All' and now this crazy eye thing of Steffen Jobs, the world was conspiring to make me grow a full beard.

The simple solution to all this, putting an eye patch over it, was according to the mad professor, "The worst thing you can do." But at least doing so gave me a sense of control over the latest little extra mind that had taken up residence in my skull. But long term I knew I had to get used to it. So, I started talking to it, berating it on occasion. Oh, not in a crazy way, just in the same way a man might berate his arthritic knee when the weather turns cold, and I seldom did so out loud. But I would be lying if I were to say I wasn't starting to question my sanity a little. All things considered. *'Still, it's better than that damn spider, Harry old son,'* I told myself daily, while never quite being convinced of my wisdom in this regard.

But anyway, as I was saying, they came and told me Wells wanted to see me. The 'they', in this case, was my Russian 'friend' Vladimir. As much a peacock as ever, and I may add preening with petulance having been asked to act the messenger boy once more.

Which I may have pointed out, a little.

In my defence, Putin was and remains an utter arse of a man. Needling him put a little shine in my day and small victories are small victories, after all.

Having had to climb all the way up to the top of the monastery to collect me, the be-tasselled Muscovite was rather stiffly trying to catch his breath as he passed on his message. He was also far from pleased that I didn't simply jump to it. Instead, I thanked him for giving me the message, while showing no intention on rushing off to see Wells before I finished the cigarette I was rolling at the time. Vlad was predictably stiff and irritable in his rebuttal of my lack of urgency.

As I recall, I said, as I didn't need a guide, he could "toddle off by all means." Which wasn't the sort of reply he was expecting, I suspect. Indeed, he failed utterly to hide his disapproval, but as I wasn't feeling much obliged to respect anyone at the time, I can't say I cared overly. Besides which my new eye was playing up more than usual, and I was buying time to steal my nerve before I risked the walk back down the stairs to get to the main entrance.

Vlad stood before me for a full minute, as I lit my cigarette and proceeded to smoke it, before he coughed loudly, announced he would "await me at the bottom" in a tone which suggested he didn't expect to be kept waiting for long. He was an airship captain, after all. His rank alone demanded I treat his instructions as orders and not doing so showed no respect whatsoever for his authority.

As I had damn all respect for Putin's authority, I took my time and rolled another cigarette first, enjoying the view for the first time, as I was keeping the arse waiting, and found myself idly wondering about the strange mist that seemed to be rising from the ground at the far edge of the valley. Though it was a truly idle bit of pondering and I remember dismissing it at the time as just another of those odd little things with the weather thereabouts. Even if it did strike me as a little late in the day for such a mist to be forming. Fog normally rose in the centre of the valley around the small river that passed through it, and then when it did it was an early morning thing. Not a little past noon with the sun reasonably high in the sky. But as I said I paid it no mind and pulled on my eye patch before my new eye tried to examine the end of the valley in greater detail. Putin's nostril hairs had been the final straw as far as putting up with the damn thing was concerned right then.

I smoked my cigarette, shrugged to myself, then flicked the butt out over the edge. Not giving the strange mist another thought as I headed down the steps to where the priggish little Wanna-be Cossack was awaiting my pleasure with very little of his own.

All in all, looking back at it now, I suspect that was a major blunder on my part…

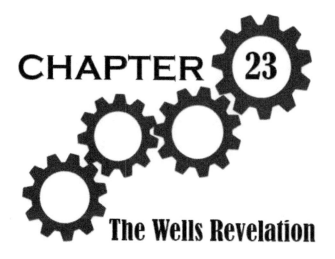

CHAPTER 23

The Wells Revelation

Wells' inner sanctum was much as it had been the last time I'd been there. The same reek of stale tea, crumpets, incense and yak hair that you get when east meets west and doesn't quite get along.

Wells himself was sitting behind a large imposing desk which I didn't remember from my previous visit. I suspected it had been liberated from one of the captured liners outside. When we entered, he was studiously poring over some documents. Peering at them in a fashion which suggested his spectacles didn't work quite as efficiently as they should — all the while quietly ignoring his newly arrived guests.

At my side, Vladimir stood to attention, as stiff and formal as you like. Ramrod straight as they used to say.

Chest pumped out. Moustache waxed within an inch of its life. Trying, not very successfully, to not show that he was irritated beyond belief at being kept waiting on another's pleasure. Even if this time he was waiting on the man who was his rank superior. Though he seemed more impatient than usual for all he hid it well. He had somewhere to be and something to do if I was any judge, though that said, Vladimir never did like waiting on anyone's pleasure. I suspect because he believed other people should be waiting on his and felt cheated somehow that he hadn't risen to the great heights he believed he was due. He was the kind of man who believed he should be a great and respected leader, that he should be a man to lead nations, not a man condemned to be a lowly airship captain and a pirate at that. This, I'd come to suspect, was partly what made him such a stiff-limbed prig of a man, though saying that I also suspected were he ever to find himself in a position of real power, he would still be a stiff-limbed prig obsessed over and above anything else with his own self-image.

Myself, I was more or less slouched standing up. Standards be damned, I felt much abused of late and had little desire to show much in the way of respect to anyone by this point. Besides which, my new eye was itching like an airman's crotch after shore-leave in Vancouver. Manfully resisting the urge to scratch it was taking all my willpower frankly. I removed my eyepatch once more and was relieved that, for the moment at least, my alien eye seemed to be behaving itself.

A good five minutes went past, with Vlad unmoving in his stiff Russian fashion while Wells pored over his documents, which I was failing to read upside down. Not for want of trying, I should probably add. Poor spy I may be, but enlightened self-interest alone made me prone to consider gathering a little intelligence a worthy exercise at this point. Unfortunately, whatever the documents were they were written in a code of some kind and utterly indecipherable to me. It was that or some language so foreign it didn't share a common root with any other despite using the Latin alphabet.

Finally, when I'd become bored with waiting, I coughed loudly, causing Wells to look up and apparently notice us for the first time.

"Ah, Mr Smyth, so good of you to visit," Wells said with smooth understatement. Smiling broadly, he let his gaze cross to my escort, nodded towards him absently and added dismissively, "That will be all, Captain Putin. Don't let us keep you."

Vladimir saluted with precision. If he felt aggrieved at such a dismissal, he kept it to himself, though I saw his moustache twitch a little with discord as he turned and marched, with a certain degree of stamping, out of the office. Though in my augmented peripheral vision I caught a glance of a slit of a smile crossing his lips for a moment, which seemed oddly out of character for him all considered. My eye stopped misbehaving again a second later, and so I didn't think much of it at the time but looking back I suspect he was only too pleased to get about his own business. Of course, such business as he was about didn't bode well for anyone, but I didn't know that at the time.

"Odious man…" Wells commented as Vladimir left the room. Causing me to raise a wry smile. Wells sighed in response to this and muttered just loudly enough for me to hear, "Strange to think that in another timeline he is a man of great power, though he is no more odious in that version of the present either, I dare say."

I raised an eyebrow at this. Not that I had a bloody clue to what he was referring. It sounded like gibberish to me if I'm honest. It was more the case that I found it hard to credit that a loathsome self-obsessed bully like Vladimir could ever amount to much. But then on occasion I'm a tad naiver than I willingly admit. Thinking back now on all the self-obsessed bullies in the halls of Westminster, I'm embarrassed I even questioned the suggestion.

"Captain Putin is a man displaced by time, for the better in his case. Sadly, such is not always true of such men," Wells went on to explain or attempted to. I can't pretend that I'd any great interest in his mad theories back then. Wells, even from the briefness of our association at that juncture, struck me as a man with many a mad theory, which were due only a modicum of credence at the best of times. Still, that said, I could only agree with his assessment of Putin, if anything 'odious' was an understatement.

My host shuffled his papers and squared them up before dumping them in a tray to the right side of his desk. Then he offered me a seat, and rang a small brass bell, doubtless to call for tea. Wells was ever a good host in that regard.

"Why am I here?" I asked after I had seated myself. Not the most original line, I will admit, but I wanted to cut to the heart of the things. Wells wanted something from me, that much was clear, and, truth told, I was sick of loitering around on the fringes. I'd been misused by The Ministry, and despite myself, over the last few days, I'd decided if Wells was going to do them some damage, I'd probably enjoy aiding and abetting his endeavours as long as there was only minimal danger to myself and maybe some coin to be made.

Feel free to call me a mercenary bastard, by all means, but if the cap fits, one may as well wear it.

"Why are any of us here, Mr Smyth? Why indeed."

I groaned inwardly, suddenly not looking forward to what was framing up to be another pointless conversation with the ever-evasive Wells.

"Our mothers had intercourse with our fathers," I snarked back at him by way of reply. A coarse retort, I'm aware, and one below even the likes of me, but I was feeling a tad irritable, and my left eye was counting nasal hairs again, which was a closer inspection of HG Wells than I wished to undertake.

For the record, Wells had very hairy nostrils. Hirsute even. I guessed being the most wanted man in the Empire left him somewhat short of time to pluck at them with tweezers. But I digress, and it's even further from the relevant than I normally wander...

He laughed, that special kind of gentleman's club laugh. The '*We wouldn't say that in the company of ladies, but it's all gents together here,*' laugh only British men of the smoking jacket classes have managed to perfect. Well, men and Hettie Clarkhurst, which is more or less the same thing, but I'm sure you know the kind of laugh I mean.

"Quite so, quite so…" he retorted to my quip as the tea was laid before us by one of the servants.

It was British tea, silver service and everything, which probably offended the locals a little. Though the Raj has been doing that for centuries, so it seems foolish to worry about such things nowadays.

As the servant scuttled off to wherever servants go, Wells picked up his bone china cup, sipped at his tea and pulled an odd face. Then he took a sugar cube in the silver tongs and dropped it into his cup. A strangely bizarre thing to do, it struck me at the time. '*How does a man not know if he wants sugar in his tea before he sips it?*' I found myself wondering.

I, for my part, pride myself that I'm a man who knows how much sugar he wants in his tea. So, I took a sip of my own. Finding it surprisingly bitter, I added another sugar myself.

"The local brew, it never is quite as you expect it to be, but then so few things ever are what you expect, Mr Smith, are they? Or shall I call you Harry?" he asked with what I felt was a somewhat irksome smile.

"My name is Hannibal…" I began, half out of habit, only for him to raise a hand to interrupt me and, adopting the knowing tone of a Peeler, he corrected me.

"You are Harry Smith, son of Lizza Smith of Roecock Road, Hackney. A lad from the East End and a gutter lout some might say. It doesn't really matter what you call yourself 'Mr Smyth', that lad from the East End is still who you are. I firmly believe a man should never be ashamed of his roots, Harry. They, after all, make you who you are…"

"Who says I'm ashamed," I bristled, somewhat red-faced if truth be told, my blood was up, and the urge to punch Wells in the face was nothing to do with any mechanical spider in my eye this time. I knew exactly who and what I was, and I didn't need anyone throwing it in my face.

"No one, Harry, just the look on your face," Wells replied evenly, then after sipping his tea once more he smiled. "I knew your mother, Harry. She was a good woman, proud with it, never a dirty step or an unwashed window at her home, no matter what."

Well, about that he was right enough, my mother would die before she let the windows get grimy or, god forbid, have a dirty doorstep. Appearances were important. We might not have had much, but she made damn sure clothes were clean, and dust was swept away. Leastways, that was true before the gin took her. She always cleaned the house before she opened the gin. Trouble was she always opened the gin before she worried about feeding us. But it didn't matter so much if your bellies were empty to her mind, as long as your clothes were clean. '*We may not 'ave much, son, but what we 'ave we'll damn we'll look after, lad, or you'll feel the lash of ma tongue,*' came her voice across the years, as I thought on this.

"How did you know my mother?" I found myself asking. I was suspicious now. In the back of my mind, a light was dawning. If The Ministry knew that Wells had known my mother, then everything that had happened made a damn sight more sense. They had to have a reason to believe I could get close to Wells. That particular 'Why me?' had been bouncing around for some time.

"Lizza was the granddaughter of an old friend, who in turn was your great grandfather Albert. He used to work for me many years ago. You could say I owe him something of a debt. A debt which latterly I've repaid through you," Wells told me.

Now unsurprisingly I struggled to get my head around that little snippet. I'd never known my maternal grandfather, let alone his father. Hell, I didn't even know who my actual father was, which had presented its own problem back in the days of my youth. Family trees mattered in the East End, mattered as much as they did in noble households, I'd wager, if for more prosaic reasons. In the East End, if your father was part of the firm, well then the firm had a place for you. Be it the shipyards or the gangs.

Some East End gangsters traced their family firms back to the days before Her Royal Highness Queen Steam Knickers sat on her clockwork throne. Tradition and heritage mean more than you'd imagine among the working classes. There was a weird sense of pride that went with it. If you got tapped up for protection money by a thug, it was better somehow if you knew he came from a long line of thugs – men who took pride in their work. Blackjack handed down from father to son for generations. East End villains were in a weird way their own kind of nobility, the gangs, in essence, existing as a neo-feudal society all of their own. As I said, a lot of local pride was involved. No one wanted to be mugged by someone who had no family behind them. Common thugs were just too, well, common for want of a better word, and the 'families' took a dim view of incomers plying their trade on the family's patch unless they were getting a hefty cut from the business. You had to be part of the family or have connections with them if you were going to try and make a living on the shady side of the street. Many a fool has embarked on a criminal career in the East End and ended up wishing it was the Peelers who felt their collar. The gangs dealt justice in more rudimentary ways, and more than one gang boss had a pig farm on the side where the swine were often as not well fed. There was a certain pride about that too.

Ron and Reggie's Mile End Bacon, best-fed porkers in the East End…

I grew up knowing who the villains were, who to be respectful around, and which of my playmates were 'connected'. Even now, years after I left the streets of my childhood, I knew a few contacts who'd proved useful over the years when I came across the odd trinket here and there. I wasn't of the families, but I was Lizza Smith's lad, and as such the East End has a long memory.

But as for my own heritage, well, truth told, my old mum never really talked about her family at all. Can't say I ever asked either. She was dead before such questions really occurred to me.

Wells though, he was in his early forties, late forties at the most. So how the hell could he have known my great grandfather? Much less employed him some time in the way back. The whole thing struck me as ridiculous. Clearly another symptom of his obvious delusions. However, that said, my ears had caught hold of one word in the hogwash Wells was speaking. One particular word, a word which sharpens the ears with dreams of avarice…

"Debt?" I inquired, which caused a thin smile.

"Yes, Harry, but one I've already repaid, as I said, why else do you imagine you were accepted into a good school like Rudgley. Boarders fees all paid up and everything?" he said to me, still smiling. It was, I must say, a smile I was starting to take a disliking to. Besides, in this case, I knew better…

"It was state funding for orphans; I received a grant after my mum died. So, it had sweet nothing to do with you," I replied with a certain belligerence.

"Oh, yes, the state funds for orphans of the Empire. They picked your name out of a hat, no doubt. Certainly, there were no manipulations behind the scenes; no favours called in by some mysterious benefactor to get you that grant. Really, Harry… I mean, just how often do you think a lad from the East End goes to public school on a state scholarship. No, Harry, those funds were set up for the orphans of servicemen. Men who die in service of the state, junior officers as a rule, though the odd decorated private soldier's son might sneak in. A fund designed to raise another generation of soldiers for Her Majesty's Armed Services. A way to look after the sons of the valiant dead. Did you know those funds are raised by the services themselves? A charitable concern centred around annual dinners to honour the memories of dead comrades and give their sons a start in life. Not for East End lads whose mothers die of the gin. Sons with a soldier's heritage, which given even dear old Lizza wasn't entirely sure who your father was, you, my friend, are not."

"You can damn well leave my mother out of this…" I snapped back at him, though my anger stemmed from things other than defending my dear old mum's honour if truth be told. I was well aware of my paternal heritage, or lack of it, more's the rub. I'd accepted it long ago and made peace with it. But that didn't mean I appreciated it being thrown in my face by anyone, much less a bloody duffer like HG Wells.

"I wouldn't dream of disparaging the woman, Harry. Lizza Smith was a woman with many fine qualities," Wells replied, though he did so a little too easily for my liking.

I gave him a hard look. I was still angry, with the world in general and with Wells in particular, but I bit my tongue, sipped tea and took a couple of long breaths, then tried to shift the subject away from my parentage. Besides which, despite my anger, I was more than a little curious about one question in all this which his revelation had sprung to mind.

"So, tell me, Wells, how exactly does a man like you manage to manipulate state funds?" I asked, and in doing so brought that smug, irritating smile back to his lips.

"Oh, that wasn't particularly difficult. I didn't always hold up here in Tibet, you know. This is something of a recent development. I've many connections in the corridors of power, or I did have at one time. I've pulled a few strings here and there. Had a quiet word in a few ears and called in a favour or two. A man must pay his debts, Harry, no matter how old they are, and god knows something needed to be done with you. You were going off the rails a little even before your mother passed on. I knew because I owed your family a debt, so I had eyes upon you even back then. When Lizza passed, I made sure you didn't fall through the cracks and set you up in a good school, gave you a decent start in life and whatnot. It was the least I could do really." And there was, it seemed to me, a dreadful smugness in his tone, which irked me more than anything.

I sat there silently for a while. Sipping my tea, taking all this in and in the process found myself thinking back to my school days. To cold showers and endless cross country runs through even colder drizzle. The disdainful attitude my peers took to the East End oink foisted on them by the housemaster. The beatings handed out by the masters and my peers alike. The bloody awful food. The endless Latin, Geometry and Algebra. The bullies. The cold nights spent shivering under paper thin sheets. Oh yes, school days, those wondrous bygone days of desperate misery and humiliation.

So, I sat there thinking about my school days and all the degradations handed out to the snot-nosed scholarship boy that everyone despised.

I sat there thinking of Rudgley bloody school, and 'the best years of your life,' as they always say...

I sat...

I thought...

Then I punched HG Wells as hard as I could in the face.

CHAPTER 24

Reunions...
Just Like Old Times

"Well, having been to public school myself, I guess I deserved that," Wells said as he nursed a bloody nose with a monogrammed handkerchief.

For my own part, I was sipping my tea once more and, much to my surprise, not being restrained by the guards. I hadn't, for example, been leapt upon by said guards, beaten to a bloody pulp and then dragged off to a cell below the red stone walls of the monastery after feeling the sharp end of their shock batons. Indeed, all those guards were doing was looking on somewhat passively with bored expressions. This struck me as something of a revelation, and I wondered for a moment if perhaps Wells wasn't quite as in charge as I'd assumed after all. But then I reasoned that it was equally possible he'd instructed them not to intervene if I reacted badly to certain revelations. So, I was no wiser than before, all considered. Regardless of this, having got the punch out of my system, I saw no reason to push my luck. The wave of volatile anger I'd been struck with leeched away, to be replaced with a cold kind of logic. But, if nothing else, a few mysteries had started to make some kind of sense at least.

"That's why The Ministry tapped me for all this, isn't it?" I said. Which you may consider to be stating the obvious, but sometimes the obvious needs stating, I believe. If only to yourself. In any event, Wells confirmed my suspicions.

"I presumed as much when I discovered their plans, yes," Wells replied, still dabbing the blood form his nose.

"So, this is all your fault then, I lost my eye to that damn spider because of you…" I said, logic giving ground to anger once more. I banged my fists on the desk, which hurt my knuckles more than punching Wells in the face had, but it was at least a wiser way to vent my anger. Not quite as satisfying though, I will admit, but wiser all the same. I suspected the leniency of the guards had limits I didn't want to test.

"Yes, yes, Harry, it was indeed all my fault," Wells snapped back, the calm mask of his demeanour slipping aside for a moment as a more irritated side of him rose to the surface. He continued much in the same vein, becoming slightly red-faced, letting his opinion of me slip past the mask of civility. An odd kind of disappointment to his tone. "Indeed, Mr Smyth… Because of me, they didn't just string you up… Is that the reason for your petulance on the matter, would you have preferred to swing from the Tyburn tree, to have danced a jig on the end of the rope. Tell me, would that have been your preference?"

He had a point, though I didn't say as much. Instead, I glowered for a moment, stewing a little which doubtless showed in my one remaining natural eye. Then, naturally, instead of admitting my own errors, I rallied towards anger…

"I was only going to hang because I joined the bloody Royal Air Navy, and I was only a damn officer in that misbegotten organisation because of you. If I hadn't been in the service, I'd have never been arrested in the first damn place," I snarled, slamming my fist down on his desk again, no more wisely than before, splitting the skin on my knuckles into the bargain. Wells' moustache bristled, and he jabbed an accusing finger at me.

"Yes, boy, you were an officer, and I dare say you could've been a gentleman if you had chosen to be so. But you didn't choose that path, did you? You foreswore your oaths and engaged in petty larceny, smuggling, carousing with criminals. Gambling yourself into debt and then trying to steal your way out of it. Selling out your good name for want of thirty pieces of silver and god only knows what else."

I opened my mouth to cut him off, but he just continued with his irritatingly cutting rant.

"All I did for you, Harry bloody Smith, was give your sorry arse a chance to make something of your damn life. But you know what? Considering the choices you made, I'd have been as well to leave you to rot in the East End. Judging by what you made of the life I gave you, if I had left you there you'd have ended up waiting to be hung for thieving anyway, like a hundred other common street thugs, I've little doubt. God's man. Take some responsibility for your own damn actions… I put you on a course for a life of honor and high regard. You ruined the opertunity you were given all by yourself." He slapped his hand down hard on the table hard to emphasise his point.

It dawned on me then that Wells was angrier with me than I'd ever thought possible, all things considered. Not for being a spy for The Ministry but because he'd taken a chance and tried to raise my station in life, to repay a debt to an old friend. And what had I done? Wasted it on drink, cards and general thievery. Until I gotten myself caught and sentenced to the jib. Later and with hindsight, I could see why that may have irked him somewhat. Of course, at that moment I wasn't thinking quite that clearly, and the definition of what amounts to a wasted life is subjective after all. Frankly, I didn't consider it wasted at the time, nor do I now, truth told. Besides which I was feeling both petulant and angry, so I was rather sharp in my reply.

"Balls to you. You interfered and screwed up my whole life, you utter arse."

"You made your own choices, Harry, regardless of anything I did," he snapped back, his tone aloof and dismissive – staring back at me over the rims of his glasses and looking for all the world a disappointed schoolmaster dealing with a poor student.

I simmered for a while, biting back replies which were less than gentlemanly. He had me over a barrel in some respects. As he had pointed out, I was actually far from a gentleman in any event, but we are, I think, what we pretend to be, leastways what we try to be. I'd like to think there was some small victory in preserving my decorum once I'd recovered it. But small victories, well, they are often so small they barely count as a draw, so small victories be damned. After a while and with little in the way of manners, I asked the question that was now bugging me the most. "What is it you want of me, Mr Wells?"

He looked up from his tea, a slow cynical smile on his lips. "Nothing, nothing at all, except, perhaps to give you an opportunity. I find myself now in your debt if only ever so slightly, and a man, as I said, must pay his debts. You agreed to have the surgery on your eye, twice in fact, and while I may admit some minor culpability in the reason you needed that surgery. Saving you from the noose I'd consider to be its own reward. Nevertheless, I remain indebted to you for this."

"Saffron…" I said, as the connection stuck me.

"Indeed, my granddaughter has her own little spider to be dealt with. Jobs tells me the latest surgery went well?"

"That's a matter of perspective…" I joked though I suspect he didn't get it. At that precise moment, the 'perspective' I saw with my new eye was a wide-angle visa of the whole room, distorted in much the way things are if you're looking through the bottom of a jam jar… A moment before the eye had been determined to make me look through a crack in the shutters, though all I'd seen was a thick veil of mist beyond. The fog had it seemed grown thicker in the half hour or so I'd spent with Wells.

"Preferable to the alternative, I'm sure?" Wells half stated, and half inquired. The note of concern in his voice clear, he may have had only passing regard for me, but he cared a great deal about his granddaughter. If that is, that was truly who she was.

"There is that, certainly," I conceded.

"Then in your debt, I remain, and as such I shall make you an offer. I need a captain for the Jonah, one whom I can 'trust' to a degree and who knows the ship and it seems to me you're a man with few options before him, Harry… Or indeed, Hannibal, if you prefer. While I suspect your loyalties are as malleable as your honor, your loyalty to yourself is one I'm sure can always be counted upon. Indeed, of that, I've no doubt at all. Besides which you've certain skills, and I would suspect a few dubious contacts which may prove useful to us. Let be honest here, I don't see anyone else beating a path to your door. You're not a popular with The Ministry, I suspect, which gives us something in common. I doubt you have many other options to consider."

There was some truth in that last bit. I was done with The Ministry and no doubt I was a wanted man back anywhere within the British Empire, which was after all a fair portion of the globe. All the same, I was somewhat incredulous. Even letting his jibe about my loyalties slide, it was a strange offer to make to a man who until very recently had been an agent of the crown. Or at least an agent of a dubious organization who operated on behalf of the crown. I had, after all, been used as a stalking horse and as a weapon with which to strike him down even if I'd little say in the matter.

I was, therefore, and to put it mildly, somewhat taken aback. "You want me to captain an airship for you? To actually join your little outlaw navy. You want me to turn guns on the crown's own, my former comrades in arms? You're seriously asking me to be a part of all... all... whatever the hell this all is?" I asked him.

"Oh, my dear Hannibal, are you going to be tiresome now and talk about honour, loyalties to the crown, your sense of justice and responsibility?" Wells said dismissively, sounding remarkably tired all at once.

His dismissive tone wasn't entirely misplaced. I'd been about to do just that. In truth as much for the look of the thing as anything else. That need to keep up the appearance of a straight-backed officer of the crown that Rudgley School had beaten into me, both figuratively and actually on many occasions.

'An Englishman must do his duty to crown and country.'

We'd heard the school's masters repeating that phrase by rote so often I'm surprised me, and the other lads didn't murmur it in our sleep. So, the words were already on my lips before Wells told me he considered it tiresome. Not that I'd have believed a word I was saying or expect Wells to do so. But there are appearances to uphold all the same. The guards may look bored, but they were natives, and native tongues would always wag. It didn't do to seem less than forthright in defense of the crown, even if I believed it all so much hogwash. Such was the thinking bred into every Englishman from birth. We were, as we'd always been told, a superior breed of men. Stiff-lipped and rigid in our ethics, men who could be relied upon to stand while Johnny native crawls off to hide at the first sound of gunfire. Men who held themselves to a higher standard because we were men of a higher standard.

Which, I may add, is also so much horse shit.

But just because I knew it was horse shit didn't stop it from being something bred into me. The Empire had been founded on that belligerent spirit. We, the British, ruled because we deserved to rule. It didn't matter if that was a lie, it didn't matter if we knew it was a lie, all that mattered was making sure the natives whose lands we ruled never realised it was a lie. So much so in fact that we could ill afford even to allow ourselves to realise it.

Even the lowest guttersnipe in the East End knew at their core they were a British guttersnipe. As such, they were worth ten of anyone born in a slum anywhere else in the world. No matter how empty your belly, it was a British belly, and you may bitch and moan between yourselves about the hunger, but you'd never admit to it in front of Johnnie foreigner.

Yes, I know, as I said, utter horse shit…

Despite the inbred impulse to parade out such twaddle, I deflated quickly. Wells had taken the wind from my sails. Besides, I was busy being shocked they would give over command of an airship to me, an enemy spy, albeit an unwilling one, while my mind raced, thinking several things at once.

"No, not at all, I don't believe I owe any debt to the crown anymore, all things considered. I'm just surprised by your offer is all," I told him, which was true enough as it goes. But of course, what I was thinking was more along the lines of how easy it might prove to subvert whatever crew he landed me with. Or for that matter, just alter course a little here and there until I could find a good place to vanish. After all, if he was willing to give me of all people a command, it stood to reason he must be short of actual airmen, or competent ones at any rate. Also, a man with an airship could find a lot of ways to make money. Oh yes, subvert the crew, which at best would be a few rebellious native lads I could probably buy with a bit of braggadocious bluster and a few false promises. What were they in the end but a few bandits and pirates after all? Whatever loyalty they may have, it was undoubtedly to gold rather than some golden ideal, and there was gold aplenty to be made beyond the reaches of the Empire, pernicious though it may be. Some of the tinpot dictatorships in the disunited states would pay well for the services of a gunship and crew, though such a berth could get a little hairy, I imagined. The former states were all a bit too fond of their little wars right now. Illicit cargos, gun running, and the odd bit of smuggling were more my style. A ship and crew, why that was all a man needed. It was a big sky out there. The Jonah's Lament may be a beaten-up company tramp, but with the right kind of investment, a couple of good scores, and I could have her running fast and smooth, she was a gunship, after all.

Oh yes, I don't mind telling you, the possibilities were fair racing through my mind.

There was another consideration too for I'd no doubt whatever Wells had planned would mean going up against the Royal Air Navy. Not those scraggy old East India companies' ships but real ridgeback RAN crewed craft. A prospect which didn't inspire me with confidence or any deep longing come to that. But if I appeared to go along with everything, well, once we got out of these mountains, I was sure I could find the right cloud bank to get lost in. Possibly, if I didn't fancy the life of a privateer, well, at worst I could cut my losses, subvert the crew, and fly her down to Delhi to make a gift of it to the High Commissioner. That might buy me my freedom. Hell, if I played it right, it could get me a knighthood. Services to the crown and all that. It would mean selling out Wells, but what had he actually ever done to earn my loyalty really? Sure, he might have paid for my schooling one way or another, but I never asked for that, did I?

But even as I thought about all this, I realised there was one thing that niggled at both those plans. The question of her, his daughter, or granddaughter, or whatever he claimed she was. Saffron Wells… That was an infatuation I'd yet to rid myself of. And yes, I know what you're thinking, beyond Cairo and my time aboard the Empress on the way out to India, that unfortunate incident with several bottles of Raki and her boots, and whatever few moments I had spent in her company since, I had no real grounds for any infatuation with the woman. Or indeed reason to think she had given me more than a second thought in all that time. But she had those eyes, the kind that will make a man a fool every time, and if I've one true vice, it's strong women… Okay, I have lots of vices, but I'm sure you understand what I mean… And, well, were I to betray whatever narrow confidence her grandfather placed in me, I doubted somehow she would be overly forgiving. Indeed, vengeful was the word that sprang to mind. It was a strange duality when I thought about it; I'd hate to disappoint her almost as much as I'd hate to have her out to seek vengeance upon me.

But, hell, there would be other girls. A handsome man, which I still considered myself to be, a man fresh from India with a knighthood and a big reward from the High Commissioner himself. I dare say there may even be a reception at the palace for such a man. Such a man could catch the eye of some young debutant, with a rich father, titled perhaps… Fortunes had been made before by heroes returning from the colonies, as I'm sure you're aware, so I thought to myself, *why not me?* And wondered if the old fool realised the mistake he was making?

As for my old friend, 'M' and The Ministry, now there I will admit, was a rub, but a shadowy organisation like that… They'd probably be happy with the success and let bygones be bygones. After all, I was sure I could swing it, so they'd believe I'd given up my eye just to gain Wells' confidence. A risk taken in pursuit of my mission, a sacrifice for the greater good, for the Empire. Why they'd laud me too, I'd no doubt.

So yes, as I said, I was thinking fast, and about as dishonourably as could be. If these thoughts of mine shock you, then you really haven't been paying attention to my tale at all… Or perhaps you're just aghast at my avarice-driven stupidity… For which I can't say I blame you.

But then you're reading this in the cold light of day and can, no doubt, see all the fallacies in my chains of thought I utterly failed to contemplate as I sat there sipping tea with a man I was now planning to betray at the first opportunity presented to me. It would be wrong to say these didn't occur to me at the time; I was just choosing to ignore the obvious, like the fact The Ministry would just quietly do away with me once I was no longer of any use to them. And the loyalties of the crew, well they would be unlikely to bend far quickly, no matter how flexible they may prove to be. And while there may be call for a gunship and crew in the more disparate parts of the world, that didn't mean they would keep its captain. And, importantly, there may well be other women in the world, but none of them were Saffron Wells, and my infatuation with her had far from run its course…

Besides, Wells, mad as the proverbial hatter though he may be, was no man's fool…

"Of course, there will be some restrictions…" Wells said.

'*And here it comes,*' I thought to myself.

"I am well aware you cannot be trusted as far as I can spit. Though I trust your sense of self-preservation alone will keep you in line, after all, no one wishes to see you killed…"

The threat, which was not even thinly veiled, seemed strange coming from Wells. He wasn't really the Machiavellian type. Nor was he some penny dreadful villain to offer threats between steepled fingers while smiling in an unsettling manner. He didn't even have a white cat to stroke or any other prop to suggest the sort of disinterested villainy that could have a man killed at a snap of his fingers but was currently just too bored to do so. Instead, this was a threat coming from a mild mannered, middle Englander, a minor bank manager who gave every indication he was feeling apologetic about the necessity of the threat and was mildly embarrassed at the necessity of making it.

Somehow that made the threat worse.

"Of course," I uttered, bluffing for all I was worth. Pretending that my implied demise was of little importance. I suspect Wells wasn't fooled at all. He was smiling at me, the kind of smile that knows when the punchline is coming, and I had a sinking feeling…

"As luck would have it, an old friend of yours has agreed to serve as your first mate…"

"Doesn't a captain normally choose his own officers?" I inquired innocently, while my mind raced with the possibilities, an 'old friend'. I didn't have any old friends, not anymore. Enemies, hell, I had plenty of those. But friends, my friends had always been the type of callow fly by nights who'd disown you the moment you got arrested for murder and treason. Not that I blamed them overly, it's exactly what I'd have done in the circumstances.

"I'm sure they normally have a say in such matters, yes, but you understand I am sure that in the circumstances I thought it best to select your crew personally. Besides it's not like you can fly a ship on your own, is it? You could get lost or lose sight of the task at hand, and that wouldn't do at all. No, a firm right hand at your tiller, well, I would be remiss if I weren't to provide you with someone we could trust to have both our interests at heart," he explained, still smiling, the blameless smile of someone who knows they've got you by 'the dangler's' as my old mum would've put it.

"That's very thoughtful of you," I said, and it was. His thoughts were clearly, '*I don't trust you as far as I can throw you, Harry…*'

"Yes… I am sure," he said, with an air of amusement to his voice. "We've found you a couple of good officers who are willing to fly with you and help you stay on course. Your first mate is not an airwoman herself, but she is a very capable woman. I am sure you will get along perfectly, you are quite well acquainted after all. Almost intimately at one point, or so I am told." Wells failed to hide the chuckle at that last nugget.

There is something very disturbing about a man wanted by half the secret police in the Empire and beyond, chuckling. That's not overly important in the grand scheme of things, I know, but I feel I should mention it all the same.

"She…?" I said, while my thoughts unsurprisingly went to '*intimately*'? I hadn't known a woman intimately since before my arrest and I was sure none of those were ladies Wells was acquainted with. He didn't seem the type for that kind of lady… My mind raced ahead of his answer, as it sometimes does. It went something along the lines of '*The closest I've come to knowing a woman intimately recently was that night in Calcutta with Bad bloody Penny, surely he can't mean...'*

"Hannibal, it's so good to see you again," said a feminine voice with a distinctly American accent despite me being aware she was not actually an American at all.

'Well, of course, it was, who bloody else would Wells shackle me with...?' I thought to myself. And then, well, then the world became an explosion of pain and noise.

Because reunions, they really are just like old times...

CHAPTER 25

The Ukrainian Gambit

A lot of things happened at once. When I say a lot of things, well, on this occasion I'm the very master of understatement...

Bad Penny, as I continued to think of her, apparently thought it best to subdue me a little, just in case I'd an adverse reaction to her appointment as The Jonah's first officer. So, she gave me a dig on the back of the skull, no doubt, to her infallible logic, so I'd reflect on what a wise appointment it was. The blow was gentle by her standards, so it didn't quite knock me senseless. Doubtless, she thought it would serve to remind me just how easily she could kill me if she had to. I'll admit, looked at that way it made a certain degree of sense, at least from her perspective, which was, of course, the perspective of a psychopath.

Her timing, however, could perhaps have been a little better because the merest smidgen of a second before her fist came into contact with my bonce, the outer wall of the room exploded inward due to, what my years of gunnery officer's experience told me, was a bloody big gun being shot at it.

A storm of brick, dust and god only knows what else flew through the room, shards of rubble striking the back of Wells' chair hard enough to knock him to the ground. People were screaming, shouting, and running around like lemmings. Not that I could hear much due to the ringing in my ears. Which might have been caused by the explosion, or it could just have been due to being hit around the head by a mad woman.

Luck alone had sheltered me from the initial blast, as Wells had been seated between me and it. Given the shards of stone embedded in the back of his chair, I'd had been very lucky. Which wasn't the case when the second shell hit and blew a new hole in the wall a few feet to the left of the first.

Still dazed and confused between the first concussive blasts and Penny's punch, I'd started staggering to my feet just before the second blast hit. Bad Penny saved me from that blast by dumping me to the ground behind the shattered remains of the table.

I was still struggling to regain my wits, had ringing in my ears, felt shocked and confused, and was sheltering beneath a psychopathic woman with razors for fingernails, when the unknown enemy started to burst in through the breaches in the walls.

Wells' guards were slow to react. So was Wells, and for that matter even the proverbial one. As for myself, I was barely reacting at all. The battle inside Wells' sanctum was bloody and swift. It was also fast going against team Wells. The team on which I had inadvertently found myself by warrant of being in the room when it was attacked. I may not have considered Wells a friend or an ally, but he wasn't the one doing their best to kill me right at that moment and running and hiding didn't seem to be an option.

Bad Penny was the first to try and stem the tide. She was up and fighting before the Wells guards had collected their wits. But even the deadly viper of a woman she was, it was for a few moments her alone against a dozen or more well-armed assailants. The odds were far from in her favour.

My recollections are somewhat dimmed by the concussion, and I'd never actually seen her in a full on fight before, but the overwhelming impression I got could be summed up with the word 'bloody'. Her blades were fully out before she reached the first man. This unfortunate's throat was sliced open before he could bring his weapon to bear. The clouds of dust and general confusion weren't aiding her, yet she went through them like a hot knife through butter. Three more were down before a concussive shot of some kind hit her a glancing blow and sent her cartwheeling back across the room.

Those guards remaining had gathered enough of their wits by this time to start fighting back too, but of the six that had been stationed in Wells' office, only two were standing by this point. I scrabbled around for something, anything in all honesty, I could use to defend myself and managed to grab a fallen guard's harpoon rifle, but as I turned it on the melee, I realised I could barely tell friend from foe in all the dust and confusion. Besides I was damned if I knew how to arm the bloody thing. I tried a shot at a likely target, who I was almost sure was one of the assailants, but the trigger just locked itself out. Some kind of safety feature no doubt, but honestly what's the point of a gun you need an instruction manual to fire? Cursing my luck, I turned it over in my hands and clinging to the barrel held it like a club. Blunt force is as much your friend as anything if it's all you have. So, I fought to find my footing and looked around for a safe wall to put my back against as more dust and crap fell from the ceiling.

There were more explosions outside. My new eye took it on itself to suddenly focus wildly through the dust around the breach. I got the impression of an airship out there, its guns trained down upon us. A flicker of recognition passed over me as my eye refocused again and I suddenly realised that I knew who the attackers were. Knew them quite well; in fact, I'd been playing cards with several of them only the evening before.

Another guard went down to shots from a Ukrainian's gun. The last of them charged our attackers, with the kind of idiotic bravery you can only admire, and only admire for a moment. The guns found him, and he flew backwards.

Shouts from inside the monastery could be heard above the noise, which may have been help on its way to us, but it sounded distant and remote. Bad Penny was groaning in a corner, down but far from out, but also far from getting back into the fray in the next few seconds. Which left me, alone among Wells' people, standing near where he was staggering to his feet, a prone struggling form, as about eight Ukrainian airmen turned their nasty-looking guns to bear on me.

I had a useless gun, held like an equally useless club, in my hands, blood pouring from my head, no strength in my legs, and I was as confused as I possibly could be.

Surprising as you doubtless don't find it, I didn't at this point scream, "Come on then you bastards, let's be having you…" or anything else brave but foolhardy at them. Instead, I recall saying, rather timidly, "Yuri? What the fuck is going on?" while standing there trying to gather my shaken wits. As he, of all people, was standing front and centre of our attackers, with his rifle trained on me.

Yuri, who I may add, had lost half a hundred rubles to me the night before at cards, a game I regretted having palmed the king of spades to win, given I was standing before him and seven of his buddies holding a club when they turned up for a gunfight.

Yuri smiled at me, a smile that was all beard and broken teeth. Luckily for me, it seemed he didn't bear a grudge. If he had then I dare say the only answer I would've received was a volley of Russian rifles. Instead, the Ukrainian engineer kept his gun trained on me while two of his crewmates stepped forward, grabbed Wells by the arms and started to drag him back towards the breach. Then with a grin and a nod of the head, he said to me, "We take Wells now, yar. Maybe you want come with us, yar? We play some poker tonight, and you drink vodka with Yuri, yar? Captain Putin says we go back to Russia now. Go back heroes to many rubles and as much vodka as we can drink. Is good, you come, up to you English man, yar?"

Yuri was already turning away before I could answer this far from tempting offer. There was heavy pounding on the doors behind me. Help, it seemed, was close now if only I could stall the Russians a few moments.

"Wait…" I yelled, not really knowing why I yelled it, truth told. Perhaps some inner desire to for once be the hero I wasn't. Though I suspect it was more bewilderment brought on by the concussion. "Can we just, I don't know, take a moment and think about this?" I said in something between a shout and an incoherent mumble.

Yuri, turning back towards me, just shrugged his shoulders, a little Ukrainian fatalism crossed his dirty features, and with a look that said 'too bad', he raised his rifle to point at me once more, and then with the smallest modicum of regret crossing his features he said, "Sorry, friend Hannibal, but we go now," and pulled the trigger…

CHAPTER 26

Chaos Reigns

Of all the things to save me at that moment, it was my new eye. Its focus snapped to study in the minutest detail the movement of Yuri's trigger finger as it tightened on the lever. As I saw my doom before me and he pulled it back, time seemed to slow for the briefest of time. Whether this was the effect of the eye or the sheer amount of adrenaline pumping through my veins, I don't know to this day, but I hit the deck in the split second before the gun went off and the shot went just wide, through my coat sleeve and grazing a patch of pure white pain across my upper arm.

The Ukrainian didn't take the time for a second shot. If he had, I wouldn't be telling this tale at all. As it was, the shock was enough to spin me onto my back and crash my head once more against the stone floor. But what's the third concussion in a couple of minutes between friends... And now I was down, I bloody stayed down, because there was sod all I could do right then that would have made a damn difference save get myself killed, and I'd definite opinions on avoiding that if at all possible.

They'd dragged Wells all the way to the breach and had attached some kind of chain to his belt by the time the doors burst open and Saffron, leading a dozen or more of the insignia guards, came rushing in. Two of which went down to the retreating Ukrainian's guns as they stepped through.

Penny had struggled back to her feet, and I heard her let out a howl of frustration as the hoist to which they had attached Wells dragged him out through the breach and up into the air beyond. She crossed the room in an inhuman fashion, three or four steps to travel twenty yards, leaping at the last to stick her blades through one of Yuri's friends as he was hooking himself up to another hoist. Saffron or her guards shot two more, but it was already too late, as Yuri and the others were gone the way of Wells, no doubt to a reward of vodka, rubles and card games aboard the hulking Iron Tsar that was already pulling away from the monastery.

I staggered back to my feet, blood gushing from the thankfully superficial wound on my arm. It stung like buggery, but no more than that, and on the bright side it gave a false impression that I'd fought hard to defend Wells. Even in my less than fully coherent state, I was aware this would be a wise conceit, better to let Saffron and anyone else who cared believe I'd put up some resistance.

Penny, as ever a fly in the ointment, might recall otherwise but I had to hope she had been out of the game just long enough to believe I'd done something to defend her master. At that moment she was too busy taking pot shots at the retreating airship with a rifle she grabbed from a corpse. That and yelling curses after it which would have scandalised polite society to hear them issuing from the mouth of a lady.

Saffron strode over towards her and grabbed the American by the shoulder. "Don't," she hissed, her own rage held back by the merest slither of control. "You might hit him," she added.

I looked through the breach and saw that Wells, Yuri and several others still hung from cables trailing off the retreating airship, hoists slowly winding them in. My artificial eye decided of its own will to be helpful and zoom in on Wells' face for a flashing second or two. He looked startled but otherwise fine, considering he was dangling from a cable below an airship running at full tilt off into the wild blue. Of course, he was probably half concussed himself.

"He's okay," I heard myself saying, half to myself, but loud enough for Saffron to hear.

"How do you know?" she asked accusingly, and in answer I pointed to my silver eye. I'd not told her, or anyone other than Jobs what the eye was doing, but I surmised they probably all knew. A guess that was confirmed when she nodded back to me and said, "I see…" the edge in her voice was palatable. Controlled anger barely held at bay and threatening to explode at any moment. "What else can you see up there?" she asked.

I looked up again, but my eye obtusely refused to help this time, but it didn't need to, the answer was obvious. The Ukrainians were loyal men, loyal to money at least, and loyal to their captain for all they hurled the odd barb at him behind his back. Loyal mostly to his rubles and his stock of vodka, but loyal all the same. More loyal in fact than any of us had imagined.

"Vladimir…" I said, with a degree of certainty. He would've just about had time to get to his ship and move it into position after he escorted me to Wells. Indeed that made a horrible kind of sense when you thought about it, which I did afterwards when my head had cleared itself enough to allow some abstract thinking.

If he needed Wells alive, then he needed to know exactly where he was in the room and to know that he would still likely be where he was thirty minutes later when he started firing shells at the wall to breach it.

I could almost admire the nerve of that. Those shots had to be remarkably precise in order to breach the walls and leave the one person you wanted alive, all so you could capture him relatively unharmed. His strike team had been surgical too. In fact, too damn surgical for a group of men led by an engineer. Those kinds of tactics were the kind of tactics we taught to the Special Airship Service units at Horseguards. Which meant that Yuri and his friends weren't conscript airmen but Russian special forces. Which opened a whole new can of worms. It also explained why Putin was happy to play the lapdog, cunning bastard that he was. Play the sniveling lackey long enough and wait till you have your main chance. Everything about the Russians was a carefully constructed lie. I'd wondered how an arse like Putin had pulled off a mutiny, and now I knew. His crew had never mutinied at all, and that explained too damn much, to be honest, and none of it good…

But I'd other things on my mind right at that moment and didn't piece all that together till much later. Right then I was surveying the valley below, which was as always a bloody ants' nest, but now one utterly upturned. Chaos reigned below us. Crews were running towards airships, and a mad panic abounded. Even more, I realised, than I should have a right to expect. The explosions and bloody violence in the monastery were one thing. But the chaos below was already too advanced for that to be the cause. A sinking realisation struck me all of a sudden as I let my gaze fall on the mists surrounding the valley.

'*Oh shit…*' I thought, as recognition sank in and I realised what I was seeing. I'd seen it before, on a much smaller scale of course, but I'd seen it all the same. '*Oh shit, shit, shit…*' I suddenly knew with absolute certainty why Vlad had chosen to act when he did. After all, if you are going to kidnap the leader of a military force of fanatics from the centre of his power base, you're going to need a distraction to keep those fanatics busy while you get away. And what better distraction than to invite the enemy of your enemy to a play date in the mountains…

"The Ministry…" I said, pointing to the figures appearing out of the mist. A mist they dragged along behind them. A mist billowing from below their feet. "Oh shit on me, Sleepmen…"

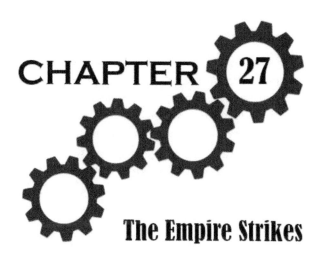

CHAPTER 27

The Empire Strikes

I was wrong of course; it wasn't The Ministry. Well, not just The Ministry. It was a full blown British imperial strike force.

Coming out of the mists I saw the nose cones of small airships. Airships I recognised instantly as RAN strike craft. Short range, fast ships that were carried by much larger craft. Which could only mean there were several carrier ships out there in the mountains; carriers and troop ships, so a few escort craft as well.

There were Sleepmen taking point as the ground forces moved up the valley floor, the strange fog-like gases billowing out from under them as they came. Behind them came platoons of red-uniformed troops wearing gas masks, marching in formations too tightly regimented to be mere company conscripts. I couldn't see the colours they flew, but I could hazard a fair guess it was one of the guards' regiments. Who else would 'M' call on for a task like this but the guards.

Scattered among them were special weapons teams, carrying rockets, harpoon launchers and tesla arcs. All the modern anti-airship weapons the infantry had in their arsenal. It was a wonder they had got so close unseen, there were so many of them, though that mystery was also solved later when we realised who had taken charge of the midrange patrols Wells had out in the mountains.

Vladimir had planned his final moves carefully.

We watched them start to come through the fog from our vantage point, still shocked by this sudden turn of events. Bad Penny was still raving at the sky while Saffron took on a cool calm collected look that spoke of a colder rage burning within. Then the first shots of the real battle were fired.

Main cannon fire from the strike craft arced towards the nearest of our airships. The Russian ex-liner that was in the middle of being refitted as a gunship.

I say 'our' because right then at that precise moment I knew exactly which side I stood upon. The side that was about to be destroyed by the combined forces of the British Empire. It wasn't a side I really wanted to be part of, but I'd little doubt it was the only side that would have me right there and then.

If only that liner had finished its transformation, it might have stood a chance against the fairly pitiful ordinance of the strike craft. Against an armoured ship, at long range, the shots would be less than wasp stings. But as it was, they tore through the aft air sacks in one volley, and the craft was crippled in a moment. Whatever crew were aboard were attempting to cast off and gain some height, while others still swarmed to get aboard. It should've tried to turn and bring its broadside to bear, but there was neither time nor space to do so. The swift little airships were coming in too fast, bearing down with their guns once more. I saw a second volley from three of them smash into the underframe of the liner before I turned away and started to run.

I heard the explosion a moment later which must have been one of the fuel tanks going up, raining burning oil down on those who were fighting to get aboard.

I stopped before I had crossed the shattered remains of the room and shouted at the others to follow me. Some of the guards followed, but Penny and Saffron stayed watching through the breach.

"Damn it," I cursed and ran back to them. Grabbing Saffron by the arm, I told her to come with me.

"No, I'm not going anywhere," she snapped back with steel in her voice but damned all reason.

"We can't win here. All we can do here is die, and this is not the time nor the place for that," I argued with no small passion because staying alive is one thing I definitely have a passion for.

"What do you care?" she snarled at me, and for a moment I thought she would gut me with the blade in her hand.

"I don't," I replied truthfully. "But no one is getting out of here unless we all get out of here. Your grandfather wouldn't want you to die here for no reason, and how the hell can you rescue him if you do?" I growled, as more explosions rang out, and the sound of small arms fire filled the air. I didn't have time for this, none of us had time for this...

"He's right; we have to get out of here. It's the only way we save any of this..." my dearest Bad Penny shouted over the chaos. I never thought she of all people would agree with me, but she did and her words it seemed carried more weight than mine, as Saffron nodded to her.

"Right, you're right, but where…?" Miss Wells said, for some reason suddenly looking at me for leadership, which said much for her state of mind right then. Or else she knew the right time to trust a gutter rat is when you're planning to flee for your life. I racked my brains and tried to remember which ship was furthest from the assaulting forces. The answer, which struck me suddenly, was obvious, and somehow, I should've known what that answer would be without even thinking.

"The Jonah, she's the best hope we have…" I shouted and didn't wait for them to agree. By the time the words had left my lips, I was already running. While thinking to myself, '*That's bloody typical isn't it, Harry, just bloody typical.*' The irony of Wells wanting me to play the captain of the one ship I suspected could get us free of the mountains fast enough, was heavy. But I guessed captain I was going to have to be. Fate's a fickle bastard, don't you find?

The Jonah was smaller and lighter than the big liners and the larger gunships in Wells' fleet, while she was tethered far enough away from the bulk of the craft and the invading British that we stood a chance of getting her in the air and underway before they brought her down.

At least, that was if our forces put up a token resistance worth a damn. If I were them, I'd be raising white flags and hands about now. Luckily, they were made of sterner stuff, though how stern I suspected was going to be put to the test rather rapidly. But by the sound of the fighting, none of them had thrown in the towel as we emerged on the far side of the monastery and ran straight on down the steps towards the main field. Before we got to the bottom, I heard a string of explosions that could only be the final death throes of the Russian liner, which was all the encouragement I needed to run faster.

The running battle was starting to turn in our direction as we ran across the sodden ground. While plenty were making a stand of it, plenty more were now running for their lives and not caring a great deal about the lives of anyone who got in their way.

All considered you might be wondering why I gave a damn about Saffron Wells and why I'd even bothered to argue her into making a run for it. Chivalry and a genuine regard for the woman aside, it was pure survival instincts on my part. I doubted anyone would give a damn if Wells had made me captain of The Jonah or not just before his kidnapping, but at least if I'd his granddaughter in tow, there was half a chance I'd get aboard.

By the time we reached The Jonah, a couple of its crew had already got the gist of the better part of valour and were busy cutting guide ropes. Several of Wells' special guards were barring our way. But they stepped aside once they recognised Penny and Saffron, allowing us to scramble up the gantry.

"Get the damn engines started," I yelled, and ran for the bridge. Getting there I found half the crew didn't seem to have a clue how to get a craft underway quickly, while the other half were still too dumbstruck to do anything useful. I pulled one man over to me and told him sharply to go help cut the guide ropes, then bawled at another to go help the engineer start the engines. And got a blank stare for my trouble.

"Did you hear me? Go help the engineer," I screamed at him, no doubt with a wild look in my eyes.

"He's not on board," the man replied in faltering English, an ashen look on his face.

"What?" I yelled.

"He was at the temple," he told me, pointing out through a viewing port to a building to the side of the monastery proper. It was a good five hundred yards away and already swarming with British troops, fighting a fierce hand to hand combat with locals. I half spied my 'friend' the black robe teaching several of them the finer points of swordsmanship, which caused me to revise my opinion of him somewhat all considered. He and his trainees were putting up the stiffest resistance and teaching some red jackets a lesson in hand to hand combat, but they backed away from Sleepmen whenever they got too close. The strange hulking figures billowing flog like gas must've seemed like Rakshasa's demons to them. God knows they scared the living hell out of me.

"Crap…" I shouted, pulling my eyes away from the battle outside and looked around at the crew for anyone I could bully into going to get the engines started. Only then did I realise that most of them weren't crew at all, just people who had scrambled aboard The Jonah for safety when the first explosions started. I ran to the port side windows to look down at the gantry and saw more people running to get on board.

Too many of them.

Far too many.

I looked around for the one person I trusted, for want of any other word, to stop the flow of refugees. Unable to see her I ended up just shouting, "Penny!" instead.

"That's not my name…" came a snarled reply from the crowd behind me.

"Damned if I bloody care right now," I snapped back and pulled her over to the port windows to point out the refugees now coming to blows with the guardsmen at the gantry. "Stop anyone else getting on board for god sake or we ain't going anywhere."

She blinked at me, then realisation flooded over her fast. I'll give Bad Penny this much; she was quick on the uptake. She nodded to me and made for the top of the gantry. If it were anyone else, a short, slight girl like her would have presented no barrier at all, been next to laughable in fact, but Penny was already showing her claws, literally, and it would be a brave swine who tried to get past her, I didn't doubt, and a luckier one who did.

"Saffron, do you know how to pilot this damn crate?" I shouted because frankly, I didn't know who else to trust beyond the ladies I'd run there with.

She looked at me, still in something akin to shock. I think she'd been mostly dragged along by anger so far – the rage was all that was keeping her moving.

"Saffron!" I shouted again.

This time she responded.

"Yes, I can."

"Good, soon as the lines are cut and you hear the engines fire up, get us some height and head south-west," I shouted above the furor of another chain of explosions that was probably a second airship going up.

"Vlad went north," she snarled, all her anger focused suddenly on me.

"I know, but we need to get free and clear of all this first, for god's sake. We can worry about Vlad afterwards," I countered, not caring if she believed my reasoning or not, just as long as she did what I told her to do. South-west would take us away from the main British force at a right angle, and if I knew RAN tactics, they would have craft lying in wait to the south-east, on the most direct course away from the fighting. And we sure as hell wouldn't catch Vladimir if we had to dodge through the British skirmish lines. Not that I gave a fig for catching Vladimir. All I cared about was getting the hell out of there. Vlad could take Wells all the way to Moscow if he wanted and be welcome to him. I just wanted to get out of this mess alive, and south-west was the best hope of that. If that was, I could get the damn thing started.

"Right fine, we'll do that, but what the hell are you going to be doing, Hannibal?" she shouted back at me, already pushing her way to the main console.

"I'll be starting the damn engines," I called out after her while pulling open the hatch that led down to the engineering deck below us. All the while desperately trying to recall everything I knew about airship engines.

Unfortunately, there wasn't a great deal to recall…

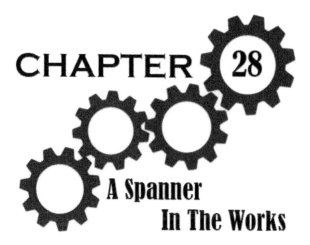

CHAPTER 28

A Spanner In The Works

The engine room was cold, which I took as a bad sign. Engine rooms should be hot, humid places, in which you struggle to breathe properly — populated by big men in vests, with lots of tattoos and greasy hair. Men who bawl out orders to other big men in vests with lots of tattoos, covered in grease, all of whom knew exactly what they are doing. A cold engine room meant the engines hadn't been turned over for a while. Which I knew damn well meant they'd be all the harder to start. The room was also lacking any greasy tattooed men of any description, which worried me even more as I didn't have the first clue how to start the main engines. There were two engines for a start; big twin diesel-powered affairs that ran the length of the chamber. The main console sat at the end I'd entered and had a confusing array of gauges and buttons on it.

None of these, I noticed, was a large green button with a big sign saying 'start' inscribed next to it.

There are times in your life you have sudden moments of utter regret. Like when your father dies, and you regret that your last words to him were uttered in the midst of a shouting match after you rolled in drunk at four in the morning. Or that pang of regret you feel, for never getting up the courage to ask out the barmaid at '*The Three Flags*' when you discovered from one of your mates she is a bit of a goer… Moments which get all the worse when you discover a few weeks later that Elwood asked her to marry him after you'd finally had a one-night stand with her the night before.

Actually, scratch that last one, I don't regret that at all.

But anyway, at that particular moment in The Jonah's engine room, as I stared at the dials and switches before me with an utter lack of comprehension, I was regretting not paying a blind bit of attention in Mr Woolford's engineering class on Wednesday afternoons.

You see, the chief engineer's job was, in my opinion, a dead-end placement that kept you in a dank, sweaty engine rooms surrounded by greasy men with lots of tattoos. Now, I knew a couple of my fellow cadets to whom that idea doubtless held appeal; but it held sod all attraction to me at the time. But until now I'd never found myself stuck in an engine room, in the middle of a battle, in the Himalayas, staring at the one thing that would give me a smidgen of hope of escape, and being at an utter loss. I dare say had I suspected when I was a cadet, even for a moment, that such an event would occur in my future, I wouldn't have spent my time in that class sitting at the back, reading illicit magazines full of pictures of the kind of girls who served the drinks at '*The Three Flags*'.

As it was, I was wracking my brain trying to remember anything useful I might have picked up through general osmosis over the years. While also flicking random switches in an equally random order. I doubted that would help at all, it was better than doing nothing.

Well, in theory at least.

There was another loud explosion, which was bloody loud even through the walls of the engine room. The whole room shook violently with the concussion, and I was sent flying into the wall at the side of me. It didn't take a genius to work out that was probably another airship going up, and one all too close. I clambered back to my feet and started pressing buttons and flicking switches in a frantic panic. Shouting loudly at the controls box in none-too-mild hysteria. Something along the lines of, "God damn it, one of you bastards has to do something." While hitting buttons with my fist and half wrenching dials around.

"Ye know when ye start questioning the parentage of controls they tend to get the hump, laddie," said a voice with a heavy Scottish accent from somewhere behind me.

This, I felt, was possibly the least useful advice in a pressure situation I'd ever heard. It also caught me utterly off guard and almost shredded the last of my nerves.

I looked around sharply to find whoever was speaking but what I found was no one in sight. For a moment I thought I'd finally gone mad or hit my head one time too many and pushed my concussion over the edge. A moment passed, till another loud explosion and the sound of small arms fire dragged me back to the urgency of the situation. And I found myself asking, rather loudly, with a degree of desperation that there was a small greasy man with arms full of tattoos hiding between the engines, "Who the bloody hell is there?"

"Nar is there any need for that ken of language lad? I ask yer. Politeness costs nothing ya knows," said a small speaker mounted on the wall. Just above where I'd just been hurled by a concussion wave.

"Where the hell are you?" I asked, for politeness may indeed cost nothing, but I was under pressure and somewhat exasperated. In fairness, it was also far more polite a question than I intended.

"Argyle, and I'll thank ye ta watch ye tone."

"Argyle?"

"Yes, what of it, you called for remote assistance, so I assume ye need help with yer engine, laddie."

"Argyle?" I said again, not really believing this was happening. Also, I was now dimly aware there was something not quite right about the accent. I couldn't place it at first because it was emanating through a speaker that distorted it all the further.

I stared at the button on the wall next to the speaker.

Then it all clicked into place, as the sign next to it said intercom. But before I could say anything, the voice coming through the speaker started again. "Are ye hard of hearing, laddie? Yes Argyle, in Scotch-land…" said the voice and started to snicker a little to itself, while in the background I could just pick out another snigger.

"For crying out loud, we are under attack; I need these damn engines started. Get your arse's out here now," I shouted, wondering how anyone couldn't know what was happening outside by now.

"What?" said the voice which was suddenly somewhat less Scottish.

"We're under attack and need to get the engines started, or we're all going to bloody die!" I said as calmly as I could.

Which wasn't very.

"What?" said a second voice.

There was another explosion, closer still, and I was knocked over towards the speaker, where I yelled something profane. Though the shockwave of the explosion probably saved my life as several high calibre, ballistic projectiles pierced the engine room wall and exited through the other side, the holes they left leaving little pin spots of light shining through the air, which in other circumstances would have made for good mood lighting.

"Get out here now, for god's sake!" I yelled. And to my relief, a small hatch in the floor popped open, not far from where I was slumped on the deck.

A man's head appeared, swiftly followed by the rest of him, still clutching a mostly empty bottle of Grant's whisky. Just behind him came a second man, looking no less drunk, the pair of them somehow managing to fall out of the hatchway despite it being level with the deck. They looked worried. In other circumstances I might even have had some sympathy for them. I've been drunk and found myself needing to sober up in a hurry enough times in my life to know how they felt. But never, admittedly, because half the British army was busily trying to slaughter everyone in a three-mile radius, including me.

Well, there was that time in Soho, but let's not discuss that right now…

Anyway, while the world was busy going straight to hell all around us, I suddenly found myself in charge of two Indian engineers who'd decided today was the day to camp out in a crawl-way, drink as much of the old captain's whisky as they had managed to scrounge up and play silly bastards over the intercom.

All things considered; I'd like to report I was remarkably calm about all this. I wasn't of course, but I'd like to say I was…

"Now, how do we start these damn engines?" I asked over the noise of gunfire.

The most senior-looking of the pair pointed at the console where I'd been randomly pressing buttons and said something which was either "pre-ignition coils" or in Urdu.

Either way, I didn't understand what he was saying, but if it got the engines started, I'd take it.

"Do it," I shouted, and he stumbled over towards the console and started messing with the buttons and switches. Something clicked, then whirred, then made a chugging sound. But, entirely predictably, nothing else happened.

"Now what?" I shouted with some desperation.

"You need to turn both cranks," he said, pointing at heavy-looking levers attached to wheels on either side of the engines. His co-drunkard was staggering over to one of them. So, I lurched unsteadily to the other, for while I was stone cold sober I'd taken enough blows to the head that day that I was feeling damn unsteady on my feet.

I grasped the handle and turned it clockwise. Or tried to but it didn't budge.

"The other way…" said the drunk at the main panel, who at least seemed to have a grasp on the urgency now.

I yanked at the lever, cursing whichever mad bastard designed it to crack counter intuitively. This time it turned, and once it reached the top of the arc it thundered down, and there was a loud groan from the engine.

Then silence.

I cracked it again.

Then a third time as I heard the first engine, the one being cranked by the other engineer burst into life, spluttering and coughing life but life all the same. It was a start, but I still needed to get my engine going as well, I needed as much power as I could get, to get us out of the mountains.

I cranked again, heard the engine burble… and then another strafe of bullets pierced the walls around us, hitting the man by the console and sending him splattering across the room.

Desperate now I tried once more, and to cap the whole sorry business off, there was a loud snapping sound as the handle came off in my hand.

"Shit," I said, or something equally profane and decided *'one engine will do, Harry, one engine will have to do...'* and started running for the ladder that would take me back to the upper deck and the control room.

"What shall I do...?" came a plaintive half drunken cry from behind me.

"Patch him up and get that other engine running," I yelled vainly as I climbed. Before the whole room lurched heavily to port as the last of the moorings was cut, and I swung round, crashing into the wall. My head hammered against a bulkhead and I fell to the deck once more.

Then, just for a change of pace, and probably because it hadn't happened to me for a few days, my world went black...

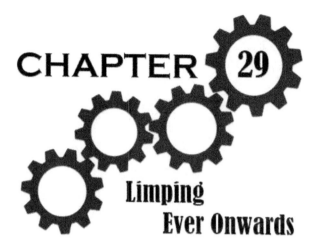

CHAPTER 29

Limping Ever Onwards

I occasionally wonder to myself what happens to the world when I black out. I mean does it bother to fill the intervening time between blacking out and my regaining consciousness. Or does it just leap forward to the next point of awakening? I guess what I am wondering here is, is my propensity to be knocked out just a cheap narrative device employed by some omniscient consciousness to move the story forward? The universe, if you will, taking a narrative leap forward to skip a load of tedious filler?

I say this because I once went on several dates with a solipsist. Sadly, the relationship fizzled out because she refused to accept that I existed, philosophically speaking, when I wasn't with her. I say fizzled; it actually ended with a bang when she caught me in bed with her roommate. I argued that I couldn't have just had sex with another woman, because by her own reasoning neither I or the other woman had any existence beyond that which she could perceive. Therefore, as she didn't perceive us in 'flagrante delicto' as we'd finished an hour or so before she came back unexpectedly, I hadn't actually cheated on her.

As I recall she threw several things at me including a vase that, I'm sure you'll be shocked to learn, knocked me out. When I woke up, I'd been dragged out into the street in nothing but my underwear… I was young and foolish at the time. So, I actually thought she might've calmed down when I came back a few days later to collect my things.

Long story short, she hadn't…

But to move on from fond reminiscing of my colourful past endeavor's… When I awoke after this particular bout of unconsciousness, or narrative leap-frog if you prefer, I was lying on a bunk, being ministered to by, of all people, my own favourite Bad Penny. As awakenings go, finding a woman you know has extendable razors for fingernails and a grip that could crush Brazil nuts, gently applying a wet towel to your forehead is not one I'd recommend. It is, however, something that wakes you up quite swiftly once you realise what's happening.

"He's awake," the diminutive psychopath shouted across the room that turned out to be the captain's cabin on The Jonah. Before throwing away the damp cloth and clearly having decided now I was conscious her job as nursemaid was over, she got up and stalked across the room to slump herself down in one of the chairs, in a surprisingly pouty way for a homicidal maniac.

I was lying on the small cot at the back of the cabin, which also served as the captain's quarters. Space on an airship of any kind is at a premium. Even their captains rarely got two rooms to call their own.

Stiffly, I sat myself up, resting my back against the wall and felt my neck click as I did so. My head was throbbing with a headache yet to come, which is much like the ghost of a hangover that had yet to make its presence felt. Everything seemed too bright, despite the room being unlit, illuminated only by the sunlight coming through the small portholes on either side of the cabin. I was in short feeling ill-used. All the more ill-used as it wasn't because I'd been drinking to excess the previous evening.

Flashes of memory came to me. Blood and oil in the engine room. The shifting of the airframe. The mad panic of our escape. '*If we escaped…*' I corrected myself and tried to take in my surroundings, which wasn't helped by my left eye deciding that a point of focus was optional.

As I came around, slowly, trying not to focus on Penny, mostly because I found her presence as disturbing as ever, I started to get a feel for the movement of the ship, thanks to the vibrations I could feel through the wall I was leaning against. We were in the air and moving with a disturbing amount of juddering. I could feel the strain the airframe was under; something was definitely not right. My air-sense told me that much. Not that I claim to have the keenest of air-sense in the world. I knew engineers who could tell you if a rivet had popped on the rudder by putting their hand on a support strut. But it was keen enough, and I knew The Jonah reasonably well from the short time I'd served on her. The pitch of the engine noise was all wrong for a start; that was the source of the juddering I mentioned a moment ago. There was also something in the way the airframe felt like it was straining to starboard, while being forced to port. I could feel the superstructure fighting against itself, straining and groaning.

'*Damn,*' I found myself thinking, as I was able to guess at the likely cause. "We only have one engine," I said aloud, more to myself than anyone else.

"That's the least of it," someone said. It took me a moment to realise it was Penny despite her being the only other person in the room. I was still not entirely with it...

"I'm on my way up." Another voice cut in over a speaker, Saffron's at a guess, though it was that distorted it was hard to tell. I realised my ears were ringing, more after-effects of concussion, I assumed. As was the uneasy feeling in the pit of my stomach. I felt like a cadet on his first day in the air, yet I hadn't felt airsick in years. I found myself wondering if I'd done some permanent damage to myself in our flight from the monastery, gods knew I'd taken enough knocks on the way. I took a breath and tried to focus more clearly on the problems I could deal with, rather than worrying if I'd permanently cracked my head somehow.

"What else is wrong, Penny?" I asked, without really thinking about what I was saying.

"That's not my name…" she sneered back at me in what was becoming a familiar pattern. I sighed heavily and held my head, which felt like a foreign object to me as it pulsed with pain.

"Whatever… Just tell me what else is wrong with the bloody ship? How long I've been out? Where the hell are we? And is anyone after us?" I asked, not really wanting to deal with her moods right at the moment, but wanting to know as much as possible before Saffron arrived in the cabin. I'd a feeling talking to her would go even worse than talking to her pet psychopath, which was saying something. But Penny could be unreasonable in a very reasonable way most of the time. At least I knew what I was going to get from her, true it was generally laced with spite, sarcasm and anger, but I was used to that. Saffron was capable of being a whole lot more vexing, and unlike my relationship with Penny, I still held a fool's hope that it was worth caring what Saffron thought of me.

"Everything, two days, somewhere over West Bengal, we hope, though in truth god only knows, and apart from half the British fleet presumably, no one right now. Not that that matters much as we will be lucky to stay in the air much longer..." Penny replied, answering my flurry of questions with a flurry of answers. I tried to take them all in, but my head was pounding now, and the urge to vomit was only getting worse. A fit of dizziness hit me, my vision swimming, or half of it swimming, at any rate, the other half had been swimming to start with.

"Two days?" I found myself asking, trying to focus on questions to take my mind off how ill I felt.

"We found you in the engine room after we got underway, you were out cold and welting blood. Though you got off lightly compared to the other two that were in there with you," she replied, with no real sympathy in her voice. I doubt she would've been overly bothered had I not made it out of there alive.

"They're both..."

"Dead, yes. And one engine is shot to hell. Luckily one of them got the other working."

"That was me," I said, though at the time I couldn't recall if that was a lie or not. I could remember just enough to know I deserved some damn credit for once. But Penny dragged the wind from those sails fast enough...

"No, it wasn't, this was after you blacked out, the first engine got shot to pieces when we ran into the blockade ships. Lucky for us, your man got the second working, we found him holding this huge spanner and bleeding out and babbling something about a damn idiot breaking the main crank..."

The ship lurched again, and so did my stomach. I bravely fought down the contents of an empty stomach. '*Two days*,' I found myself thinking again.

"Okay… that was me… But whatever, why are we over Bengal? I said go south-west?" I asked her, having managed to sort all the geography out in my head despite it spinning.

The door of the cabin crashed open violently as I was saying this and Saffron Wells entered, clearly far from happy.

"We did go south-west, you bastard, straight into their blockade, but I'm sure you wouldn't know anything about that now, would you?" she shouted, which, I'll admit, was another indicator as to her mood, if I'd needed one. One look at her face told me I didn't. She was angry and looking for someone to take it out upon.

So guess who was the prime target for that rage?

Go on, guess…

"Shit, why the hell would they be there?" I muttered half to myself, sure I knew I'd been guessing at the time, but it had been my best guess unless the fleet was a lot larger than I expected.

"Did you know…?" she shouted again, stalking over towards me, all hail and thunder. Whatever frustrations she'd suffered in the past couple of days, she was clearly more than willing to take them out on me. I can't say I blamed her much, even at the time. Let's face it, I was the obvious choice. The Ministry's spy in the camp, unwilling or otherwise. What reason did she have to trust me when all was said and done?

"No, but it was a shot in the dark. By rights they should have been massed due south," I replied, trying to keep both my voice and myself calm. The last thing I needed or wanted right now was a slanging match. I barely felt up to conversing at all.

"A shot in the bloody dark. It nearly damn well got us all killed, you bastard…" she yelled. Stopping just short of hurling something at me.

She stared at me, red with anger, her eyes full of fire and hate; damn but they looked wonderful…

And then…

Then the wind went out of her sails. I suspect because she knew enough to know that it would've been insane of me to run them into a trap. She might not trust me, but if I'd wanted to aid in their capture just scuttling the engines completely would've been a damn sight more effective. She just needed to vent her rage.

She sighed heavily, slumped down into the chair behind the captain's desk and held her head in her hands a few moments. Collecting herself after her initial outburst. Pushing her rage back down and letting a colder cooler logic take hold.

I waited a while, staring at the decking, breathing slowly and trying to get control of my nausea.

When I looked up, I caught sight of Bad Penny smiling, a nasty little smile as she watched me. I half suspected she had hoped the argument would boil over into violence. No doubt she would have enjoyed watching Saffron beat the hell out of me. God knows I was in no state to resist if that was what it came to.

"Okay, so you hit the blockade and turned south-east, but how did we outrun them on one engine, and why are we still heading south-east?" I asked after the atmosphere in the cabin had found some pretense of normality.

"The Russians…" Saffron replied, a note of despondency creeping in her tone.

"What? Vlad came back? I asked incredulously.

"No, not The Sharapova, some other Russian gunships. They hit the blockade at the same time we ran into it," she said.

"That doesn't make sense. Why would Russians attack the blockade? Are you sure they were Russians?"

"The big Romanov Imperial Eagles painted on their side were a bit of a clue…" Penny injected sneeringly.

"Russians," I said, thinking aloud, or trying to, my head hurt enough as it was without trying to straight all this out. But then after a moment I realised the most obvious conclusion, one I hinted at earlier, because now everything added up, I told you I'd get there in the end. "Russian… Okay… That only makes sense if Vladimir was never a dissident at all but was working for Kremlin all along. Which means he was playing us all. But even if that's true, if the Russian navy attacked the Royal fleet, that's an act of war against the Empire, that's a hell of a shit show to start. Why the hell would they risk that over Vladimir… Oh…" Another thought struck me, and not a pleasant one, as it made everything I'd been tied up with so very much worse.

Saffron half smiled at my 'oh', but said nothing; I guess she wanted to see if I could work it all out on my own. Penny meanwhile just leered at me, clearly aching to vent some frustrations of her own.

"It's not about Vladimir, is it? It's Wells, it's all about Wells. Whatever the British want him for, the Russians want him just as bad. They want him enough to risk all-out war between them and the British, and they have been dancing around that for decades. They must have been planning this for months, years possibly. But why? What is it they want? What the hell does Wells have that is so damn important?" I said, still piecing it all together as I spoke.

"You mean you don't know?" Bad Penny asked, sounding genuinely surprised.

"Of course, I don't bloody know. You think The Ministry told me anything? They just packed me off with a mechanical spider in my head and pointed me at you lot. You think they thought for a minute it was worth telling me why? You think anyone has bothered to tell me bloody anything? For all, I know he's Queen bloody Victoria's favourite chicken fetishist. No one has ever bothered to tell me a damn thing." I was angry now. Not with the two women in the cabin, though they would do right then, but mostly at the world in general and everyone in it. I was in the middle of things I didn't understand, and the whole world was falling apart because of it. I'd been abused, beaten, stabbed, knocked senseless more times than I could count, tied up, shot at, almost been blown up by the biggest bomb in history, caught up in the middle of a bloody full-scale battle and despite all that, no one had yet had the common decency to tell me what the hell it was all about.

Penny, by this point, was laughing, laughing hard, and quite obviously at me, which didn't help one bit. "They never told you why they were sending you to India? Why they wanted Wells? That's priceless. Honestly, that's bloody priceless. Poor little Hannibal, not even trusted enough by the very men who sent him out into the world to know what they were sending him to do…"

Saffron, on the other hand, just remained silent, staring at me, weighing me up, and I suspect not entirely believing me even now.

Another shot of pain ran through my head, but I did my best to ignore it. Being the butt of Bad Penny's humour did not help with my anger.

"Russians and Britain are going to bloody war with each other over this. Bastard Sleepmen, The Ministry, this whole damn mess. For the love of god, can someone just tell me what the hell they're all after? What the hell is it they want?" I implored.

Penny continued to laugh. Then Saffron sighed heavily and looked straight at me, and with nothing but a serious expression on her face she told me something I couldn't bring myself to believe.

"It's the time machine. They're all after my grandfather's time machine," she said.

I looked at her, lost for words, between the thumping in my head, the lurching of the ship, and the incessant out of kilter drone of that one lone engine, already on its last legs, all contributing in making me feel sick to the stomach, and now she was telling me this!

I looked at her and tried once more to add it all up. To make sense of everything I was being told. Sense of the world going to hell in a handbasket over something utterly impossible. Then I asked the only question that now occurred to me at all.

"The what now…?"

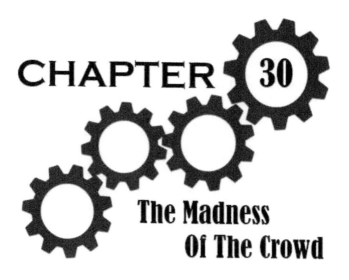

CHAPTER 30

The Madness Of The Crowd

We were nigh on drifting, the prevailing east wind blowing us out over the Bay of Bengal. Our one remaining engine was sputtering, coughing and barely giving out enough power to give us any control, our fuel reserves all but gone, mainly because bullet holes through the upper tank had pissed out most of our fuel before we got out of the mountains. We were lucky that diesel didn't take to flame, or we would never have got out of the mountains at all. So, I'd ordered them to shut the engine down till we needed it.

Then, when they ignored the order, I pleaded a bit and told them that until we had some destination in mind, we were better saving what we had.

My authority as captain of our little craft was, as you can probably guess, non-existent. Saffron was in charge, Bad

Penny her second, mostly because no one would willingly disagree with her after witnessing her hold off two armies at the monastery. One of refugees desperate to escape and the other one determined to kill us all.

The crew, such as it was, was made up of those who had been lucky enough to be aboard when we got to her, and a couple of Wells' guardsmen who'd helped Penny hold off the waves of the desperate and the deadly. Only a couple of them were actual aircrew, one a gunner, who would have been useful if we had a working gun, which unsurprisingly we didn't due to expending all the rounds we had in our desperate escape. The other was a navigator who would have been a blessing, if only we had fuel for power and a destination to aim for that was worth a crap.

We were also losing altitude…

Not dramatically I should mention, a few dozen feet an hour, which could mean nothing. Changes in air pressure could cause that, and out over the ocean, air pressure had a way of shifting. But with the main engines down we weren't re-pressuring the canopy gas as we should have been. Also, the pumps forcing air into the ballasts were down and a dozen other things were going wrong, all little things on their own but these things add up, so losing some buoyancy was bound to happen. But still, I thought it best not to mention it when I first noticed, in case it was something more sinister. We could re-pressure on fuel reserves once we figured out where we were going. But if we had leaks, even small ones, it was going to become more of a problem.

I was staring at the alt meter about three days after I had first awoken in the cabin when I reached the inevitable conclusion, the one I had been avoiding coming to…

We had leaks… More than one…

Considering everything I'd been told in the last seventy-two hours, leaks almost seemed a mundane problem, because if I believed only half of what I'd been told, then we was mixed up in world-shattering events, and if I believed none of it, well in that case I was surrounded by lunatics. I wasn't sure which was worse. I was sure, however, none of it was good. But to recap a little…

"The what now?"

Saffron sighed, the kind of sigh you expect from someone when you're about to have one of those conversations. A conversation that they know you're not going to believe. One in which they know you will end up disputing everything they say and clearly think them mad. It was also a sigh I'd gotten used to hearing of late.

"His time machine. My grandfather is from the past, and they think that with it they can reshape the present," she said, which I barely followed as a chain of logic. Not least because the idea of someone from the past coming to the present in a time machine seemed absurd. People with time machines, it seemed to me, would naturally go to the past and come from the future, not the other way round. Except when I thought about it, it made exactly as much sense the other way around… But at the time I was trying to dismiss the whole idea flippantly.

"Everyone's grandfather is from the past; that's how grandfathers work…" I said. My head was still pounding, which wasn't helping a great deal as I would rather have been curling up in a ball and started rocking myself back to sleep at this point, as opposed to trying to follow a weird chain of logic, that failed at being logical in the very first instance.

Saffron looked at me in disgust, clearly not in any mood for my wit. I could tell she was on the verge of another rant, so I tried to head it off, mainly just to spare my head, and because while I may not believe all I was being told, it struck me that she and others did, and it would be nice to know what was going on for once, because at that moment it seemed to me the world was being dragged towards catastrophe by madmen, and me along with it. If, I reasoned, I knew what was behind it all then I might at least stand half a chance of getting out of their damn way…

"Fine, okay, putting my cynicism to one side, you're saying Wells is from the past, and both the Russians and the British, want his time machine, and that's what all this has been about from the start?"

"Ostensibly, yes," she said, biting back her irritation.

"Okay then, so the reason they believe this is? Why? Because it's not exactly easy to believe…" I asked, trying to at least seem to be open to the idea. Which I may add, I would've been far more open to if I were discussing it in a bar with a couple or three good scotches down my throat and a fresh glass in my hand. Sadly, that was not the case, though I could've cheerfully killed for a stiff drink around about then.

"Because he is the 'Architect of the Present' and they know it. This present anyway."

"The what now?" I asked while becoming aware just how annoying that phase was starting to be, to me if no one else.

"The 'Architect of the Present'. It's a title Queen Victoria once bestowed upon him for his services to the crown. He'd been guiding the Empire for years at that point. It was an open secret he had a means of knowing what lay in the future and so was able to guide events so the British Empire stayed in control of everything. His Ministry was tasked with guiding everything from behind the scenes, avoiding wars, moving people about so their future changed, he and his partners guided the fortunes of Britain, France, Russia… everywhere. They had a hand in everything that happened."

"Hang on, his partners?" I asked, wondering who else was involved while feeling I just missed something important. My head really was throbbing at this point, and it was hard to think clearly.

"The other Architects, but they don't matter right now, there is only one of them that's still around. I doubt we can find him anyway. What we need to do is get my grandfather back from the Russians…"

"No one will help us," Bad Penny interrupted, with another nugget I missed at the time. I'd blame my pounding head, but in truth it that was an easier nugget to miss, a subtle note in the tone of her voice was all that would've given me the slightest inclination of what she actually meant.

Saffron turned to stare at Penny, and something passed between them I'm sure because I closed my eyes for a moment, trying to numb the pain by force of will and when I opened them again, Bad Penny was stalking out of the cabin. If words had been exchanged, I'd missed them entirely. But the way the door slammed behind her, spoke a note of petulance, but then my nerves were not the only ones on edge.

"Okay," I said after a moment, feeling I'd the edge on my headache for a little while. "Let's put that little problem of getting Wells back from the Russians on one side for a moment. Not forgetting the British probably have the same idea and ain't fond of us either. I need to know more about all this if I am going to be of any help. So enough of keeping me in the dark, okay. Explain what's going on."

I said all that while not wanting to know as much as I already did. What I wanted was to be on a beach somewhere just below the tropic of cancer, sipping cocktails and contemplating grass skirts. But if that wasn't a possibility, and frankly I doubted it was, knowing more about what all this was really about was probably one of the few things that would keep me alive.

Saffron turned back to me with a snarl on her normally pretty face. "Getting him back is all that matters right now," she said.

"Then let me help you… But I can't do that unless I know more," I said, which was disingenuous to a degree. I was indeed happy to help, because right now it seemed like the only option I had, and winning her trust was important to me for more than one reason. Though winning that trust was never going to be easy. "Please…" I added because it couldn't hurt any.

She looked far from convinced. I can't say I blamed her. Instead, she just stared at me in silence.

"You said Old Iron Knickers handed him a title for services to the Empire, him and his time machine. What exactly did he do?" I asked, trying to get her talking again, and not entirely convinced she was not just winding me up at this point. And let's face it 'what did your grandfather do with his time machine?' is one of the stranger questions you can find yourself asking a girl.

"He arranged things, differently, better, at least he thought so at the time. That was before," she told me, not that she was making much sense to me, but it was better than silence at least.

"Before?" I prompted, hopefully.

"Before he realised the mistake he'd made and tried to fix it, but it was too late by then. When they found out what he planned to do, they forced him out of The Ministry."

"Wait, The Ministry? That Ministry? Wells was part of The Ministry?" I was shocked by this intelligence, as I'm sure you can imagine. "The bloody Ministry, those bastards. 'M' and his cronies. That bloody ministry?"

"Yes," she said simply, adding, almost as an afterthought, "I thought you knew."

"He was part of The Ministry?" I repeated. In my defence, the news was taking some sinking in. I'd known The Ministry were at the heart of everything. Always manipulating things behind the scenes. But finding out the man I'd been sent to hunt down for them had once been part of The Ministry himself was too much. "The same bloody Ministry that put that damn spider in my eye?" I snarled. "In both our eyes?"

"Of course. It was my grandfather that founded it…" she said. It was at this point the conversation started to go downhill a little.

According to the alt meter, we had dropped another thirty foot in the last twenty minutes. It was too big a drop to just be a change in air pressure. Drifting as we were, it wasn't like we were moving fast enough for this to just be a natural dip.

Watching that alt meter had become my new obsession in the last couple of hours. I knew too well what it meant. Thirty foot wasn't much in the grand scheme of things; we were still a good five hundred feet above the Bay of Bengal after all. But a leak in the air sack could only get worse. Eventually, the pressure forcing gas out of whatever small holes was leaking it would cause the holes to rip wide open. At which point our slow descent would become more of a plummet.

Watching the alt meter was, therefore, a tad disturbing, as the needle slowly moved back down the dial. Yet somehow it was easier to focus on that than all I'd been told over the last three days since I'd awakened in the captain's cabin of my first and probably last command…

All the same, I was going to have to do something about the leak, if I could, at any rate. This was a prospect that didn't thrill me greatly, for all it focused the mind…

The gist of what I'd learned, if you chose to believe it, was something like this, though you'll have to forgive me if I miss out some important points. The concussion I'd been suffering was faded by then, but it had hung around for a long time and I may be confused on some of the details. In all honesty, I hoped that is the case at the time. But let's see if I can explain what I was told...

History, not the dull irritating subject you sat through dreary Wednesday afternoons back in your school days, but actual history. Well, according to HG Wells, its broken. If you're wondering how you can break history, Saffron explained it something like this.

In the spring of 1894, or at least an 1894, not my 1894, the 1894 I didn't bother learning anything about at school, but some other original 1894 in which Wells lived, Saffron's grandfather had been working on an idea for a novel which he planned to call 'The Time Machine' when he happened upon a moment of inspiration. A way to actually go about making such a device.

Now, obviously, when she told me this, I said such an idea was ridiculous. So, she gave me a hard stare by way of a reply, then started trying to explain how it worked based, no doubt, on how Wells had explained it to her. Unfortunately, second-hand explanations are never the easiest things to follow. So, you will have to forgive me for not explaining them third hand to you now. Besides, frankly, I didn't follow a word of it and how it worked didn't seem particularly important. Not compared with what he did with it once he got it working.

Time, Wells told her, comes down to a matter of causal effect, and so, if you disconnect the cause from the effect, you can alter the flow of time. Do that in the right place, and it flows down the next available route, do so again, and the same happens. The flow is constant, but like the flow of a river you can paddle against it or with it, if you have the right kind of paddle, and Wells time machine was his paddle...

And Wells had found a paddle, so he went paddling.

I guess I understood why he would because if I could nip into the future, I would. If only to find out who was going to win the Grand National for the next twenty years. So, Wells took his paddle if you'll forgive me overextending that metaphor, and he went forward in time, and that is where the story gets a little difficult to believe... because there he witnessed a horrific future about to befall mankind.

Okay, I know, none of this is easy to believe, but trust me it gets harder...

In 1914, which if I remember my history correctly was the year of the first great peace festival at Versailles, where the Accord de Paris was signed by all the major western powers, ensuring peace for the next fifty years, based on agreements to respect the colonial rights of all concerned. But in his 1914, Wells witnessed a great war of some kind. A war in which the great powers were at odds and started failing, a great war that lasted four years and left Europe in ruins. By its end, Bolsheviks had run riot in Russia, killed off the Tsar, and a single-party state replaced him based on insane ideas, like the equality of all men and each doing what they could for the benefit of each according to their need, or some other claptrap.

If that doesn't seem crazy enough, couple of decades later an Austrian anti-Semite rose in of all things a united Germany and plunged the world into another horrific war. While this Germany was ultimately defeated, the war left behind a shattered world. A cold war followed whatever the hell one of those was. As far as I could gather from Saffron's explanation, it had something to do with iron drapery. This pitched the eastern European states headed by Russia against the western nations led by of a still United States of

America. A USA which hadn't plunged into the internal strife of the 1890's that led to their disastrous second series of civil wars, but had risen to eclipse the other western nations and become a new superpower, which is another name for an empire but without all that tedious occupying of other countries, instead you just buy them up. All the while, the star of Great Britain was gradually fading, and weapons were created that could destroy whole cities, in ways that made even the bullet train at Hiroshima seem humane, which I found particularly hard to stomach. This then was a world where humanity was tittering on the brink of annihilation. Having created a means of its own extinction it had neither the will nor the leadership to step back from it.

Wells saw all this, and, according to Saffron who was playing for melodrama I suspect, he wept.

So having found the future a place to despair, Wells, so he claimed to Saffron who believed all this even if I didn't, ever a proud Englishman, came to believe that it was the decline of the British Empire that led to all the horror he had witnessed. So, when he returned home to his own 1894, he determined he must find a way to change the course of the future and avoid the nightmare that awaited the world. This epiphany led to a second. That the Empire in which he lived had started to fall when Queen Victoria died.

Yes, died, for this 1894 was a very different 1894 from the one we know.

Wells, in this strange 1894 where Victoria didn't sit on the throne, believed the British Empire's strength held other powers in check. Its wealth, its power, its influence, were the rock on which civilisation was built. He decided while the Union Jack flew in the four corners of the earth, the world as he knew would be safe. So, Wells had determined, to maintain it this state of grace, Queen Victoria needed not to die in 1876.

So, like you do, Wells popped in his time machine once more and went back in time with a plan. He sought out another writer he knew of, a man called Haggard, a man with his own secret. A man who had written a story based on a truth wrapped up as fiction, which he had vouched safe to Wells over drinks one night in 1925, at their club. Again, this was not our 1925, but a 1925 in Wells' original time stream, Wells having popped forward to ask Haggard about a novel he had written some years before, and if any truth lay within it.

Yes, I know, it gets more confusing and harder to believe every passing sentence. How do you think I felt?

Anyway, this Haggard vouched the truth of his tale about a mysterious burning pool in Africa that granted eternal life. Which apparently was not actually in Africa or guarded by a four thousand-year-old queen's army. But the tale about a flame that burns forever in a cave and gives forth life, well it was true, after a fashion, but Saffron didn't know the details of where and what it actually was. Somethings Wells didn't even trust his granddaughter to know apparently, which struck me as convenient…

This, however, is apparently the secret of the long life of our own eternal queen, old Brass Knickers herself. But putting my own disbelief on one side, if true Sticky Vicky, and one or two of her most trusted advisors have been gifted long life form this eternal flame, because Wells went back to the 1850s, far enough to make himself one of those advisors, armed as he was with knowledge of the future. He arranged for the British army to seize control of that cave, and apparently made sure Mr Haggard never wrote his story or found the cave himself.

Unfortunately, this led to a whole new set of problems because of somethings called paradoxes. Now I have no idea if paradoxes are some odd kind of mammal that drops from the sky in boxes or what, but they are bad apparently, and they fit into the whole time is a river, it flows, analogy, by acting like mini whirlpools.

Yes, I know, this confused me too.

If it helps, I'd as hard a time believing all this as you're no doubt having now, but as I said, Saffron believed it, she believed everything her grandfather had ever told her. Vouching that he himself had made use of that same secret pool to gain the kind of longevity that blessed old Seldom Bloody Amused.

If there were grains of truth in all this, I struggled to find them. Save for the evidence of Queen Victoria's long life, but personally I still believe that's down to British science and technology, not some bloody magic pool in Africa.

But anyway, according to Saffron this was when Wells really got busy. He and several others he recruited set up the first incarnation of The Ministry. Then they set about making other changes to history, at least changes from Wells' perspective, for the rest of us History is just a boring subject in school, because, as I understand what Saffron explained to me, we are in the new flow Wells created.

The Ministry under Wells' direction started 'fixing' the flow of time, so it suited the Empire and kept the enemies of Britain's new glorious future at bay. Little things that he and the other 'Architects' changed, pebbles to form dams or prevent them more to the point, to keep everything flowing along as he wanted it.

A man called Marx in 1870 was advised to move to New York rather than settle in London, his ticket across the Atlantic paid for by the crown, which stopped Russia ever falling to his followers. Americans, they reasoned, would despise the politics Marx suggested far more than Europeans. This was responsible for the fall of the

American dream, the internal bickering of the states, and that's what led to the second civil war. Apparently, Wells considered this a great irony, because in his own original time flow, the American's fear of communism was what led to the frosty war about iron drapery, and kept the United States united, apparently.

Wells had told Saffron that had been a mistake on The Ministry's part. America, it seemed, needed external enemies to stand united against. With no great communist evil to face down, it had turned in on itself and fallen into the chaos that reigns there in our own age. But the loss of American unity was Europe's gain and allowed Wells to go meddling in Europe.

The Germanic states were kept disparate through careful diplomacy. Instead of uniting into one nation strong enough to threaten the peace of the world. Which, unbelievable though it may seem, they had done in Wells' original history.

They made other small changes. A man called Adolf was given an art scholarship in Vienna, where he painted horrible pictures that would have never caught on, but for The Ministry buying them through third parties. He enjoyed many commissions, and success as an artist kept him too busy to pursue any of his strange political ideas. Mostly the paintings were burnt after they were purchased and when he died of syphilis in the early fifties, The Ministry bought up what was left and burnt them too. He was forgotten entirely in less than a decade apparently. Her grandfather seemed to find this particularly amusing for some reason.

Up and down the time streams, changes were planned, changes were made, and time flowed forward on a new path. A new path which saw the British Empire stay rampant in its supremacy. Peace and stability were assured... and the flow became what you doubtless recognise the world we lived in. Which as you know is far from perfect, but at least it sounds better than the weird future Wells claimed to have witnessed. Though I guess we will never know how that would have worked out in the end.

It's at this point Wells apparently went rogue. Or a little nutty, or a lot of nuts, a whole bag of nuts perhaps, though judging by everything Saffron swore he had told her, he was nuts to begin with.

Apparently, Wells came to an epiphany. Time needed to flow back to its natural course, more and more of those whirlpool things I mentioned were showing up, and the more he meddled, the worse it got. While the river itself, he came to believe, had stagnated. This is because empires need to rise and fall, wars need to be fought, powers need to peak and wane, and to everything, there is a time.

He came to believe that in his meddling with the natural course of time, he had changed the destiny of mankind and we had stagnated with it, both in terms of technology and of culture. That future that had once so horrified him now seemed a distant memory of a golden age. The wars and disasters of the 20th century had, he believed, been the growing pains of a truly global civilisation. He had sought to bring about the changes he had witnessed after the wars that never were, without the conflict that drove those changes in the first place. And in doing so, the human race had barely advanced at all in the last hundred and fifty years.

As he believed he had broken time, he therefore had to be the one to fix it.

Remarkably the British Empire and The Ministry he had founded to protect it, disagreed with this idea. Quite violently in fact, and he had fled the Empire some years ago. Then from scratch he started to build a new organisation with the help of no one. But when he fled, he had left his time machine behind, taking only a few vital components with him and these he had hidden.

All of this was utter hogwash of course, but by the time Saffron had finished telling me all this I was convinced of three things.

Firstly, the British and Russian governments, who had a stake in the status quo, believed it, and both wanted Wells and the parts of his machine.

Secondly, Wells must be the greatest con man in history to have convinced two great powers he could travel through time and alter events.

Thirdly and importantly, Wells was also utterly and completely off his bloody rocker...

But none of that mattered to me right at that moment, three days later, stood on the bridge of The Jonah's Lament, however, because the alt-meter I was watching had just dropped another twenty feet, and I'd no choice but to go outside and try and patch a hole in an airship, drifting over the Bay of Bengal, at the mercy of the elements.

It had also just started to rain because just to top it all off, it was monsoon season...

CHAPTER 31

Then Along Comes The Rain

Falling…

It always seems to come down to falling…

Just like that same damn dream I'd been having for over a year. I was watching the sky fall away from me. Then as I twisted through the air, saw the ocean racing towards me.

Everything I'd been through, the court case, the death cell, The Ministry, that damn spider of theirs in my eye. Sleepmen. Egypt. Calcutta. Crazy razor-fingered women, trying to kill me. Japan. Want to be Shoguns and bullet train bombs, Wells and his damn rebels. Great Britain and the Russian Empire going to the brink of war, all over some damn impossible time machine and there's me getting caught up in the middle of this whole insane shit storm. And now here I was, falling into the Bay of Bengal from a sodding airship in the midst of a monsoon…

Frankly, it was past time I considered my life choices…

There may be worse ways to die than slamming into the ocean at maximum velocity, but right at that second, I couldn't think of many. Water, for all it may seem like a reasonably safe option as a place to land when you fall from an airship, isn't far removed from concrete when you hit it travelling at 122 mph. It's a bone-shattering impact at best, but if the impact doesn't kill you, and if you don't lose consciousness, then you best learn to swim with broken bones. Of course, you might even survive that if you're lucky, if cramp doesn't hit you, if you're not bleeding internally, or externally come to that. Oh yes, you might manage to stay afloat for a while before you needed to consider niceties like sharks. So, as I said, while there may be worse ways to die than falling twelve hundred feet into the Bay of Bengal, at that particular second, as I saw the ocean rushing towards me, my mechanical eye choosing that moment to zoom right in on the crests of waves and the odd fin, I honestly couldn't think of any.

Luckily my lanyard caught, and I felt it spring back on me. Leaving me swaying in the breeze a mere ten foot below the canopy.

Of course, I had a safety line and harness on, did you think me an utter fool…? Actually, perhaps it's better if you don't answer that…

Though, for swaying in the breeze, you should be reading, being lashed about in a gale while hanging ten feet under the airframe canopy. I was also hanging on a piece of fraying cord that I'd scrounged up from a pile of discarded ropes a few minutes before. So, in fairness, it didn't inspire much in the way of hope beyond a short respite from my impending doom.

I'll also not mention the rope burns you get from a harness as it jerks you to a halt. Strapped as of course it was, across my unmentionables. Let's just say the pain I had just experienced made me feel that plummeting to my death may not entirely have been the worst option.

"Hannibal, you alright down there?" came a cry from above.

I managed to twist myself round by pulling on my harness and grabbing the lifeline enough to look up at Saffron, who was hanging out of the cargo door with one hand to look down, while I was swinging about like a departing guest at Tyburn.

"A little help wouldn't go amiss," I shouted back over the wail of the wind.

I'm not sure whether she heard me or not, but as I managed more by luck than judgement to avoid being hit in the face by the rope they slung down for me a moment later, I assumed that they had.

It took me a couple of attempts to grab hold of it and with Saffron still hanging out of the cargo door to watch me, someone else started pulling me back up towards her. Once I reached them, I pulled myself over the lip and inside once more, trying to preserve at least some dignity in the process. I expected to see a half dozen crew members on the other end of the rope. A captain must maintain a certain aloofness after all.

It wasn't half a dozen men who had hauled me back in, of course, just the one skinny little 'Not-Actually-An-American' girl. Which, from my perspective, was somewhat worse than being pulled in by my crew.

Doing my best to hide my utter relief at not falling to my doom, I regained my feet and adjusted my uniform more in hope than expectation. I'd no doubt I presented a far from the dashing figure, and mostly I was just trying to adjust my safety harness so it stopped biting into my skin and other parts of me. I winced a little as I loosened things up.

"My thanks to you, Penny," I said, trying manfully to disguise my embarrassment at having fallen in the first place.

I'd not even fully climbed out on to the running-board when I fell. I'd merely caught my foot in the safety line and managed to trip myself.

"That's not my name…" came the usual retort in what'd become a regular quid pro quo between us. The sneer on her face suggested she currently found this less amusing than I did. I'd grown increasingly fond of calling her Bad Penny by this point. At least, in the lighter moments of our association, those moments when she wasn't trying to kill me, beat me to a pulp or lacerate parts of my body. Occasionally she would even smile when I used it; I think perhaps this was because it had the suggestion of a pulp novel villainess about it and this appealed to her more than she would willingly admit. Though as often as not, it just made her scowl at me.

Most women of my acquaintance tend to look a little ugly when they scowl. Penny, however, wasn't most women; there was something undeniably attractive about her when she scowled at you. Mildly terrifying if you'd ever seen what she could do when she was angry, but attractive, nonetheless. If I was pushed, I'd say it was the way her lips turned up at one side, and her nose pulled ever so slightly to the right. It was adorable, frankly.

Adorable, in the way a puma looks adorable, just before it tries to rip your face off.

"Okay," I said to the two ladies, once I'd gathered my courage once more, which sadly did not involve a glass of whisky. "Let's try that again, shall we?"

I made my way back towards the cargo door, through which cold rain was lashing. I peeked out into the rain at the running-boards, which still looked too damn narrow, wet and ill-repaired. Remarkably, they had not improved in the few minutes since I last tried to clamber onto them. Not that I expected them to do so, but it would have been nice, just for once, for a small bloody miracle to happen. I had involved the Lord when I fell the first time, after all.

I found myself making a mental note that should I survive this doomed venture and somehow remain captain of this or any other airship, I'd bloody well make sure the crew kept the damn running-boards in good repair. I don't know how familiar you are with airship design. So, I'll try and keep this simple, as who wants a lecture at this stage of events? I doubt you want to hear it any more than I want to give it, but some semblance of explanation may be in order. Leaks on an airship are a common hazard. Much like ocean-going vessels always have a leak somewhere, airships are always leaking. Unlike their aquatic counterparts, they leak outwards. It's not too much of a problem as a rule, because pressure pumps constantly run to redress the balance of all those little microleaks. However, if the airframe is damaged, by a high-velocity armour piercing round, for example, you can leak gas faster than you can replenish it. This is considered a problem, as I am sure you can imagine.

Unlike an ocean-going ship, you can't just send someone down into the bilges with a welding rod and some steel plate. You have to plug those leaks from the outside, and, as you will no doubt unsurprised to learn when you're a thousand feet up, that's not a job for the faint-hearted. This is also where running-boards come into it; they're nothing more than ledges really. Ledges that run horizontally along the ships every seven foot or so. With guide wires underneath them so you can attach your safety line to the one above you while you are walking the board below.

On the most modern ships the running-boards are wide enough for one man to pass another safely, while the guidelines are an intricate system of inter-locking pulley switches that keep you connected to the airframe with your safety line at all times.

The Jonah wasn't a modern ship. Big surprise there...

So anyway, I climbed out on to the airframe and started to edge my way along the boards. All the while rain lashed at my face, and gusty winds buffeted me constantly. Within a few moments, my arms were already starting to ache, as I clung to the guide rails running above me and did everything I could to avoid looking down.

I hadn't gone more than a few yards along the board when Saffron climbed out after me. I'd tried to dissuade her from joining me on this fool's errand, but both she and Penny insisted on doing so. I'll admit I didn't try too hard because if anything I was secretly relieved by this. Searching the whole of the outer skin for leaks was going to be a thankless task. Three of us had more chance of finding whatever was leaching our buoyancy than one, and it meant less time out there on the airframe than doing this alone. Which if nothing else would reduce the risk of exposure because typically we didn't have the right kit for this. Linemen, those specialists trained to do this kind of thing in Old Iron Knickers' navy, wore thick, fleece-lined leathers, with heating coils that kept them warm. A thousand feet up, even when you weren't in the middle of a monsoon, the air was cold. With wind and rain, it could be bitingly cold. Ice crystals could build-up on an airframe in no time, even in tropical regions.

The ladies were lither than I or seemed so at least. Saffron moved about on the airframe with the same grace she possessed in the ballroom of The Empress the first time we met. While Bad Penny, well, she might as well have been out for a stroll for all the lack of concern she exhibited. When I reached the first junction point, where ladder bars led up and down the canopy, I looked back and noticed to my alarm but utter lack of surprise, Penny hadn't even bothered to wear a harness and line.

The first junction was a real test of nerve. As I said The Jonah wasn't a modern ship, and the only way to move from one safety rail to the next was to unclip fully. Most harnesses in these enlightened days come with two safety lines, that way you only ever had to unclip one at a time, thus stay attached even when you moved between junction points.

Naval linemen working an old ship like The Jonah, in utter disregard of regulations, tended to cut the second line off a harness, so as not to impede progress and allow them to work faster. I had heard such men joke between themselves on this score, deriding any among their colleagues who used a two-line harness. 'A good linesman doesn't even need a harness' you would hear them brag. Which was certainly true in some cases, though a bad linesman didn't need one either, not for very long anyway...

Unsurprisingly, given my luck, the harnesses we had managed to find aboard The Jonah had all belonged to 'good' linesmen. So not one of them had a second safety line. Hence the aforementioned test of nerve at the first junction.

Tentatively I unhooked myself, holding on to the ladder bar with my other hand, then reached over myself to clip it back to the new safety rail. Just as I was at my most unbalanced, a change in the wind caught me, twisted me around and made me lose my footing. That nightmare about falling came back to me once more, as for a fleeting second, that lasted an eternity, I hung on by one hand until I managed to swing back around and grabbed on to the cold, wet rail with the other. Then I pulled myself up and found my footing again, clamped the safety line back in place on the new rail and clung tight to the ladder for a moment while I caught both my breath and my nerve.

"Steady there, flyboy..." Penny shouted above the wind, her lack of even a modicum of concern for me oozing with her every word. I looked back and saw her laughing to herself. But Saffron, at least, looked like she gave a damn.

"You okay?" she asked me.

"I'll live," I muttered, and started to climb up the ladder, dragging my lifeline behind me. Still doing all I could to avoid looking down.

I was headed for the upper hull. The leak could just as easily be on the lower half, but The Jonah did at least have armour down there, so chances were the upper section was where the damage lay. Also, it happened to be a whole lot easier to go crawling around on top of an airship, rather than go swinging around underneath the damn thing. Besides the gondola ran most of the length of the lower hull anyway. So, playing the odds, we were going to check the upper section first in relative safety.

Relative to hanging from a harness over a thousand-foot drop that is...

I continued to climb. Progress was slow but steady and as I got past the outward arch of the airframe, it got easier. Luckily the main safety rail ran straight up at this point, with only a few gates it in that I needed to push the carabiner through.

Of course, that meant if I fell, I would rail down several metres of the ship before my fall got arrested. If it got arrested... another quirk of older craft was that if you fell the full length of a drop there was always a chance the carabiner would jar itself through a gate and let you fall another full length. If that was, it didn't rip the rail completely free of the airframe. Another reason for those regularly mandated maintenance checks The Jonah had noticeably not had...

Finally, I crested the top of the airframe where it levelled out until it was almost flat. The rain was still lashing down and the wind threatened to knock me from my feet, but I managed to drop to all fours and move the safety line over to the main runner. On another day, with the sun shining it would've been almost pleasant up there. You could even have taken a deck chair up and a cooler of beers and chill out for a few hours quite happily. I knew a few gunners who would do just that when a ship was in port.

Today was not such a day.

When I stood back up, I was reminded by the wind just why this wasn't a good day to go crawling around the top of an airship.

I glanced around, looking for any obvious signs of a leak, but sadly they seldom have neon signs pointing to them. I sighed to myself. '*Best get this done, Harry,*' I thought to myself, already looking forward to a nip of the previous captain's whisky when I got back in. I'd managed to find a bottle stashed in his desk the day before. It was rather pleasant to drink Captain Singh's whisky after how I'd been treated under his command. When I had downed a finger or three the night before I'd wondered vaguely what had happened to the old bastard. Not that I'm the vindictive sort, but I held out hope that a court martial for losing his ship was the least he suffered. His whisky tasted all the finer for those thoughts.

"Any chance of a hand here, Hannibal?" Saffron said from somewhere down the ladder.

I went back to look over the edge and saw she was struggling with her carabiner. It was caught on one of the runners behind her, but she couldn't see it from where she was.

"You're caught up," I shouted, for which I received a withering look.

"Just wait a moment, I'll get it for you," Penny shouted up from behind her, as ever eager to help her darling Miss Wells. I shrugged. It seemed as good a plan as any, as there was little I could do from where I stood.

As Penny climbed, there was a deep groaning sound, and the whole ship yawned to port, the whole airframe twisting in the wind. For a moment I almost lost my footing entirely and had to grab onto a guide rail for support.

The ladies fared worse than I. The sudden shift of the wind caused Saffron to swing around on one hand. Penny clinging on for dear life, and if I'd had the time, I would've wondered if she was now regretting the lack of a harness.

The ship lurched again, and Saffron crashed back on the airframe, luckily with the presence of mind to grab hold with both hands once more, but not before her head had been slammed into the ladder itself.

Penny actually fell back several rungs before grasping hold on one of the rungs again, thanks no doubt to her mechanical arm, because if anyone else had tried that they would have dislocated their shoulder. The ladder beneath her grip bent sharply with the sudden force of arresting her fall.

Things were quickly getting out of hand.

In a fit of heroic daring-do, I dragged my safety line closer to the edge and leant right over to offer Saffron my hand, which she gratefully accepted. If such an act seems out of character, remember that I was captain of this doomed vessel by her grace alone. I didn't relish returning to my crew without her. I doubted somehow, I'd remain in charge for long if that happened. Though calling them a crew was stretching it. If I'd a real crew it would've had a couple of linesmen in it and I would not have been out there in the first place. But besides that, it was Saffron and Saffron was Saffron. If you ever met her, you'd understand there are moments when self-preservation has to be put to one side, because even the best of us are slaves to our hormones at times.

As I helped her up over the lip, I saw the blood pouring down her face. She had a nasty-looking cut where her monocle had dug into her when she hit the ladder; the glass lens had been smashed in the process, so she might have had a stray shard of glass or two embedded in her as well. Yet Miss Wells' face was impressively impassive about the whole thing. I remember being not in any way surprised that she wasn't letting a little blood faze her.

As I hauled her up and onto the platform area at the top, I glanced down and saw Bad Penny was climbing the ladder again, though she had slipped quite a way back. '*No chance of her falling to her death,*' I thought and found myself surprised that I didn't think that a bad thing. Psychopath, she might be, but right now she was a psychopath on my side, and my side was looking a tad thin as it was of late.

Seeing as Saffron was now safely on top of the airframe, and seemed fine enough all considered, I determined I should get on with the search for leaks. Though you'll have to forgive that my gaze lingered upon her for a moment or two first.

"Are you okay?" I asked her, as ever a fool's question.

She looked up at me, one hand pressing down on her head where she'd been cut in order to try and stem the bleed. The strap on her monocle clearly wasn't helping so she pushed it aside, before pulling it off completely for a moment, and examining the broken lens with a rueful gaze.

"I'll live…" she told me, and I nodded in reply before turning back to the task at hand.

I hadn't got far in my search when I heard the shot. Even in a gale the sound of a gun being fired close by is distinctive, particularly if it's a few feet behind you.

I turned back around slowly. To see Saffron standing there, unnaturally still and solid looking in the wind. A pistol in her hand that was levelled straight at me. On the deck at her feet her bloody monocle lay discarded. While I was staring down a barrel, it was her eyes that grabbed my attention.

Two very different eyes.

One normal, light brown and shining.

The other black as night, with little flecks of red that pulsed, growing dim then bright, almost as if the creature within that eye was breathing. The same kind of creature I'd once had in my own eye. One of Gates' nasty little mechanical spider creatures. Not so little anymore.

Something the professor had said about my own spider came back to me, about how the device had been growing into the eye, and down the optic nerve. Growing until it could gain full control of its host. I suddenly had a chilling feeling that was nothing to do with the wind and rain. Saffron's spider had grown. Even while Jobs' monocle kept it dormant, it had still been slowly growing, and now, here of all places, it was free.

"Ah Mr Smyth, what a disappointment you turned out to be. I am afraid I will have to rescind your stay of execution. But before I do, tell me, where is Mr Wells now?" said a voice that was almost Saffron's own. The words, however, they were someone else's entirely. I didn't need to guess whose words they were; I recognised the dismissive tone and the arrogance behind it. And I knew, without any doubt, the spider was completely in control of her now. As for the spider, that was under the control of The Ministry, and The Ministry was under the control of the man speaking to me through her lips, 'M'.

I pulled my own gun and levelled it at the woman who had only moments before been Saffron Wells. Now she was fully 'M's creature. I wanted desperately not to have to pull the trigger, but I was all too aware that the woman before me was gone. I couldn't get past the irony of it all. I'd feared for so long that William Gates' damn spiders would be the death of me. I just hadn't expected it not to be the one in my own eye. I thought that doom had passed me by when my spider had been ripped out before I could lose myself to it. I should've thanked Steffen Jobs for that, rather than punched him in the face. But a spider in the eye was still going to be the death of me. Just not my spider, but the spider in the eye of Miss Saffron Wells.

I levelled my gun on her, knowing I wouldn't fire, and waiting for 'M' to do so.

Which was when Bad Penny finished her own climb and came over the edge of the canopy to see me pointing a gun at the woman she loved.

Things really started going badly at that point…

CHAPTER 32

The Spider In The Eye

"Bastard…" Penny yelled, which took 'M's creature off guard. Whatever the spider had done to her, it clearly now heard as well as saw. If I'd had time to wonder, I would have wondered how long 'M' had been sitting waiting for Saffron Wells to take off that monocle. He must have had the patience of a spider himself.

She/he/it, I'm not sure what I should call the creature that had until a few moments ago been Saffron Wells turned to face this new interruption. Surprised, no doubt, because the creature had lain in the dark so long waiting. If we'd any advantage, that was it, 'M' was still playing catch up and while he had control of Saffron's body, he had so without really knowing where it was and who was about. So Bad

Penny had the jump on him/it/her, whatever the correct pronoun is for such an occasion.

Except of course she didn't...

She wasn't questioning the parentage of Miss Wells, or the puppeteer pulling her strings. It was me she'd seen holding a gun on someone she loved. I was the 'bastard' and I was the focus of her rage.

"Oh, shit no..." I managed to shout as my psychotic friend crashed into me. Covering the distance between the rim and myself in less time than should've been possible, bypassing the real threat entirely on the way. She thundered into me and knocked me flying, sending both of us sliding towards the other side of the airship.

'M' fired again, whether at me or Penny, I've no idea. But the speed of Penny's assault must have thrown out his aim. I tried scrambling for a handhold, but the rain made it like grabbing for soap in a shower. So, I slide out across the airframe and plunged over the side.

Luckily my safety line caught hold and I was slammed back into the side of the ship. Winded by the impact, my eyes watering, it took me a moment to gather my bearings.

My pistol was gone. Either laying on the top of the airship or over the side completely and down into the Indian Ocean. It hardly mattered which, chances were I would be joining it soon, if my line gave way, or was cut.

"What the hell is going on?" snarled a familiar voice to my left. "Why the hell did you pull a gun on Saffron? Have you got a bloody death wish?"

I turned to see Penny hanging off the side a few yards from me. It took a moment for me to realise just how she was hanging there. With no safety line to arrest her fall, she had clawed at the airframe for purchase. If anyone else tried that they would be currently falling into the ocean. But

Penny had real claws which were dug into the aluminium skin of the gas envelope.

I could've commented on the irony of her being part of a team looking to fix leaks and ending up puncturing the gas envelope herself. But I was a bit distracted at the time to notice, as I suspect was Penny.

"It's not her," I yelled back.

"What?" she shouted, the look in her face suggesting she was getting ready to take another leap of faith. I had a horrible feeling I knew what direction the leap would be, and who she would be leaping at.

"It's not Saffron; it's the spider. It's the spider," I yelled at her, only the last of it was drowned out by something that sounded like a foghorn going off far below us. "What the hell?" I remembered shouting.

For a second Bad Penny was distracted, looking down at the ocean below us. Then as her gaze snapped back up, I saw that she was smiling, of all things. "It's no one," she said.

"What?"

"No one…" she replied, and that was the last thing she said at all, as I heard a gunshot once more and watched as a bullet tore into her shoulder. She fell back, her bladed nails ripping four tears straight down as she fell away. My eyes followed her fall.

"Penny…" I shouted after her.

With one eye I watched as she grew smaller until she finally vanished into the sea. The other eye, Jobs' eye, watched her face all the way down. The strangest look upon it, she was smiling. And still mouthing a reply I never heard. I cannot say for sure, but I like to think it was 'That's not my name…'

Despite the noise of the wind, and the hiss of escaping air, I still managed to hear the cocking of a pistol's hammer. But I ignored it while I watched Penny drop into the ocean.

It was not like I could do anything about it. My pistol was gone, all I had was my cutthroat in my boot, fat use that was going to be as I hung there on my safety line.

Besides, I think I felt I owed Bad Penny that much. Or something anyway. I couldn't explain why, but I felt close to her somehow. Despite the fact all she had ever done was threaten me, knock me out and scare the living crap out of me. Sometimes the enemy of your enemy is your friend. And sometimes an enemy is the closest thing you have to a friend in the world. At least you know that they care enough to hate you.

I turned my gaze back upwards to see her/him/it looking over the edge at me, her/his/its pistol cocked and ready, pointing at my head.

"Now, as I was saying before that, whatever that was, interrupted our little chat, Mr Smyth... would you be so kind as to inform us where we would find Mr Wells? Is he on this delightfully fragile craft by chance? Tell me and perhaps I'll just shoot you in the head rather than just send you screaming to your death. Really, you have been such a disappointment to us. I had such high hopes you might be enough of a sniveling little bastard that you would play your part in our little game. So, come now, tell me, where is Wells?"

There was something particularly wrong with those words been spoken out of Saffron's mouth. The way her voice was twisted and wrong. Her vocal cords must have been screaming in pain. I wondered if she was still in there at all, or if the spider really had full control. Had her mind been snapped or was she still there behind the twisted visage that had been her face, which was contorted now by an alien mind's invasion. Its movements were wrong, its expressions too. But I had to wonder if perhaps she was in there, still fighting against it.

"Really, Hannibal, you're testing my patience. Where is Wells?" she/he/it asked again.

What could I tell it? What could I say? Should I beg for mercy, or claim I was working for The Ministry all along? I could lie, I could always lie - lying is the easiest thing in the world. You've been listening to me all this time, and for all you know everything I have told you is a tissue of lies. I did tell you at the start, right where we began, that I'm a liar, a thief and a scoundrel. Why should you believe all this? Perhaps you don't, perhaps you take this testimony as no more honest than that I gave in court the day they condemned me to the gallows.

I can't say I would blame you for thinking that.

But right there, right then, I couldn't lie to save myself. Not while I stared up into the eyes of a woman, I want to claim I loved, though I'm not sure I truly know what that means. Staring up at her face and watching another speak through her mouth, that damn foul spider in her eye giving control of her body to a man like 'M'. I couldn't lie to save myself while that other eye, the eye that Professor Job gave me, had focused itself on Saffron's right eye, her own human eye and I watched in the most intimate of details as a tear formed within it and ran down her cheek.

I could not lie to save myself, and I would be damn before I betrayed her now by answering that question. The one she/he/it repeated one more time.

"Come on, Mr Smyth, tell me, where will I find HG Wells?" she/he/it said and sighted down she/he/its pistol at me.

So instead, I laughed, oh how I laughed.

What else is there to do sometimes but laugh? I was dead no matter what I did, so why the hell should I make my last act yet another betrayal? There'd been so many of them over the years.

So I laughed, while I came to a decision, reached down to the top of my boot, and the small leather sleeve waiting there.

I laughed and decided in that moment that I wasn't going to lie to save myself, or for that matter tell them the truth and betray Saffron. A woman locked in a cell that was her own body. And I would be damned three times over before I let that self-important obnoxious officious self-aggrandising swine take my life by the hand of his prisoner. Not when I had one last option, one last roll of the die. After all, there is always that one choice that is ever open to you, and I was as ever self-obsessed, conceited and full of myself. So as I was going to die that day, I would die by my own act alone, no one else's.

Because, as it turns out, and I surprised myself when I came to this conclusion, there are indeed worse ways to die than falling a thousand feet into the middle of the India Ocean.

I grasped my trusty cutthroat from my boot and slid it open. And did what the doctor did when I first came into this world.

I cut the cord…

And fell…

THE END?

Well that would be telling

But Hannibal Smyth will return in

'A Squid On The Shoulder'

ABOUT THE AUTHOR

Mark writes novels that often defy simple genre definitions, they could be described as speculative fiction, though Mark would never use the term as he prefers not to speculate.

When not writing novels Mark is a persistent pernicious procrastinator, he recently petitioned parliament for the removal of the sixteenth letter from the Latin alphabet.

He is also 7th Dan Blackbelt in the ancient Yorkshire marshal art of EckEThump and favours a one man one vote system but has yet to supply the name of the man in question.

Mark has also been known to not take bio very serious.

Email: Darrack@hotmail.com
Twitter: @darrackmark
Blog: https://markhayesblog.com/

Printed in Great Britain
by Amazon